My Bermuda Namesakes

Namesakes

To Shreen –
Here's to future
projects! (And visits
to Cornwall).
Love,
Maggie  x x

Maggie Fogarty

Copyright © 2012 Margaret J. Fogarty

The right of Margaret J. Fogarty to be identified as the Author of this Work has been asserted to her in accordance with the Copyright, Designs and Patents Act 1988

ISBN: 1480283673
ISBN-13: 978-1480283671

ACKNOWLEDGMENTS

Thanks to Jacqui Port, Annette Mirfield and Bermuda Sun journalist, Ray Hainey, for agreeing to be my 'test' readers – your feedback has been much appreciated.

To Samantha Johnson, neuroscientist and brain rehabilitation counsellor for Brain Injury Community Re-entry, Niagara, Canada. Her advice has been invaluable. Also to Dr Tim Hull, Consultant Neuropsychologist and the Brain Injury Rehabilitation Trust team at West Heath House, in Birmingham, England. Thanks as well to my long term partner, Paul Weall, who has worked for the Bermuda Police Service as a digital forensics consultant. It was this role that gave us the opportunity to spend a wonderful year living in Bermuda, where the idea for this novel was born. Finally heartfelt thanks to Paul Bacon, Kevin Mulhern and to all of those inspirational friends, colleagues and family. The names are too numerous to mention here but you know who you are.

Bermuda Calling

I don't really know what drew me to Bermuda. Perhaps it was the magazine pictures. Or perhaps it was the film about the Bermuda Triangle I remember watching as a kid. Or maybe it was just fate, something that was just meant to be.

So here I am staying on this achingly pretty mid Atlantic ocean sub tropical island which is just 21 square miles and is known for its pastel coloured buildings with their trade mark white lime washed rooftops. From space it must look like an elaborate pink, lemon and white iced celebration cake.

It's much hotter and more humid than the rain sodden city of London I've just left behind but somehow this place already feels like home. Maybe it's the familiar mix of American and British influences. Red post boxes meet California style beaches. Afternoon tea meets coffee and Oreo cookies. CNN and BBC World. You get my drift.

I'm staying in a one bedroom cottage in an area called Paget and it has a small terrace with a view of the glistening turquoise sea. I could stare at that view for hours and never tire of it. I've only been here for a week but have managed to see most parts of the island by travelling around on the pink and blue buses with my friendly landlady Pauletta.

Sometimes I go on my own by taxi tour if I feel up to it. Pauletta has suggested that I hire a scooter – she'd feel a bit sick about saying that if she knew why I'm here.

You see I'm not just here for a holiday although that's part of it. No, the main reason is to help my recovery and to meet Dr Raymond Silver. I'm told if anyone can improve on the new me it's the amazing Dr Silver. The Bermuda sea and sunsets are bound to help too. Not sure I'm ready to risk the Rum Swizzle cocktails just yet but maybe soon. Maybe.

It's just before midnight and I'm busy writing everything I've done today in my electronic diary. It's my lifeline and I can't miss this routine however tired I feel. So here I am making copious notes on my laptop and making sure that I back everything up. Back up and then back up again for good measure. I also take a photo of myself to remind me what I was wearing today. Only then can I go to sleep to the whistling sound of the Bermuda tree frogs outside and hoping that the night terrors don't come to me tonight. Please God.

Chapter 1

That Was Then

Just to introduce myself. My name is Josie James or 'JJ' as I like to be called. I'm 32 years old and until the day that changes my life forever, I am living in a one bedroom flat on the rougher side of Islington, north London. It isn't far from where I grew up and I can still travel home for some of my mom Carol's cooking and to see my younger brother Jeff. It is a comfortable existence, probably a bit too comfortable truth be told.

At the time I'm working for a small graphic design company in Covent Garden doing a bit of everything really. It is that sort of company, just about keeping its head above water and everyone having to muck in when the occasional big deadline looms. While I enjoy the work most of the time, it isn't what I'd imagined doing when I graduated from art school hoping to become the next big name in the design world. When my thirtieth birthday comes and goes I decide that this is about as good as it is going to get for me. A case of putting up or shutting up.

Tim has been my boyfriend for nearly a year. We met at a work training day and we sort of just clicked. He reminds me a bit of younger Bob Geldolf, all tousle haired, lanky with bags of nervous energy. Friends joke that we are the living embodiment of opposites attracting. Me average height, long dark curly hair and well toned from my regular gym classes. Him rangy, scruffy, mousy haired and a bit unhealthy looking.

On the day that everything changes, we meet up for lunch at Dinos Deli just around the corner from where I work. He's got the day off from his job as a production assistant at an independent TV company but still manages to turn up late. Typical. When he arrives I've already started on my favourite mozzarella and tomato panini.

"You've got cheese on your chin" Tim leans over to give me a kiss and licks off the drizzle of melted mozzarella which is resting on my chin.

"Always been a messy eater you" He winks and sits down. Well sort of slides his 6ft 2 frame into the red plastic seat almost taking the matching checked table cloth with him.

"And you're a clumsy prat" I joke "and why so late anyway?"

He then begins an elaborate and probably untrue story about late buses and tube delays. I smile and decide that he'll be paying for lunch.

An hour and a shared bottle of red wine later we decide, yet again, to leave things for a bit longer before moving in together. This has been our regular 'shall we, shan't we?' conversation over the past few weeks. Perhaps this is all for the best because of how things have turned out. More about that later.

The next bit I can remember in vivid

technicolour. The images are frozen in time like those old garish film posters I adored as a kid. I kiss Tim goodbye and buy myself a fresh orange smoothie from the juice bar on the corner. I spot my boss, Richard, who is on the other side of the road and step off the pavement to join him.

Then the next bit. The almighty screech, the smell of burning rubber, smoke and the feeling of warm liquid around my head as I'm lying on the ground. The juice container squashed in my hand and a smell of oranges mixed with petrol. After that it all gets a bit hazy. I remember the piercing sound of sirens, my boss leaning over me and then feeling more dog tired than I'd ever felt before. I just want to sleep but Richard keeps telling me I need to stay awake.

"Keep your eyes open JJ. Just for me. The ambulance is on its way. Come on, can you hear me?" I can see the worried look on his face but I really just need to sleep. Disappear into blackness. Into absolute oblivion.

So that is the first day of the new chapter in my life and all because I stupidly step out into the path of a speeding motor cycle. Afterwards it is weeks in hospital – though I don't remember too much about that – before moving into the brain injury rehabilitation centre.

It is inside this ugly red bricked building on the outskirts of London that I learn I have severe brain damage.

"So Josie. You understand your condition? It's called frontal temporal brain injury." Dr Shirley Peters, my brain injury specialist at the rehab centre, peers over her glasses to check my reaction.

I nod. Sounds so precise, so clinical when put that way.

To you and me it means a head injury caused when a motorcycle crashed into me and left me for dead. It also means that I now lead the perfect life if you can believe all those self help books. You know the ones where they say you should live in the present to be truly happy?

Well I'm living in the present all right. Every single day. Ask me what I did yesterday and without referring to my daily diary I won't have a clue. You see my new brain is like a blackboard that gets wiped every day and I start afresh the next morning. No recent past. No regrets about what I did yesterday.

It's a funny old thing the brain. Dr Peters explains to me that my short term memory is shot to pieces. It's strange because I can still remember things from way back. Holidays with my mom and dad and younger brother. I can remember my friends from school, college, work colleagues and can still do graphic design if I try. I can recall the shock and grief I felt the on the day my dad died of a heart attack. I still know how to read, write and add up. All of that stuff is hard wired deep into my brain. It's the little day to day things that I can't remember now. Like what I had to eat yesterday, the things I did and what I chose to wear. So that's why I have to keep a diary. It's why I have to carry it with me and make sure that my diary notes are backed up on my computer. This is my everyday life we're talking about here, a record of all of my yesterdays.

Just to give you an idea, here's one of my diary entries for January 10:

"Mom and my brother came to visit today. Mom kept moaning about the trip across London and asked why 'these places' are always built miles away from anywhere. She should try living here. My little bro Jeff brought my favourite sweets and a travel magazine. He said I should start thinking about a holiday for when I get out. Well, it's worth fantasising.

Tim arrived just as mom and Jeff were leaving. He looked sad and hardly said a word. He kept saying that I've changed and he can't cope. Personally I don't think the real me has changed. I've just got a dicky short term memory and it gets tiring having to write everything down. So I made a big decision today. I asked Tim not to visit for a while. Just need some space from him. He didn't argue which says everything really"

By the next morning my brain won't remember any of this and if anyone asks me "What did you get up to yesterday?" I need to consult the diary. Without it I'd be lost.

Funnily enough, Bermuda is the first place I look at in the travel magazine my thoughtful little brother has left and I'm mesmerised. Nowhere else stands out in the same way. Afterwards I spend hours trawling websites and looking at Bermuda holiday movies posted online. I write down loads about the place and reminders to re-read everything and make more notes.

When work decides to offer me redundancy, I grab it with both hands. But how to persuade Dr Peters at the rehab centre that I am safe to travel on my own? As it happens, it is the good Dr herself who comes up with the answer.

"I know it looks beautiful but it is 4,000 miles away" She's staring at my wall covered in pictures of Bermuda. Elbow Beach, the main town Hamilton, the older St George's part of the island, Horse Shoe Bay. There is hardly a space left to fill.

"And you'll need to continue your treatment if you go there. You realise that don't you?"

I nod. Best always to appear compliant. But my mind is made up.

"I think it would do me good to travel Dr Peters. I've got to go back into the big wide world at some time" I hold her gaze hoping that it signals resolve.

She sighs.

"Yes but why Bermuda? Couldn't you just go to the Lake District or Wales? It would be a lot easier"

I don't reply. Our eyes lock for a few seconds, just enough to let her know that I'm not going to give up on this one.

"Well the good news is that a top brain specialist works over there. But he's not cheap and you'll have to pay for yourself. I can't see the NHS stumping up for treatment in Bermuda even if it is a British territory" She looks down at her notes.

"He's called Dr Raymond Silver and he's doing some pioneering work with brain injured patients. If you insist on going, I'll contact him and see if he's interested in taking you on"

I give her an appreciative smile.

"Thanks Dr Peters. I'll google him and get some background"

"Can't promise anything mind you" She writes

something hurriedly on her file before being ushered away by a nurse to deal with Sue, my next door neighbour at the centre, who is apparently standing stark naked in the corridor - yet again. Well she isn't known as 'Sue the Stripper' for nothing

My diary entry for March 16 says.

"Bermuda here I come. Looked up Dr Raymond Silver and made loads of notes. I'm beyond excited. He's dealt with lots of people like me who have brain injuries from road accidents. He's bound to be interested in my case. I'll make sure of it. Need now to become an expert on Dr Silver. Feel it won't be long till I'm out of here".

And my prediction turns out to be right. May 20th 2011 is the start of my big Bermudian adventure. Little do I realise what awaits me as I feel the warm sun on my face at L F Wade International airport and then spot the large sign being held up by my smiling landlady Pauletta.

"Welcome to Bermuda Josie James".

Chapter 2

And This Is Now

My first week on the Island has been amazing. The truth is that I really am living in the present over here. Big time. I have no past connections to the place and my short term recall problems mean that I have to take each day at a time. Things have improved a little since I had my accident over a year ago. Occasionally I now get snatches or flashes of memory from the previous day. I find this usually happens if I've seen or experienced something that affects me on some sort of deep emotional or sensual level – a stunning landscape, a beautiful painting, building or even a delicious meal. It's as if that memory part of my brain is slowly starting to wake up. There's only a tantalising glimpse, a short flicker of what went before. But it's there and Dr Silver thinks that's a good sign.

Dr Raymond Silver. He's a legend if you can believe all that's been written about him. The morning I meet him I pour over all the background stuff I've collected about him. It's frustrating to know I have read it all before but keep on having to come back to 'refresh' my memory. It must be like some of those people who have Alzheimers disease or dementia. No wonder they keep repeating themselves, desperately trying to hang on to the threads of what is left of their memories before they disappear forever. I can't even do that because I don't have a decent thread to hang on to once I've gone to sleep. I do sometimes dream though. Disconnected, nightmarish dreams that take me right back to the day of my accident. I smell petrol. Hear sirens. Feel needles going into my arms and legs. Wake up in a cold sweat. That's another strange thing. I can remember these dreams. So how do you work that one out?

Dr Silver finds this a particularly interesting aspect of my condition. We're sitting in his large airy office that is part of his own family home. It is a typical island colonial style house painted in pastel yellow with a large front garden and what I'm told is an avocado tree growing in the middle of the lawn. The grass grows much thicker and coarser over here and it's like walking across a dense carpet. His office has lots of certificates on the wall and pictures of Dr Silver receiving awards. I know he's been given loads of those for his pioneering work with brain injured patients. On his desk are photos of his wife who looks very glamorous in a streaky blondish film star sort of way and toddler twin boys smiling shyly at the camera wearing matching red T shirts. He tells me his boys are now about to start school.

"So JJ, you can remember these dreams, these nightmares?"

He is sitting straight backed on a large brown

leather chair at the side of his desk. Clearly he is one of those doctors who doesn't want to be seen sitting behind a desk. Not that I'd mind if he did.

He's tanned with a serious but good looking face and has thick salt and pepper hair. I know from reading up on him that he's aged about 40 and comes from Boston. He's clearly confident enough not to be worried about covering up the grey flecks and his taut build suggests someone who makes an effort to work out. He's tall but not awkwardly so like Tim. I decide that I like Dr Silver. He has a cheeky sparkle in those brown eyes of his that hint of a good sense of humour. But today the talk is serious.

I nod at his question about the dreams.

"Yes, that confuses me. I mean I have to write down everything I do before I fall asleep but I can remember the dreams. At least the repetitive bad ones anyway"

"Hmm interesting" Dr Silver is making notes but still managing to keep regular eye contact with me. He is also recording our chat with one of those mini devices which sits perched on the end of the desk, red light winking.

"And you say that you are starting to get the occasional short term memory without the help of your diary?" He glances up from his notes to check that the machine is still recording.

"Yes. Not anything detailed as such. Just a hazy recall now and then. Like the other day when I saw the most incredible sunset from my terrace. It was awesome and the next day when I woke up the image was in my mind first thing."

"Well JJ that's a good sign I think. It could be an indication that you are starting to recover some short term memory. We'll just have to wait and see."

Dr Silver asks if he can see some of my diary entries.

"It would be good to see how you record things. I've developed a technique that has helped a lot of my patients to keep a better memory record"

I'm distracted by the sight of a green and red lizard climbing up the outside pane of the window behind Dr Silver's desk. He glances across to see what I'm staring at.

"Oh Lizzies. You'll get used to those over here. That's what comes from being in a sub tropical climate"

And with that our session comes to an end. I leave some copies of my diary notes with him and we agree to meet up again in three days time. I walk out of the office into the sort of searing heat that you only get in England once in a while. And today I decide that I must think of a way of meeting some new friends over here. My landlady is great but I need to meet some more people and I don't want Pauletta feeling that she has to be my constant companion. I haven't told her yet about my accident and brain troubles but I will do soon. Otherwise she'll keep banging on about renting that scooter.

I jump on the crowded pink bus that goes into Hamilton, the main town in Bermuda. Front Street, the shopping thoroughfare, is jam-packed full of visitors today as a cruise ship has just arrived at Hamilton Docks. An American couple asks me what is the best way to the bus station. I think about looking at my street map but then decide to play the stranger-in-town role like them. It's not a total lie. I just don't want to have to get to grips with the map as it takes a little time for my brain to take in the details and to trace the hand written arrows and notes I've dotted all over it. Anyway, they look like a couple in a hurry.

Marco's, just off Front Street, is one of those little Italian style coffee shops that reminds me of my much loved Dino's Deli in London. The coffee is good and they make their own home made banana bread which is to die for. At least that's what my diary reminded me of this morning.

Today Marco is alone behind the counter.

"Ah JJ. Good morning. The usual?"

I've only been here for just over a week and already I've been spotted as a regular customer. Pauletta keeps telling me it's a small island and I'll have to get used to people recognising me on a daily basis. If you could come up with the pole opposite of London, this is it.

"Morning Marco. Seems like I'm getting hooked on that banana bread of yours"

This pleases Marco who treats me to an even bigger smile.

"I'll tell my wife. She makes it herself. An old family recipe." He pats his protruding stomach. "As you can see I love it too"

I choose a seat close to the window so I can people watch. Marco arrives with a large cappuccino and a giant slab of his wife's creation. I tell him I don't think I'll be eating lunch after this lot.

He shrugs

"You just need to eat later in the afternoon. Think of this as brunch" And with that he is off to deal with some cruise ship customers asking if he does "tea and English scones" If he's offended he doesn't show it.

So back to my immediate problem. How do I make friends in Bermuda? I could join a club of some sort but I don't want to meet too many people at once. Otherwise I'll have to try to figure out how to remember them all. Ideally it would be good to meet just two or three people to start with. That way I can keep tabs and get to know them well enough to let them into my world. To let them know this stranger in a strange world.

It is only when I arrive home that the penny finally drops.

I've just got out of the shower when Pauletta knocks on my door. Originally from Portugal she has lived in Bermuda for over 30 years. She is a short skinny bundle of energy with a shock of auburn dyed hair and wearing a little too much eye liner for the weather here. It's a hot sticky afternoon and the eyeliner has started to run. Being English and polite I say nothing. Instead I fix my gaze on the copy of the Bermuda phone book she is holding.

"Hi. You ok? I've got two of these so thought you might like a copy. It lists a lot of the restaurant menus with the prices and everything"

I say thanks and mercifully she doesn't want to hang around today. One of Pauletta's so called 'little chats' can take up the best part of an afternoon.

I start to flick through the phone book. I wonder

if anyone with the surname, James, lives on the island? Actually there are quite a few. Ok, let's make this a little harder. Are there any of my namesakes, Josie James'?

My full name is Josephine, the same as my maternal grandmother, the one I never knew because she died before I was born. I start to scroll down the J's and find just two Josephine James'. One lives across the other side of the island in St George's, a quaint almost English style town with one of the oldest churches in the western hemisphere. The other lives within walking distance of Hamilton.

I stare at the phone numbers. What if I were to just take the plunge and give them a call? The namesakes thing would be a good ice breaker. I practice my approach front of my dressing table mirror noticing at the same time how my skin is starting to turn a light brown with a smattering of freckles appearing around my nose.

"Hello my name is Josie James and I'm from London. I'm over here in Bermuda for a few months and noticed in the phone book that you have the same name as me. I'm interested in tracing my family history and I always like to look up people with the same name when I'm travelling. Would it be ok if I met you while I'm here?"

Hmm. Sounds a bit cheesy, creepy even. Perhaps it is best not to sound over rehearsed. A casual call might be more appropriate and better just to get on with it rather than dithering.

I take a deep breath and start to dial the number of Josephine James in Hamilton.

The phone rings out several times before an answer message clicks in. Damn it.

I didn't think I'd get a recorded message. Still the voice is intriguing.

"Hi this is Josie. I'm sorry but neither myself or Callum are around at the moment. But if you leave a message we'll get back to you later. Bye"

It is a distinctive soft Irish voice. West coast of Ireland if I'm not mistaken. I dial back and listen again. Like me she shortens her name. The voice is pleasant, friendly even. Callum must be her husband or partner I guess.

Shall I leave a message? It can't do any harm and in some ways it is better than cold calling. If she's interested she'll call me back. If not then no harm done.

I dial for a third time hearing that lovely Irish accent. I take a quick breath and then take the plunge;

"Hello Josie, sorry for ringing you out of the blue but I'm over here from England and I noticed your name in the phone book. I'm also called Josie James and when I travel I like to look up my namesakes. It would be great to meet you when I'm here"

I also leave my contact phone number and email. So that's it. Done it. Told a small lie about looking up my namesakes while travelling. It has never occurred to me to look up any other Josie James when I've been to Spain, Cyprus or Greece on holidays. Back then I was with friends or with Tim and had no need to search elsewhere for company.

So better make a quick note about this new found 'hobby' of mine. I don't feel ready to approach the other Josephine in St George's yet. Let's see what this one brings first.

Later Pauletta persuades me to join her and her husband Dave for dinner at The Swizzle Inn, famous for those rum cocktails. She is trying to get me to try one – "Go on try it, you'll love it" - when my cell phone rings. It startles me as I've set the volume up on high in expectation of a call. I'm not disappointed.

"Hi is that Josie? It's the other Josie James here. You left me a message this afternoon?"

And so my namesake, Josie James from Tralee, is about to come into my life.

Pauletta is teetering across the restaurant in her sky high heels and is holding a rum swizzle.

"Who was that then. Your mama in England?"

She hands me the cocktail and grins.

"Oh just someone I spoke to today" I take the glass but don't intend to drink it. I haven't touched alcohol since the day of my accident.

"She's my namesake you know. Isn't that great?"

Pauletta looks confused.

"Namesake? Now what's that all about?"

A peculiar mixture of elation and foreboding comes over me. It's like being excited but fearful at the same time, I write later on in my diary.

Excited I can understand. The fear bit doesn't make sense. Not yet anyway.

Chapter 3

Making friends

My little brother Jeff keeps urging me to get a Skype computer phone link so I can talk to him more often in London. Today he's phoning from an old fashioned expensive landline and says it is "so last century".

"You can get one of those little cameras to attach to the computer. They're great. I talk to my mate Jimmy in Australia all the time"

I laugh and tell him that it's enough to be in a new country with my dodgy brain, let alone trying to fathom out how to work a computer based phone system. Still it's great to hear his voice as I'm really starting to miss him and mom.

Mom being mom asks me if I'm eating properly, if my flat is clean and if I've made many new friends.

"Well mom I'm going to meet someone today and guess what? She has exactly the same name as me"

Mom takes a few seconds to digest what I've just said.

"You are ok aren't you JJ? You're not just getting confused?"

"No mom. I'm as all right as I can be. I just looked in the phone book to see if there were any other people with my name over here and two came up. This one even calls herself Josie as well. She's from Tralee in Ireland and works in a bank"

"And you just called her up out of the blue?" Mom is clearly gobsmacked that I'd do such a thing.

"Er, yes as it happens. That's exactly what I did. I left a message on her answer phone and she got back to me last night. We're meeting today at Elbow Beach bar just up the road from here"

After chatting to mom and Jeff, I carry on getting ready for my meeting with Josie and her fiancé, Callum O'Toole. My main dilemma now is what to wear. I try on half a dozen outfits before settling on a red top and black linen shorts. It's not far to walk to the bar so I decide to wear some flip flops and set the whole thing off with a straw cowboy style hat – something I'd never dream of wearing back in London.

I scan my notes about my phone call last night. I know that they are both aged 28 and are engaged to be married. I know they both come from Tralee in the west of Ireland and have been living here for 18 months. I also have a photograph of them both which she sent across last night. And they won't have a problem recognising yours truly because I returned the favour.

Elbow Bar is built right by the beach, with the best tables just a short throw away from the sunbathers and the coral pink sands. The lunch crowd haven't yet arrived so the place is unusually quiet.

It is me who spots them first as they are deep in conversation. I approach them gingerly, not wanting to startle them.

"Er hello – Josie and Callum?"

They both look around and the first thing I notice about Josie is how beautiful she looks. Much better than her photograph. Like me she has dark hair though hers is longer and poker straight. She has a pale delicate Irish skin and is a lot taller than I expected – at least five feet ten inches. She is slim without being skinny and is wearing a pale blue wrap over dress. Callum, by contrast, is quite plain looking with short coarse auburn hair and a freckly complexion. He is also tall but has the beginnings of a plump belly. As far as looks go, Josie is way out of Callum's league and I bet he can't quite believe his luck.

'Tralee Josie', the nickname I've already given to her, gives me a big smile and jumps up to greet me. Callum glances across but doesn't move for now. Perhaps he's a bit shy.

"Ah hello Josie – or should I call you 'JJ' like you said last night? Great to meet you. This is my fiancé Callum"

Callum moves across and puts out his hand. His smile is reticent and I notice a tiny trickle of sweat slowly making its way down the side of his right cheek.

"Good to meet you too JJ. Can I get you a drink while the bar's quiet?"

I say thanks and order a diet coke. Tralee Josie says she'll have another dry white wine.

"I'm not driving and have the day off work. So

it's a booze day for me"

While Callum is at the bar I learn that she works for a large banking group in Hamilton and is loving it here. She and Callum got engaged two years ago in their home town of Tralee. They met when she entered a local pageant which she tells me is a bit like a smaller scale Miss World contest. I've never heard of it but I don't say as much. Callum was acting as her male 'escort' during the competition, a job which apparently involved ferrying her from one party to next, carrying her luggage and making sure she got safely back to her hotel.

"Don't tell him I let you know" she adds laughing "but I decided he was husband material when he agreed to pop out and buy me some Tampax. Now there's a man!"

I laugh a bit too loudly as I imagine him trying to buy women's sanitary wear. He glances over to signal that the drinks are on the way and then points towards the men's toilets or 'restrooms' as they are called over here.

"He's had two pints already" Tralee Josie adds. "Well gives us a few more minutes of girly chat before he gets back"

To be fair, Callum can hardly get a word in edgeways during our lunch. Tralee Josie is effortlessly chatty, a real extrovert. By the time she gets to her third glass of wine I've heard all about her big Irish family and the plans for a huge wedding next year.

So far I haven't said too much about me. I'm glad that she accepts that I like to be called JJ – unlike Pauletta who refuses point blank to use my abbreviation.

"So enough about me and Callum. Now I want to hear what you've been up to and what brings you to Bermuda?"

Callum is already looking distractedly at the lunch menu. Josie gives him a mock dirty look.

"Always thinking of his stomach him! Do you fancy ordering some food JJ?"

I'm not especially hungry but I chose a calamari appetiser. She opts for a prawn salad and Callum decides on a burger.

I can't avoid talking about the accident for much longer. So I decide to get it out of the way sooner rather than later.

"Well I just picked out Bermuda because it looked so great. I love the idea of red letter boxes and English bobbies on the beat. It's like home with a tropical twist"

"You can say that again – me and Callum can't get used to this humidity though"

Callum looks up from his burger, the beads of sweat starting to break out just below his hairline.

"Hate this humidity me – it's like being in a sauna"

Ok, now time to get the tale of the accident out of the way. Josie is intrigued and even Callum looks more than a bit interested.

"So let me get this straight" Josie takes a sip of wine while expertly forking a large peeled prawn. "Once you've gone to sleep for the day you can't remember anything about the day before?"

"That's pretty well the case" I take my small black notebook out of my bag. "See this? I jot down notes in it all the time and last thing at night I put everything onto my computer diary"

It's hard explaining my funny brain to other people. The doctors are fine because they see it all the time. But most people don't understand how I can remember a lot about the past and what I've learned over the years but can't even recall what I wore yesterday.

I tell them it's not that bad once you get used to it. Just a different way of living from day to day. In some ways it has advantages. Each day is like a new toy box waiting to be filled. And if something bad happens, I can choose not remember it by not writing it down. In this sense I'm an editor of my own life. I can scrub out the nasty bits and then forget all about it. Apart from those terrible recurring dreams which I'm stuck with.

Our lunch finished, Josie says that I must come over and visit them soon. She says that she'll cook a meal and I can see the TV recording of her debut in the Tralee pageant along with pictures from her engagement party. Callum looks nonplussed as if he doesn't really care that much if he sees me again. I think he's quite insecure and wants to keep Josie all to himself.

While Josie disappears to the Ladies restroom, I try to make stilted conversation with Callum. He's dabbing his forehead with the restaurant napkin and finds it hard to look me straight in the eye. I can't quite decide whether he's just rude or ridiculously shy. Perhaps it's a bit of both.

"So what are your plans for the rest of the day Callum?"

He shrugs.

"Get out of this heat for a start" He inspects the napkin as if he can't quite believe how much moisture it has soaked up.

"Er, sorry about that. Later on today? Not sure yet. I expect me and Josie will go shopping now. She's after a new dress for a bank charity thing she's got coming up"

"Is it one of those big charity balls where you have to wear posh frocks?"

Callum looks past me as a couple of young girls walk by our table in tight micro shorts and cropped T shirts. He then notices that I spot him ogling and quickly averts his eyes.

"Yeh, I think it's one of those posh shindigs. It's in the Hamilton Royal hotel - not keen on that type of thing myself"

This doesn't surprise me. I don't like those formal charity things either, especially with all those speeches and people trying to outdo each other on donations. What's wrong with sticking money in a tin or just posting off a cheque?

"And how are you finding not being able to work?" I already know about Bermuda's work permit situation which doesn't make it easy for the spouses or partners of existing permit holders to apply for jobs.

Callum gives another one of his non committal shrugs.

"It's not great but Josie earns enough for the both of us. My mates in Tralee think I'm a lucky bastard but you can't just be going down to the beach every day. Not with my skin" He glances down at his pinkish freckly arms.

"But I've met a good mate, Micky Doyle, and we have some great laughs. He's over here from Dublin and works in Finnegan's, the Irish bar on Front Street. He's a real character is Micky"

"The one who was in the accident?" I know because Josie has already told me about the moped accident which cost Micky his left leg.

Callum nods and scans the bar for signs of Josie.

"Yes, poor sod lost his leg when his moped ploughed into a tree. Wasn't even drunk at the time"

Josie arrives back in a cloud of perfume and newly applied lipstick. I can see why she got the place in her home town beauty pageant. Callum is already on his feet and I leave them waiting for a taxi as I make my way back home down.

As soon as I get back I start to make my notes.

"So today I've met Tralee Josie and Callum. She's great and is fantastic looking. A real live wire and lots of fun. Him a bit more serious and you have to coax a conversation out of him but we'll see. He might come out of his shell when he gets to know me a bit more. They both mentioned that I should meet their friend Micky Doyle who has had a bike accident. I hope they aren't trying to pair me off with a fellow road victim (lol). Going around to their house on June 5 and I think Micky will be there. What a pair – me with the shot memory and him with one leg. Still it should be a fun evening."

I'm just listing all the other things I've learned about Josie and Callum when there's a loud tap on the door. It's Dave, Pauletta's husband, who is wearing a BBQ apron with a 'Men like it hot!' slogan on the front. Like Pauletta he is short but much stockier and is clinging to his few remaining head hairs which are stuck together in what they call a comb over. His face is bright red and I can smell the charcoal wafting up the steps to my door.

"Ah Josie. You hungry? We have the grill all fired up. I have some great rock fish on the go."

The last thing I feel like doing is going to one of Dave and Pauletta's BBQs but hey, I am in Bermuda and it's a favourite pastime here. I don't think I can get out of it.

I say I'll be down in ten minutes and then frantically type up the rest of my notes from today.

Something tells me June 5 is going to be a big day. Meantime I have to see the lovely Dr Silver again tomorrow morning. Pauletta took a message from him when I was out at lunch. I called him back straightaway and he said he wants to see me at 10.15am tomorrow.

"I've got some exciting news for you Josie and I think you're gonna like it"

Chapter 4

Dr Knows Best

I wake up with a splitting headache. It takes me a few minutes to adjust to the sun light streaming through my bedroom blinds and to the incessant calls of the Kisskadee birds outside. When I first heard the cries of these yellow breasted exotic birds, I thought they sounded a bit like London market hawkers.

"50p, 50p!"

The guidebooks say they are called Kisskadees after their distinctive song, if you can call it that. Right now it's bloody annoying and piercing my head like a drill.

After a few minutes I get up and pour myself a large glass of water. I then glance at my computer to remind myself what I got up to yesterday. Of course, the Josie and Callum meeting. Brilliant. I notice that I'm flooded with good feelings as I read all about it. That's another funny thing about my new brain. I can conjure up emotions just by reading about what I did yesterday or even weeks before. Recalling events, people or places, kicks in an emotional response. If I read that I didn't enjoy something, then I can recreate that mood immediately. And if, like yesterday, I had a good time with Josie and Callum, then reminding myself about it brings back that feeling.

I now understand the headache. Just before I went to bed I made a note that Pauletta had given me a small glass of her favourite rum cocktail. This time I threw caution to the wind and agreed to have a taste. It's clear that I didn't like it and I conjure up immediately the sickly sweet taste of rum and fruit juice. I also read that Pauletta and Dave know all about my accident. At least I've got that out of the way. I note that Pauletta hugged me, saying that I could rely on her and Dave for any help I need and that I must take extra care when crossing Bermuda's narrow bendy roads. Somehow that instinct for self protection is still hard wired in and even more so since my accident.

Three glasses of water later and I'm ready to face the world. My meeting with Dr Silver is flagged up in a big bright red font on my computer alongside a note about the number 7 bus on the pink pole side of the street and the time it arrives, 9.45am. From a travel point of view, being on a small island makes things easy. The pink poles are for the buses taking you towards Hamilton. The blue bus poles take you to the other side of the island away from the main town.

My bus is packed with cruise ship tourists and it is standing room only. I try to balance myself and grab hold of the hand straps dangling overhead. An overweight American guy is struggling to keep upright and is moaning to his fellow passengers about having to use 'this goddamn' public transport.

"Point Finger Road" the driver yells out. I can recognise Dr Silver's road now – after several journeys I can visually recall places just as I can conjure up the faces of people I've met. This purely visual part of memory has stayed pretty much intact. But just to be on the safe side, I've asked the driver to remind me.

I arrive early and Dr Silver's wife Dianne offers me a cold drink. I opt for water with lots of ice and watch as she grabs together her things for a game of golf.

"Have you ever played golf JJ?"

"No can't say I have" I reply taking a large sip of water.

"Well if you do want to take it up I can recommend a good coach. Wow, is that really the time – better be off. See you again soon. Bye"

And then she is gone. I stare at the family photos dotted around the pristine hallway leading to Dr Silver's office. There are lots of pictures of their twin boys and a golden retriever dog which I haven't seen around yet. There is a large photo of Dr Silver and his wife wearing formal evening wear – probably at some swanky awards ceremony. There's also a picture of them on their wedding day. His hair was much darker then but the cheeky smile is the same. She looks much the same as she does now and I guess her outfit must have cost a packet. They both look glossy, happy and undeniably rich.

I glance up to see Dr Silver saying goodbye a middle aged woman who looks as though she's been crying. He turns around and spots me waiting.

"Ah JJ – good morning. I'll be with you in a mo". And with that he disappears outside with the woman muttering something about seeing her again next week.

Once we're inside Dr Silver's office he pulls out a file from his desk and plonks himself down in the large leather chair at the side of his desk. I can smell a strong floral scent which I assume has been left by his previous patient. It is mixed in with Dr Silver's own distinctive aftershave, a sort of lemony smell with something spicy like cinnamon. I also think I can detect cigarette smoke but there is no sign of any ash trays.

"So JJ, how are things with you?" Before I can answer, he leans back to adjust the blinds on the window just behind him.

"Sorry about that – sun's a bit strong today"

"I'm fine Dr Silver. Though I did try a rum cocktail last night – not a good move. I'm just shaking off the headache from hell"

He laughs, adjusting the blind a little more.

"Well I know all about those. Personally I wouldn't recommend too much alcohol during this stage of your recovery. But that's hard to stick to here in Bermuda"

"I'm not really sure if I even want to drink alcohol any more to be honest. This is the first time I've tried anything since the accident and I can't say I like it"

Dr Silver makes a quick note and just as he does this his cell phone rings out. We both flinch as a blast of the cartoon character Scooby Doo fills the room.

He grabs the phone and presses the off button.

"Sorry about that. My boys must have been playing with the phone ring tones. They are so technically savvy these days"

I smile and we spend a few minutes discussing the merits of Scooby Doo which is one of my favourite childhood TV characters. Turns out Dr Silver is also a fan though he says he prefers Top Cat. That one must have passed me by.

"Ok JJ. Let me talk you through my thoughts about your treatment. I've now read all your notes and have looked at how you do your diary. Here's what I suggest"

He opens up a large blue file, takes out a printed sheet and hands it across to me.

"Now take a look at what I've suggested you do for your memory diary. As you'll see it's a little different from the way you usually record things"

By that he means that my style is just to write everything down in a haphazard way. The way I record things is to put them down as quickly as possible with a few bullet points if I want to record specific things like what someone wore, their mannerisms and personal details. Dr Silver has handed me a detailed sheet which looks a bit like a school timetable. It is broken down into times of day and there is a section at the end that has the heading 'My best three memories from today'. There is an exercise at the end which invites me to tell a story – or "creative narrative" as he puts it – which has to include all of my best memories from that day.

He leaves me to look at it for a few minutes while

he logs onto his computer to check his emails.

"I'm not sure what you mean about this narrative bit" I say when he returns to his chair. He gives me one of his twinkly eyed smiles.

"Ok. I need to show you something before I explain that bit"

He hands me what looks like a pack of cards.

"Take a look at these. There are nine cards with an image on each one. I want you to look at them for a minute and then I'll get you to list as many of the images that you can remember"

I stare hard at the cards. There's a hat, a jacket, a shoulder bag, a cell phone, an umbrella, a hard hat, a large paper bag, a wrapped up gift style parcel and a painting.

"Now if you hand me back the cards, just write on here what you can remember" He hands me a blank sheet of paper and a black marker pen.

As it is I can only recall about four of the items. He assures me that this is quite normal even in people without head injuries.

"Most people only retain only a tiny fraction of what they see every day" he says "and if I were to ask you to come up with the same list in half an hour you'll have forgotten most of it. That's true of the majority of people"

Well that's a relief I suppose. At least I'm normal in this respect.

"But I now want you to try something else. I'm now going to play you a story. I just need you to listen carefully"

He switches on his small desk top recorder and then turns around to face away from me. He says that he doesn't want to distract me while I listen.

"Are you ready? Ok here we go"

Dr Silver's distinctive east coast American voice resonates from the recorder.

The story goes like this.

"I'm heading out wearing my hat and my jacket. It's been raining so I have an umbrella and I'm holding my mobile phone. As I rush up the road I bump into a building worker. His hard hat and lunch paper bag fall to the floor. I say sorry and I'm a bit late when I arrive to meet my friend. It's her birthday so I hand her a wrapped gift package from my bag. She's been visiting an art gallery and shows me the painting she's bought."

I concentrate as I try to visualise the scene. Dr Silver turns back to face me and hands me another blank sheet of paper.

"Now do as you did before and write down the items mentioned in the story"

Astonishingly, this time I get all nine of them. Amazing.

Dr Silver laughs as he sees my reaction.

"Now that's what I mean about a narrative. If you include the items in a story it's much easier to remember them"

I'm quite impressed but still don't quite understand how this applies to me.

Dr Silver picks up the sample diary notes I gave him to read and explains what he wants me to do.

"Your diary gives a factual account of what you have done. But I now want you to decide each day what you'd like to remember the most – your favourite memories. See here? You say that when you first met your landlady Pauletta she was wearing a bright orange dress. I guess you must have thought this was worth remembering about her?"

I nod, trying not to get too distracted by Dr Silver's serious but gorgeous brown eyes.

"With this new system you would put the orange dress into a story form. Perhaps you could write that Pauletta wears orange because it is a lucky colour and it makes her feel happy. It doesn't matter that this is made up. It's just a device – like the tale I've just told – to get you to reinforce the memory of Pauletta's dress"

I think I understand now. It's all about stimulating the visual part of the brain to make more connections.

"And will this story practice help my short term memory?" I ask trying not to sound too naïve. I understand that things won't be that simple.

"Well, let's see how we get on with it. All you need to do at the end of each day is to pick out three of the memories you think are the most important. Then weave them into your own story of the day. Be as creative as you want" He leans over the desk to switch off the recorder.

"You'll also see that I've broken down each day into 2 hour chunks. It will help you focus your diary a bit better. Are you going to be ok with that?"

I don't have a problem with his diary suggestion and he says he'll email me the template so I can do everything online. I can see it's going to be a bit more work than I'm used to.

Dr Silver then adds that he has another suggestion but that I need to go home and think about it before making a decision.

"You see I'm doing a memory experiment which involves hypnosis and sometimes a small amount of a particular drug" He shifts across in his seat to grab hold of a document which he then hands to me.

"You can read all about it in this. I'm quite excited by the results I'm getting with some of my patients and when you've read it we'll discuss it some more"

I tell him that I associate hypnosis and memory drugs with sci-fi and spy novels. He laughs and tells me to make sure I read his paper before my next appointment.

It still comes as a surprise to walk out of an air conditioned building and into the hot Bermuda sun. It's feels a bit like somebody switching on a hairdryer at the highest heat level and blasting it towards you.

The meeting with Dr Silver has left me feeling upbeat and excited about the future. The experiment sounds fascinating if a little scary. But to be honest what have I got to lose?

Just as I'm deciding whether to go straight home or to head on into Hamilton, my cell phone rings. It's Tralee Josie who sounds a little out of breath.

"Hi JJ. Where are you?"

I explain that I'm in Point Finger road outside Dr Silver's house.

"Oh great, not far then. I'm down in Hamilton and I'm just off to meet Callum and Micky at Finnegans bar. This is a bit last minute but do you want to join us? Gives you a chance to meet Micky as well"

Well that's the decision made about what to do next. At least I am about to see Josie again and that's great. I'm not so much bothered about Callum and as for Micky well let's wait and see.

As I get on the bus I smile as I hear the song on the driver's radio. She is singing along in perfect pitch. It's Johnny Nash's "I Can See Clearly Now".

Somehow it seems so appropriate.

Chapter 5

Meeting Micky

Finnegans is one of those fashionable Irish bars, popular with tourists who like to order things like 'bangers and mash' and Paddy's filled potato skins. From street level it is approached by a steep stairwell and the inside is all dark wood and green velvet-like covered chairs. There are lots of picture posters on the walls with images of the 'old country' – tipsy cow herds being offered drinks by buxom milk maids and sepia photographs of Guinness barrels lined up in ramshackle warehouses. It is only 11.30am but the bar area is already packed and the noise is deafening.

At first I can't see any sign of Tralee Josie or Callum and I've no idea what Micky Doyle looks like. I scan the bar area trying to see behind a very tall guy who is standing in front of me who could easily be a basket ball player.

"JJ, over here!" I look in the direction of the voice and I see Josie waving across from a seat at the far end of the bar. It takes me a few minutes to push my way through the sea of tourists and waiters juggling giant plates of food. I manage to make it without getting covered in beer or gravy smothered potatoes

Josie and Callum have bagged a corner seat and shift across to make room as I approach. There's no sign of their friend Micky yet.

"Hi there!" Josie greets me warmly and gives me a hug. I smile back, genuinely pleased to see her. Callum gives me one of his half smiles before looking back towards the bar, presumably on the look out for Micky. Josie is dressed more formally today in a chocolate brown linen trouser suit and white silk blouse. She still looks glamorous and I notice that despite her height she's wearing very high heeled black patent peep toe shoes. Callum looks like the average tourist in a baggy T shirt and loose pair of shorts.

I sit down beside Josie and there is already a diet coke waiting for me.

"It's so crowded in here today" she says "Hope you don't mind but I got you a coke, same as you ordered yesterday. I'm on the soft stuff too as I've got to get back to work soon. Thought I'd grab an early lunch today to avoid the crowds – so much for wishful thinking!"

I'm touched that she remembers what drink I ordered yesterday. I tend to just pick any old soft drink out of the blue as long as it is the diet version. But this is fine. Callum then gesticulates towards the bar.

"Hey Micky - Micky. Over here mate!"

The first thing I notice about Micky is his tousled dark corkscrew mop of jet black curls. He looks as though he hasn't had a hair decent cut in ages. He's shorter than I expected with an angular solid sort of build. He has dark olive coloured skin and is good looking in a gypsy-ish sort of way. He's wearing baggy denim trousers and a cheese cloth white shirt. It's only when he gets close to our table that I spot the limp.

"Jeez it's busy in here today. Glad it's not my turn behind the bar" he says shuffling in to sit beside Callum. Our eyes lock for a few seconds and I can see him sizing me up. It's Josie who makes the introduction.

"Micky, this is JJ who we were talking to you about last night."

Micky reaches across to shake my hand.

"Hi JJ. Is that what you really like to be called? Sounds like a one of those expensive juice drinks we have behind the bar" His accent is light Dublin with the beginnings of a mid Atlantic twang.

He gives me a warm grin which takes the sting out of the remark. I meet his handshake and return the smile. I notice he has very pale green eyes which stand out against his dusky complexion.

"It's just a nickname that's stuck from school days" I reply trying to sound more flippant and casual than I feel. Micky takes a big sip from the glass of beer that is already waiting in front of him before turning his attention straight back to me.

"Not seen you in here before JJ" he says "is it your first time at Finnegans?"

It's a cheesy question but I realise he's just trying to break the ice. Already I can sense that he's a lot more sociable than Callum.

"Yes, I've only been on the island for a few of weeks" I reply glancing across at Josie. "This is a busy old place though, obviously popular."

Micky gives a wave across to one of the bar tenders and takes another large gulp of his beer.

"Yes, always full here" he says "That's Aussie Pete over there by the way, who's the best barman in the place. Apart from me that is" He laughs before looking over towards Josie.

"Jeez you look all dressed up today. Off to one of your bank meetings?"

I notice Josie blushing slightly before she flicks back her long hair. The hair flicking is a Tralee Josie habit I decide.

"Nah – just got a bigwig from London visiting. Thought I'd better make an effort"

Micky is now staring back at me. I'm wearing a sheer pink floral blouse and fitted white cotton trousers. I've tied my hair up into a loose ponytail and I think I'm looking pretty damn good.

"Well JJ you're not looking so bad either. Island life is obviously agreeing with you"

I can imagine him saying this to every girl in the bar but I manage another smile and say thanks for the compliment. His chat might be corny but he's friendly enough. So far Callum has hardly uttered a word.

We spend the next half hour or so talking about my trip to the island and what brought me here. Micky listens intently as I describe my accident and the on going side effects.

"Feck. And I thought I was the unlucky one" he says looking down at his left leg. He then rolls up his trouser leg to reveal a flesh coloured prosthetic lower leg. I try not to look shocked but my expression gives me away.

"Not a bad colour match eh?" He covers the leg up quickly in a gesture that shows he doesn't want anyone else in the bar to see it. Finally Callum opens his mouth.

"Listen to him – 'good colour match' - you sound like a hairdresser" He nudges Micky who laughs and signals to his friend behind the bar that it is time for more drinks. Josie tells him to leave her out of the round.

"Not for me, I've got to get back to work" She looks at her watch. "Listen I'd better get off now. What about you JJ?"

Micky insists that he buys me another drink and I agree reluctantly to stay for a while longer. The truth is I feel uncomfortable without Josie being there but Micky is fascinating and quite good company. He's clearly a popular guy as people keep coming over to say hello and I can't help noticing that most of them are attractive young women.

Callum decides to walk Josie back to work leaving me and Micky alone to carry on our conversation. It doesn't take long before we return to his moped accident and the weeks of gruelling medical treatment.

"Jeez I've never been in such pain in my life. I mean here I am with no lower leg but I'm still in agony and it feels like the thing is still attached"

I wince in sympathy. Micky is now on his second pint and clearly wants to talk more about it.

"The thing is JJ" he continues nodding across to yet another young woman who has just entered the bar "I'm lucky to be alive. It happened on a quiet road – the car that banged into me just sped off and

I was left unconscious for god knows how long. Whoever it was knew that they'd hit me, the callous bastards"

Normally I hate swearing but I can understand his anger. A couple of elderly women sitting across from us give Micky a look of disgust and turn away to look for another seat. There aren't any and they are forced to stay put.

"Feck. Think I've just upset those two old biddies" Micky says mimicking their outraged expression.

"I think you have" I say amused by his imitation of them "Best to keep the voice down a bit"

When Callum gets back I feel a bit disappointed. It is actually been quite good talking to Micky on his own and I'm definitely starting to like him.

"Is he boring you to death with talk about the bike accident?" Callum winks across at Micky who puts two fingers up to him. "Has he told you yet about his flirting with all the hospital nurses and nearly getting punched by one of their husbands?"

Micky laughs and makes a zip gesture across his mouth. I can imagine him chatting up the female medical staff and making them giggle with his corny bartender banter.

Changing the subject, Micky asks if I'll stay with them for some lunch. I'm not sure but then cannot resist his "Ah come on JJ. Give the food a try – the treat's on me"

"I can recommend the Monte Cristo" he says handing me the huge plastic menu. From what I can gather it's a sort of egg toast sandwich with ham, cheese and tomatoes. It turns out to be a good choice but the portions are huge and I can't finish it.

"He'll eat it the greedy fecker" Micky says, passing my plate over to Callum. I can see now why Callum is getting the start of a fat belly. If Josie was here she'd probably stop him but now he's wolfing down the other half of my sandwich.

Micky is keen to learn more about my "dodgy brain" as he calls it and I tell him about Dr Silver. For once Micky goes quiet and glances across at Callum. He's still busy demolishing my left over food but I can tell that he's also been listening intently.

Micky drags Callum into the conversation.

"Hey this is a fecking fascinating condition eh Callum? A girl with no memory of the day before. Now that's what you could call a gift to mankind. Fecking great"

I'm thrown by this tasteless comment but Micky laughs loudly enough for the two elderly ladies to give him another disapproving look.

Callum glances up and shrugs.

"Don't suppose you see it that way do you JJ? I think it must be a nightmare. Me? I like to remember what I got up to yesterday. All that keeping a diary stuff would drive me up the wall"

I'm touched and more than a bit surprised by his response. Perhaps Callum isn't that bad after all. He's a bit quiet but there is a more sensitive side lurking in there. Micky on the other hand is starting to get on my nerves with his tipsy talk of "gift to mankind." I decide it's a good time to leave.

Micky makes another attempt to get me to stay for a bit longer and as he puts it to "to have a proper fecking drink". When I say no, he throws up his hands in mock surrender and gestures across to a waiter for the bill.

Back outside in Front Street I opt to walk over to Marco's for a quiet coffee and to write all about the lunch in my diary. Marco isn't around so I'm left in peace to watch the world go by and scribble down my notes.

"June 3. Today met Micky Doyle – friend of Callum and Josie – at Finnegans bar. He's good looking with the most mesmerising green eyes. Told me all about his moped accident and showed me his false left leg – as you do! He's great fun and a bit of a flirt. I'm not totally sure about him though – didn't like his loaded quip about women who can't remember things from the day before. But he was getting a bit drunk so am I just being over sensitive? Callum came to my rescue by saying that it must be a 'nightmare'. It's not that bad but it was good of him to pull Micky up. I think I might actually get to like Callum. Will have to see how dinner at Josie's goes on June 5."

I take another look at Dr Silver's diary suggestion and start to jot down things in the time categories. I also make notes about what Josie and the guys were wearing and as much as I can recall about Micky's accident.

I'm deep in thought when some raised voices outside catch my attention. There are two young black teenage boys wearing baseball caps and low slung jeans standing across the road. Another older white man in a smart work suit is waiting nearby. He seems to be with the two lads but is keeping quiet. The younger guys have their backs to me and are gesticulating at someone in front of them who I can't quite make out. Realising that they are attracting attention, the older man says something along the lines of keeping their voices down. Then there are more angry gestures and I make out the words "do something about it". The man in the suit puts his hand up as if to say "enough" and the two younger ones turn to follow him down the street.

It's only when they move that I see who they've been yelling at.

And it's Micky Doyle.

Chapter 6

My other namesake

I awake with a start and despite the heat my skin feels clammy and cold. I lie still for a few minutes and listen to my heart pounding against my chest. My mind is filled with disconnected images and noise. Cars. Buses. Foot steps. I recall a warm gritty road surface against my skin. I remember ice cold needles going into my veins and there are lots of voices but I can't make out what they are saying. My hair feels wet but there is no rain.

Here we go again. I'm coming out of the same old dream, the only dream. The one which keeps returning and sending me back to the day of my accident. And yes, I've hung onto the details even if they are all jumbled up.

The Kisskadee birds are squawking loudly outside. And slowly my heart goes back to normal. I take in my bedroom with its dark cedar furniture, the pale lemon and beige floor tiles and the white window blinds closed but still letting in bright shafts of sunlight. I glance across at the framed photograph of a smiling mom and Jeff which is resting on the small chest of drawers at the side of my bed. I take several deep breaths to calm myself down before throwing open the blinds and downing a large glass of water.

I then go to check on my lap top computer diary. As I read it I can re-live the key moments of yesterday's visit to Finnegans and that strange sighting of Micky being yelled at by two young guys. I've filled in Dr Silver's section asking me to remember my three favourite memories of the day and to place them into a type of story. I see that my favourite memories are to do with Josie, Callum and Micky – a convenient trio.

Here's what I've written.

"Beauty queen Josie arrives at Finnegans wearing chocolate brown silk and teetering black patent heels. Think chocolate and liquorice combined. I hear the shiny black shoes click loudly as she walks across the room flicking her long dark hair. Callum, her fiancé, is all shorts and tee, a quiet tourist in the town. A red head treading gingerly. And their friend Micky's hair is a mass of tumbling corkscrew curls – think Marc Bolan meets a young David Essex. Micky has a dummy left leg and enemies on the street. Could the two be connected?"

The loose imagery is just an attempt to reinforce the memories and as I scan the lines I can see each of them vividly. The one which stands out most is of Micky standing just a few yards away from Marco's coffee shop. He's just staring into space and is perfectly still, like a freeze frame photo. My diary fills in the rest of the details.

I read that Micky stays there for a few moments and doesn't notice me staring out of Marco's shop window. He then makes his way, head bowed, up the street towards the bus station. I decide to order another coffee rather than follow him and make a comment that he looks preoccupied. Funny choice of word 'preoccupied' but it's the word I use.

With no appointments written down for today, I'm not sure what I'm going to do. I could spend some time on Elbow Beach but despite the heat it's pretty windy. Then I notice the yellow post-it note on my desk with my other Bermudian namesakes contact details written down. I see the name Josephine James, St George's and a telephone number.

I'm just mulling whether to give her a call when my cell phone goes off making me jump. It's mom ringing to check that I'm ok and eating properly.

"JJ promise me that you're looking after yourself – I do worry about you being there all on your own"

Poor mom. She'd still fret even if I was living next door to her.

"Yes mom. Everything is fine and I'm loving it here. My landlady keeps inviting me to her BBQs and tomorrow I'm going to Tralee Josie's house for a meal".

"Tralee Josie?" Mom sounds confused.

"Yes, you know. The Irish girl with the same name as me?"

"Oh yes. You mentioned meeting her. What's she like then?"

I spend the next few minutes describing Josie and Callum. I don't mention Micky Doyle for now, no need to.

Mom puts Jeff on the phone and he berates me again for not having Skype. He then starts telling me about his new girlfriend Sophie. Jeff's only 17 so meeting Sophie is a big happening in his life. He tells me he has been seeing her for three weeks and thinks this is the real deal.

"I'll send you a photo sis. You'll love her. I love her."

I smile, remembering my own first boyfriend Jack Mason. That's another memory that has remained intact and can be retrieved from my past memory bank. At the time I also thought that I was madly, insanely in love and that we would stay together forever. In the end it lasted all of three months and I experienced my first broken heart. I wonder what has happened to 'Jack the lad' as my dad used to call him?

After chatting to Jeff and reassuring my mom that I'm not about to starve to death or die of heat stroke, I take another look at the telephone contact for Josephine James in St George's. Is it a bit too soon to call her? After all, I've only just met Tralee Josie and Callum. And Micky of course.

But I'm curious to find out about this second namesake and so I start to dial her number. I'm surprised when she answers after just two rings.

"Helloo…?" Even after just one word I can hear that the voice is unmistakably Bermudian with a strong emphasis on the 'o' sound.

I'm momentarily stumped for words.

"Helloo…Helloo?" She is clearly perplexed by my silence. Better get talking or she'll put down the phone.

"Oh sorry" I say "You answered a bit quicker than I was expecting. I hope you don't mind me calling you but I've recently arrived in Bermuda from England. My name is Josie James - the same as yours" I can hear her take a quick intake of breath.

"What? You're also called Josie James? Are we related or something?"

I explain my new found 'hobby' which involves looking up my namesakes and I tell her that I've already met Tralee Josie. She is clearly interested and I give her a potted version of my reasons for being in Bermuda. I tell her that I'm here for medical treatment but I don't go into details. I can save that for later.

"Well, well" she says "this is a strange way to hear from someone but we should meet up. Can you get to St George's? Or I could meet you in Hamilton if you like?"

I say that I'm fine to travel on the bus and would welcome the opportunity to go back to St George's. I tell her it reminds me a bit of Devon or Cornwall in England.

"Well I've never been to that part of England" she replies "but I'd be happy to show you around my home patch. When shall we meet?"

We decide on June 6 at 12pm and I immediately make a big note of it. I tell her that I'll send over a photo and she says she'll do the same. We exchange email and cell phone numbers and I add that I'm looking forward to meeting her.

"Me too Josie – I mean JJ. I've got a lovely garden behind my studio so we can have a picnic. Is there anything you don't like to eat?"

I tell her I'm not fussy and that I'll bring something along as well.

"No need JJ. Just bring yourself. See you soon

then – ring me if there's a problem."

She sounds delightful and I love the languid Bermudian accent. I immediately get to writing down what I've just found out about her.

"Josephine James, born in Bermuda, aged 46. Lives on her own in St George's, husband died 5 years ago after a long illness. (Stomach cancer). Lived in New York, Greenwich Village, until the death of her husband – an American called Grant – and then moved back to Bermuda. Has one daughter, 22 year old Caroline, who is at college in Boston. Josephine is an artist who paints and makes her own jewellery. She lives in a small cottage with a basement studio and has lots of relatives living on the island. Her dad also lives in St George's. Has a small terrier dog called Mutt. Likes to be called Josephine rather than Josie."

When her photo arrives I see a broad smiling face with high cheek bones and soulful deep brown eyes. She is wearing a bright red blouse and has large dangly earrings – perhaps she has made these herself? Her hair is short and straight with a slight fringe at the front. She's a bit plump but not what you'd call fat. She's also sent a picture of a coarse haired greying Mutt who has a ball in his mouth and looks really cute. No pictures of her deceased husband or daughter Caroline but I'm sure I'll see those when we meet up.

I send across some photos of me as well as mom and Jeff. Then I notice that an email has popped into my in box from Tralee Josie.

"Hi JJ. Looking forward to having you over for dinner tomo evening. Micky is going to be a bit late – has to go and see someone after he finishes his bar shift. Will meet

you at Finnegans at 7pm. Just dress casually – we'll be in shorts and tees. Josie x"

Something has been bothering me about Micky Doyle ever since I saw him standing alone in the street yesterday. I get a fleeting visual flash and this time the look on his face is one of complete fear like a deer caught in a headlight.

The only time I've seen that look was when I came around from surgery after my accident. And it was on the face of my mom who'd been told I might die.

So no doubt about it. Micky is terrified.

But about what and why?

Chapter 7

And All that Jazz

June 5. It's been ringed in bold for days and I'm looking forward to seeing Josie and Callum's Hamilton apartment. I bet it's quite a swanky place, all wood floors and minimalist furniture. At least that's how I imagine it and it won't be long before I find out for real.

My biggest decision right now is what to wear. I know Josie said 'casual' but a bit of me still thinks you should make an effort for dinner. I finally decide on a halter neck floral maxi dress and I tie my hair up in a loose bun. I apply a little make up and choose a silver sparkly necklace with matching drop earrings. As I view my image in the full length mirror I feel quite pleased. As Micky Doyle might say, I'm not looking at all bad and I'm pleased that my new found tan is deepening by the day.

I decide to get a taxi down to Finnegans and my landlord Dave gives me a playful wolf whistle as I wait on the drive for it to arrive.

"Hey – you look great. Sure you don't you want me to tag along?"

I laugh and then spot the taxi making its way up the long steep driveway. Once inside I pretend to check my phone so that I don't have to make small talk to the driver. Seeing that I'm not in the mood for chatting he switches on the radio and hums along to some gospel tunes.

When we get to Finnegans I pay up quickly and check my reflection in a nearby shop window before climbing up the steep stairs to the bar. The place is packed out again but I can see Josie sitting at the bar talking away to Micky. No Callum this time.

Josie smiles and waves as I make my way across trying not to trip up on my long dress. Micky gives me a fixed stare as if he doesn't recognise me and I can tell by his eyes that he's impressed with what he sees.

Josie gives me one of her big hugs. "JJ you look stunning - love the dress. Doesn't she look drop dead gorgeous Micky?"

Micky nods approvingly and immediately offers to buy me a drink.

"None of that namby pamby soft stuff now – how about a nice glass of chilled wine?"

I compromise by having a small wine with some added soda water and lots of ice.

"There you go" Micky hands me the drink and winks. A group of raucous tourists yell across that they need to order another round. Micky rolls his eyes and tells us he'll be back soon.

Josie is wearing a tight pink T-shirt and cut off denim shorts. Even in casual dress she looks incredible and I notice a group of young guys gawping over in our direction.

"I think we're in luck there" Josie says deliberately nodding across to them "We might even get a few free drinks out of it".

I laugh nervously hoping that they don't try to join us. They all look worse for wear and are a bit on the young side. One of them looks as though he could still be in high school.

"I can't wait to see your place" I say keen to change the subject. "And where's Callum?"

"Finishing off the cooking" Josie replies "and I hope tidying up the place. He's a bit on the messy side so I've told him he's got to clear it up"

We then spend the next few minutes or so talking about Josie's bank job. I already know she's a PA to the manager and is busy organising a big charity ball which the bank hosts every year. This time they are planning to raise thousands of dollars for a children's charity in Bermuda.

"We're talking a huge amount of money" she says "There are some seriously rich people over here and I need to make sure they donate a good bit. It's a lot of hard work but worth it. Anyway why don't you come along as well? I can get you a free ticket if you like"

I promise I'll think about it but I'm already mentally coming up with an excuse not to go. Out of the corner of my eye I can see that Micky is busy juggling drinks for the big group of tourists. Josie's cell phone goes off and I offer to buy another round while she goes outside to answer it.

Pete, the barman who Micky pointed out the other day, notices that I'm waiting to be served. He has the archetypal surfer's look, all blond streaky hair and a killer Australian accent.

"Wotcha ordering babe?" he asks while pouring

a Guinness for another customer.

"A Pinot Grigio for Josie and just a diet coke for me" I reply blushing at the word 'babe'. While I like compliments I still find them embarrassing. In truth I don't really see myself as babe material. That's more Josie's territory.

The phone call seems to be taking a little while so I sit back and take a leisurely look at the Finnegans crowd. It's hard to know how many of them are on vacation but I guess quite a few. Most of those lined up at the bar are men wearing shorts and a blaze of brightly coloured shirts. Across the way there is a large gaggle of noisy women clutching cocktails and wearing the sort of clothes that look best in a nightclub. The group of young men who have been eyeing up Josie and me now spot that I'm on my own and I begin to feel uncomfortable. Still no sign of Josie but I see that Micky is on his way back over. Thank God for that.

"Hey JJ – you've been left all on your owny boney?"

Micky ducks back behind the bar and starts to line up beer glasses ready to be filled.

"Jeez that lot over there have been in all afternoon and they're still downing the pints. I'm surprised no-one's keeled over"

I wonder whether I should mention seeing him in the street the other day but decide against it.

"Josie says you're going to be coming over to hers later?" I say watching as he expertly fills each glass to the brim "You have to go somewhere else first though?"

For a moment I see a tiny flicker of anxiety in

Micky's eyes. At least that's what I think it is. But it doesn't last long enough to be sure.

"Yep, got to do some business after I finish here" he replies "but it shouldn't take long. Make sure you save me some scran – you know what that Callum is like".

"What's this you're saying about my Callum?" Josie is back and has just caught the mention of her finance's name.

"I'm saying he's a greedy fecker and to make sure you keep back some of that great chicken of yours for me"

"Don't worry Micky, there's enough to feed an army – that call was from Callum by the way" she says turning to me. "Sorry about the wait – he was just checking the cooking times for the veg. Then we got interrupted when his dad called from Ireland"

Josie's flat is nothing like I expect. She says it was only built five years ago but the inside has the feel of a much older property with lots of dark brown furniture. It has been done out with a seaside blue theme and can best be described as cosy or even homely. There are lots of family photographs scattered around and there is a strong smell of scented candles.

"This is lovely" I say trying not to sound too disappointed that it hasn't met up with my expectations. "I love the different shades of blue"

Josie crinkles her nose. "Mmm – if you say so. I'm not so sure myself but we're stuck with the decoration. I prefer more neutrals but after a while you don't notice"

Callum emerges from the small kitchen carrying

a large bowl of what look like small crackers.

"Hey JJ you look all dolled up for dinner. I hope you're not expecting silver service"

He smiles and gives me a friendly peck on the cheek. Coming from Callum, it takes me by surprise and I don't quite know how to react.

"Here grab hold of these and help yourself" He hands me the bowl while he and Josie head off into the kitchen to sort out some drinks.

I take the opportunity to look at some of the photographs. There is one of Josie lined up with the other Tralee pageant contestants. They are all in evening gowns and waving at the camera. There's another one of Josie wearing her graduation cap and gown standing alongside what looks like her proud mom and dad.

"Ah – that's me with the parents" Josie says handing me what she says is a "very weak" white wine spritzer.

"And this is my younger sister Marie". She passes me a small silver framed photograph to look at.

I see a mini version of Josie wearing a school uniform and grinning confidently at the camera. Marie looks as though she is going to be as stunning as her big sister and I tell Josie as much.

"Ach – she better not win the Tralee pageant if she goes in for it. Now that would be taking sibling rivalry way too far"

The smells coming from the kitchen are delicious and are beginning to drown out the scent from the candles. Callum says everything will be ready in half an hour and Josie suggests that we watch a

DVD of her engagement party and "maybe a just a little bit of the pageant"

I'm not a great fan of home movies but I'm fascinated to see what a large family Josie and Callum have on both sides. No point pretending that I'll remember all the names but they are good fun and on Josie's side at least, impossibly great looking. I've never set foot in Tralee but it looks a lively place especially during the annual pageant celebrations.

Josie's signature herby chicken dish is delicious and it reminds me of my mom's Sunday roast. Over dinner I tell them about my other namesake, Josephine James, from St George's.

"Wow – so you've contacted her as well" Josie says while helping herself to more chicken. "How does she sound?"

I tell them as much as I know about Josephine and that I'm due to meet her tomorrow afternoon.

"That's great. We'll all have to meet up and have a namesakes party" Josie smiles at the thought. "Fancy that – three Josie James' in Bermuda. Who'd have thought it?"

As it turns out, Callum is quite a jazz and blues music buff. Not just the modern versions but the old stuff too. I like that because I'm also a fan of this type of music. My dad introduced it to me from an early age and I grew up with Nina Simone and BB King singing away in the background. As I got older I tried to play this down with my friends who were more into hip hop and club dance tracks.

So it is good to have someone who has the same taste in music. Again music is one of those hard wired memories I've still got.

Nina Simone is now on in the background doing an amazing bluesy version of an old folk song. It shouldn't work but it does so beautifully. I notice that once you get Callum talking about his favourite music you can't shut him up. Josie pulls a face – she's not so keen on jazz and is more of a soul and reggae fan – and disappears into the kitchen to sort out dessert.

"Nina has a great voice doesn't she?" Callum says as he leans across to pick up a jazz box set of CDs. "I'll copy these for you if you like. Do you have a CD player at your place?"

As it is I don't but I have a good selection of music on my computer. Jeff sorted that out for me before I left for Bermuda. Callum says he'll get a computer version done for me and that we should check out some of the jazz and blues clubs in Bermuda.

Josie emerges from the kitchen with an enormous blueberry cheesecake.

"And before you ask – no I didn't make it myself. It's a supermarket's best"

The combination of wine spritzers, cheesecake and languid jazz music is making me feel quite tired. I glance furtively at my watch and realise it's already 11.30pm. If Micky wants to join us he's leaving things very late.

A few minutes later Josie also notices the time.

"Hey – it's getting late. Wonder where Micky is? Do you want to give him a call Callum and see where he is?"

Callum shrugs and picks up his cell phone. "He's

probably still chatting up some girls at Finnegans knowing him"

After letting Micky's number ring for a few seconds it goes into answer mode.

"Hey Micky – where the hell are you? Get your arse over here quickly or I'll be eating the rest of the dinner" He laughs as he puts the phone down and Josie decides to put on some "more cheerful" music as she puts it. The jazz compilation is replaced by Bob Marley.

"Would you like some coffee JJ? I have some good stuff or you can just have instant if you prefer"

I tell Josie I'm happy with instant and offer to help her with the washing up.

"Not at all" she says "it'll go straight into the dish washer. Bit more upbeat this music isn't it?" She disappears into the kitchen singing "No Woman No Cry" while Callum puts the jazz CD back carefully into its allotted place. Certainly, as far as his music collection is concerned, he's a neat freak.

Josie comes back with two steaming mugs of coffee while Callum decides that he's sticking to the wine and pours himself another large glass of red. I almost spill my coffee when the door buzzer chimes loudly.

"That'll be Micky" Callum says and jumps up to press the speaker buzzer in the hallway. There's a muffled sound before Callum goes to answer the front door.

There are more muffled voices and then Callum walks in accompanied by Pete, the Aussie barman from Finnegans.

"Hiya – bet you didn't expect to see my ugly

mug again this evening" he says running a hand across his hair. "It's blowing a bloody gale out there"

It seems that Micky left Finnegans early around 10pm. Pete says he's been trying to get hold of him on his cell phone to let him know that he's got an afternoon shift tomorrow.

"Thought I'd just drop by to make sure he's got the message. So how come he's not here yet?"

Callum tries Micky's number again but this time doesn't bother to leave a message.

Josie offers Pete a coffee "or something stronger" but he declines and says that he's heading straight back into town for a hot date.

"If Micky does show up, can you tell him that he's on the 2-10pm shift tomorrow?"

It's now 12.30am and I'm really beginning to flag. Josie orders a taxi and I spend the journey back jotting down as many details as I can about this evening.

When I get back to my room I find it difficult to drift off to sleep even though I feel dog tired. So I put on some Nina Simone and concentrate on filling out Dr Silver's memory form. On the section about my three main memories of the day, I start to create a story word association around Micky Doyle's absence.

"Micky is missing. He's missing a leg and tonight he's nowhere to be found. Perhaps Micky has met a young 'miss' - a good excuse for missing dinner?"

When I read this jokey entry the following day, my blood runs cold. A worried Josie has just rung me to say that Micky really is missing. He hasn't

turned up to work and no-one has seen him since he left Finnegans last night.

And to cap it all she is about to contact the police.

Chapter 8

St George's Josephine

After I've finished talking to Josie on the phone, I re-read all my diary entries about Micky. Should I tell her about seeing the guys in the street threatening him? Just re-reading it has brought the scene back to life, although the main thing I still recall is the look on Micky's face. I can't really remember what the two young guys or the older man look like but I have written down what they were wearing.

No, it's probably best to keep this to myself for now. Micky is likely to turn up in a few hours and will be wondering what all the fuss is about. Besides today is the day I'm going to meet Josephine James over at St George's. That's more than enough to be thinking about without getting bogged down in Micky's business.

The journey to St George's involves going into Hamilton first and then getting another bus from the main terminal. The St George's bus isn't too full today as most of the tourists have set off earlier. I sit back and admire the stunning scenery and smile as two elderly local men put the world to rights.

"The island is going to the dogs man. Years ago

we never had a murder and so far we've had several shootings" one of them gripes making a disapproving sucking noise through his teeth.

His companion agrees shaking his head.

"Ooh yes you're soo right. This used to be a paradise island but these gangsters are just ruining it for everybody" They both start running through the punishments they think people should get for carrying out crimes. Apparently the island's prison is far too good for them and they should be put to hard labour with just a minimum ration of bread and water.

I smile as I contrast their comments with the passing scenes of glorious little coral sandy bays, gently swishing palm trees and garden hedges with their white and red flowers dotted throughout. Whatever the old boys think, this really is paradise. They should try living in parts of London when the rain is lashing down and the sky is the colour of dirty dish water.

Josephine is waiting as arranged at the bus stop is St George's. She looks much slimmer in the flesh and is squinting out beneath a large yellow floppy sun hat which matches her polka dot dress.

She approaches me with a shy smile and an outstretched hand.

"JJ – so good to meet you. How was the journey?"

We shake hands a little awkwardly and I tell her that it has to be one of the world's most stunning bus drives. She laughs and says that she's visited most of the Caribbean islands but thinks Bermuda is far prettier.

"I know we're not in the Caribbean but we're their soul mates and we're the best soul mate believe me" she adds before pointing across the road to a small café which looks just like a Cornish tea shop.

"Tell you what JJ. Let's go to Lena's over there for a drink and a chat first. You're thirsty I guess?"

I did take some bottled water on the journey but I do fancy a cup of old fashioned English tea. And Lenny's doesn't disappoint.

My latest namesake is less extrovert than Tralee Josie but still easy to talk to and I could listen to her voice all day. It is a mix of Bermudian with the occasional dash of New York. And her face is one of the most expressive I have ever seen. Every word is emphasised with a widening of the eyes or a variety of smiles ranging from the coy to a full on beam. It's mesmerising to watch and every so often I have to remind myself to pay attention to what she's saying.

Right from the off she wants to talk about me. And she's especially interested about why I'm so fixated with my namesakes and how many others I have contacted over the years. For a moment I'm thrown because I've only met one other and she only lives a few miles across the island.

I decide that my 'get out' is the dodgy head.

"Actually I have to tell you something" I say before going through the story of my accident. She then bombards me with so many questions that the one about my circle of namesakes is forgotten for now. When she does pick up on it later on, I simply tell her that I've got no memory of the Josie James' I've met on previous holidays. Phew.

I do tell her about Tralee Josie and Callum and I also mention Micky Doyle. But she's much more absorbed by my brain condition and suggests that art therapy might help.

"You should think about it JJ. If this Dr Silver is saying that a story or word association can help then drawing pictures could as well. I mean you have got a design background"

It's not a bad idea but the truth is I'm more comfortable with computer graphics rather than pencils or paint. I never did enjoy drawing at art school.

"You might have more of a talent than you think" Josephine says "Tell you what. Let's pay up here and I'll show you around my studio"

Josephine's cottage is tucked away down a narrow side street and looks tiny from the outside. But inside it is spacious and airy with a surprising amount of light. Yellow seems to be her favourite colour and there are swathes of it everywhere. Cushions, throws, blinds, covers – all various shades of yellow or lemon blending with the whitewashed walls.

Mutt, the scruffy border terrier, bounds over to meet us and then starts jumping up at me like a mad thing. He's cute but Josephine decides that it is better for him to be in the garden while she's showing me around the house, so scoops him up and takes him outside. He looks back at me with hang dog eyes as if to say "see you later".

There are only a few photographs but lots of wall art – mostly modern – and what look like a couple of real bronze statuettes. And the room smells of freshly cut flowers with several vases scattered around. The place exudes happiness and tranquillity, just like Josephine.

Her studio is approached by a small stairwell heading down into the basement of the cottage. Josephine points out that she has replaced the original old cedar wood door, leading out into the small garden, with a full length sliding glass one. The effect is stunning with the studio bathed in sunlight and the glass doorway creating a seamless blend into the floral garden. So now I know where all those fresh flowers have come from.

The studio itself is cluttered from floor to ceiling with a treasure trove of coloured beads, sequins, threads and various loops of silver and gold wires – all the paraphernalia of jewellery making. There is a large tray of finished items, stacks of earrings, necklaces and bracelets which are twinkling in the shafts of bright sunshine.

Josephine picks up a turquoise bracelet.

"Try this JJ. I think it will suit your colouring."

It's an exquisite mix of shiny and opaque beads and fits me perfectly. I love it.

"You can have that one" she says brushing aside my offer to pay. "Think of it as a namesake present"

I thank her for being so generous and she then shows me some of her favourite work. Her pieces are beautifully crafted and the colours are vivid.

"I've just provided a selection for a Bermuda Style magazine photo shoot" she says holding up a striking pink and gold long necklace twist "and the response has been fantastic. I've got to make another thirty of these"

I make a mental note to buy mom one of Josephine's necklaces and maybe a little something for my landlady Pauletta. Meantime Josephine slides open the glass doorway and heads into the garden. Mutt is snoozing on a makeshift mat and opens one eye. Josephine tells him to "stay, stay" and he does what he's told.

The scent is simply glorious and immediately takes me back to my teens when I had a Saturday job helping out at a little flower shop just off Islington high street. Only this time the perfume smells are infused with a deep heat which gives them a much headier aroma.

"Hmm" I enthuse sniffing the air. "Smells divine"

I learn that her favourite flowers are Frangipani and Lilies and get a quick lesson in the plants of Bermuda. I joke that I'll never remember it all and she suddenly looks concerned.

"You should really take up my suggestion of painting you know" she says patting my arm "I'm sure it would help you to remember more things"

Josephine has laid out a small table with napkins and cutlery. There is a large cool box at the side and she opens the lid taking out several foil covered plates.

"I hope you're hungry JJ"

It's just as well that I am. We start off with fresh prawns with a lime mayonnaise dip followed by thick cut slices of ham, mango salsa salad and crusty bread. There is home made ginger ale and elder flower cordial. She doesn't drink alcohol which suits me fine.

While we eat I ask Josephine about her family. She tells me all about her husband's long term illness saying that death was a blessing in the end because he was in so much pain. She came back to Bermuda to be close to her elderly father, Clarence, who lives just around the corner. He is off on a trip to the Botanical Gardens today but Josephine insists that I should meet him soon.

Caroline, Josephine's daughter, is studying sciences at University in Boston and Josephine hands me a photograph of her. She is a younger version of her mom and has the same high cheek bones and smile.

"She's a mini you Josephine – looks just like her mom."

Josephine smiles at the comparison but says that personality wise they are nothing alike.

"I'm the typical scatty artist and she's just like her dad was – methodical and logical. That's why she's doing sciences. She tries to explain it all to me but it just goes in one ear and out the other"

"I've always been rubbish at science too" I say noticing that Mutt is making his way sheepishly across the garden. He plonks himself between myself and Josephine and she gives him a small sliver of ham which he scoffs down greedily.

"I'll have to take him for a walk later. He's getting on a bit now but still loves his daily walks, don't you Mutt?" He wags his tail and sits up expectantly on the mention of the word 'walk'.

"No not now stupid. It's far too hot" Josephine wags her finger jokingly at him and throws him another piece of ham which he manages to catch in mid air.

Josephine clears away the plates while I stroke Mutt and admire the garden view. It really has to be the most peaceful place I've ever been.

Afterwards Josephine suggests that she shows me the sights of St George's from a local's perspective and hands over a white umbrella to protect me from the heat. When I first got to Bermuda I was taken aback to see people walking around with umbrellas in the blazing sun but now I can understand why.

Josephine is a mine of information about the history of the place and I can see that I'm going to be making copious notes later on. She shows me the tiny graveyard where the slaves were buried – even in death they were not allowed to be placed alongside their masters. It seems hard to believe that slavery thrived for so long on this tiny Island and the graves are a poignant reminder of this shameful period of history.

As we walk around, we are constantly approached by people saying hello to Josephine or waving across. Josephine is one popular lady and I can see why.

The afternoon flies by too quickly and before I know Josephine is waving me off on the bus reminding me that "we must meet up again soon". I'm juggling a large wrapped piece of her home made orange cake and a box set of mixed coloured paints and pencils which she has insisted that I take.

I reach deep into my bag to get out my diary to start making some notes when I notice that my phone is flashing that there is a message waiting. It's

Tralee Josie again and she sounds even more concerned than she did earlier.

"Hi JJ. Just thought I'd call to see whether you're back home. Hope you've had a good day. Me and Callum are worried sick about Micky. There's still no sign of him and it's unlike him not to call. Give me a bell when you get back – catch up later"

It's now 8pm and Micky has been missing for nearly 24 hours. I decide that I'll tell Josie about the guys making threats to him in the street as soon as I get back.

The news that Micky still hasn't turned up distracts me and I decide to leave off taking notes for now. Instead I look inside the box of paints and pencils. I see that there are some small sheets of paper inside and I take out a few of these and choose a charcoal grey pencil.

Slowly I begin to draw a street scene. There are two young men and an older guy watching on. I close my eyes and try to recall their faces. But there is nothing. Then just as I'm about to give up I get a fleeting image of something. It's only vague at first but when I concentrate even more I can see it is a snake tattoo running up the left hand side of one of the young men's necks. I begin to draw it and become fixated with recalling the detail. So I'm startled when a middle aged man sits down heavily beside me.

"My that's good" he says looking across at what I've been drawing. "Love the snake. But why have you drawn him with no face?"

A good question which I can't even start to answer. Instead I smile at him and stop my drawing in exchange for Bermuda small talk. Much easier than trying to tell the truth. Whatever that is.

Chapter 9

Snakes and ladders

I get straight on the phone to Tralee Josie after I arrive home. She answers quickly and immediately starts to tell me about her attempts to find out what has happened to Micky.

"Me and Callum have asked around all his friends but nobody has heard a thing. The police want to wait for a bit in case he's just gone off with somebody and wants to keep a low profile. But I've told them it's not like Micky."

I bite my lip before telling her about what I saw in the street the other day. She goes quiet for a minute.

"Why didn't you mention this before JJ?" she says sounding more than a bit put out.

I decide to fall yet again on the excuse of the poorly brain.

"To be honest Josie I forgot. I mean I wrote it in the diary but didn't really look at it again until you rang last night. Then I remembered"

"Of course, stupid me" she replies and I imagine her face reddening in the background. "I'm so sorry that was really insensitive of me"

Josie thinks that she should let the police know straight away and asks me if I'd mind talking to them. I say that I'd be more than happy to help as long as they see me as a reliable witness.

"Tell you what JJ, let's leave it until tomorrow as it's getting late now. I just hope Micky's ok. His mom in Dublin was worried sick when I rang her earlier"

To take her mind off Micky, I tell her about my meeting with Josephine today. It does the trick and she is keen to hear more. Going through the day is a useful refresher for me and will make writing up my notes easier.

When I finish the phone call I decide to put away the art boxed set and stumble on the article that Dr Silver gave me to read. Just as well as I'm due to see him again in a couple of days and he wants to discuss me taking part in his 'interesting experiment' as he calls it.

It makes for a fascinating read and I take a note of the main points. In a nutshell, he is combining hypnosis sessions along with a small amount of a drug – I can't even begin to pronounce the name of it - to see if he can get people with short term memory problems to recall events in greater detail.

There is a case story about a young man called 'Rudy' which isn't his real name apparently. He has similar brain injuries to me but has got problems with his longer term memory too. According to the article, written for a professional journal, Rudy has very little memory of his life before his car accident. He doesn't recognise his parents or his new wife. He also can't remember what he has done the previous day so his short term memory is shot to pieces as well. Poor guy – he sounds in a far worse way than me. Anyway, with the permission of Rudy and his family, Dr Silver has been using hypnosis and the drug to see if he can salvage anything from his long term and shorter term memories. And according to the article there are signs of improvement. Rudy has started to get the odd flash back memory from his childhood and on occasions has remembered events from the day before – things like what he had to eat and who he met and all this without the aid of a diary.

After reading the article twice I'm left thinking why not? If I can help in any way it can only be a good thing. So I decide to tell Dr Silver that I'd like to take part. I'll also show him a copy of my snake visual memory drawing as I think he'll be interested.

It's gone midnight by the time I get to bed and the tree frogs are particularly noisy tonight – a sure sign that the weather is hotting up. As I close my eyes I try to conjure up the street scene with Micky again. This time I can't recall any details of the snake image as hard as I try. I'm also unable to see Micky's facial expression any more and the whole scene is just vague and blurry, like a photograph that has been soaked in water.

When I wake up the following morning the room is stuffy and hot as I forgot to put on the ceiling fan last night. I throw open the window to let in some air and realise that there are two strong images in my mind. The first is the snake image and I can visualise myself drawing it on the bus. Then I have a strong mental picture of a beautiful scented floral garden and I'm sitting on the grass feeling happy and serene. I can't work this one out until I read my diary and I realise that it is Josephine James's garden in St George's. These images are something to tell Dr Silver about when I next see him and I put an additional note on the new diary form he has given me.

I'm beginning to realise just how much extra work Dr Silver's diary format is giving me. Not only do I have to record detailed times of day but I have to keep making up that story around my three strongest memories. I don't find this bit easy especially as I usually do most of my notes at the end of the day before going to bed. Take yesterday's memory 'narrative' tale – this is what I've written.

"Josephine James – beautiful Bermudian who loves yellow. Yellow and mellow are the words I associate with her. She makes jewels with the colours of Bermuda – coral pink and turquoise. Her garden is perfumed and peaceful. Her dog is a real Mutt in name and personality. So today's links are yellow, mellow, pink, turquoise, scented flowers and a cheeky chappy dog."

When I read this back it sort of makes sense and it does stimulate my visual memories of yesterday and the smells from the garden. But I'm not sure if I'm writing in enough detail. Nor am I convinced that a creating word association story around my strongest memories of the day is any better than my old straight forward way of recording things. Still it's early days yet and Dr Silver is a world renowned brain expert, so he should know.

I take out my art box and look again at the snake

image I began to draw yesterday. I now have a few more details to add. Today I show that the snake has its mouth open and a long forked tongue flicks out. The edge of the tongue meets the top of the young man's jaw line with the snake head leaning into the centre of his neck. It looks like some sort of grotesque necklace. I make another attempt to conjure up his facial features but still there is nothing.

My computer pings to show that I have a new email. It is from St George's Josephine as I'm now calling her. There is a picture attached of me sitting in her garden with Mutt at my side.

"Morning JJ. Hope you had a good journey back. I really enjoyed meeting you yesterday and I'm looking forward to seeing you again soon. I took this photo of you in the garden with Mutt as you looked so happy – hope you like it! And do take my advice about doing some painting and drawing. Once an artist always an artist and I'm sure you'll find it therapeutic. Anyway, catch up soon and have a great day. Josephine"

The photo is lovely and I'll print it off and buy a frame for it later. I reply straight away thanking her for the photo and tell her that I'm wearing her gorgeous blue bracelet which matches the colour of the sea view from my window. I also thank her for the art box set and reassure her that I have already started to use it. As I press the email send button I hear Pauletta calling me from the yard below my window.

"Josie, Josie – can you hear me?"

I walk out onto the balcony squinting hard against the bright sunlight.

"Morning Pauletta. Everything ok?"

She's holding a small cream coloured envelope in one hand and is balancing a large white plastic wrapped parcel under her other arm. Her face is red from the heat and the effort of holding on to the unwieldy package.

"I have a letter for you" she says holding up the envelope. "It looks like it is from England. Can you come down and get it? Only I need to put this heavy thing indoors before my arm falls off"

The letter is from England for sure and I recognise the untidy spidery hand writing straight away. It is yet another of my past surviving memories and belongs to my old boyfriend Tim who I last saw in the brain rehab centre. He hasn't been in touch until now, although I have a note in my diary saying that he has phoned my mom a few times asking about me. So mom must have passed on my Bermuda address. I'm reluctant to open the letter and decide to leave it on one side for now.

A few hours later I find myself browsing inside a Hamilton general store for a suitable frame to house Josephine's photograph, when my cell phone rings out. It's Tralee Josie who sounds excited and out of breath.

"JJ – just got a call from Callum and guess what? Micky has turned up. Isn't that grand news?"

It takes me a few seconds to digest the information.

"JJ? You still there?"

"Yes" I reply as the news begins to hit home. "That's great. Where has he been?"

It's Josie's turn to pause for a moment. It sounds

as though she is at work and someone has just interrupted her.

"Listen JJ got to go. Will get back later when I know a bit more" And with that the phone goes dead.

"Can I assist you with anything?" a helpful shop assistant asks giving me her best sales person on commission smile.

"Just looking" I reply briskly "Thanks though"

Then I notice that my phone light is flashing that there's a text waiting. This time it's a message from Callum.

"Hi JJ. With Micky now. Great that he's safe and well. He needs to have a chat with you as soon as. Are you up for tonight?"

So it looks like I'm already fixed for tonight then. On a not so hot date with Micky.

Chapter 10

A favour for Micky

Tim's letter is sitting on my dressing table unopened. I've got an hour before I have to meet Micky and Callum in town. Micky doesn't want to go to Finnegans, so we've arranged to meet at the Hoggy Poggy, an English style pub just off the main Front Street. Hopefully it will be a bit quieter than Finnegans because according to Callum, Micky wants to chat about "something important". It all sounds a bit mysterious but it won't be long before I'm more in the picture.

And so to Tim's letter. I suppose I'd better open it and see what he has to say. It might sound strange but I have not really thought much about him recently. It's not just about being in a foreign country either – when I told him not to visit me again at the rehab centre, it was as if I was wiping away his presence in my life. Considering we were talking about living together before my accident, I'm surprised how easy it is has been to shut him off.

I tear open the envelope. There is only one page inside which I'm pleased about. He has handwritten the letter so is going for the personal touch.

Hey JJ,

Hope you are settling in Bermuda. I've been reading up on the Island and it sounds beautiful. I hope you don't mind me writing but I didn't want to just send an email.

I hear from your mom that you are seeing a brain doctor over there. Sounds a good move and I'm sure you're in capable hands.

Now for the real reason I'm writing. I just want to say how sorry I am for not being more understanding after your accident. It's just that I'm not great around hospitals and I couldn't cope with you not being able to remember things. It was as if you were turning into a different person and not the outgoing feisty JJ I knew and loved.

If that sounds selfish then I apologise but I'm just trying to be honest. Perhaps it was all for the best because I don't think we were ever sure enough about moving in together.

I also just want to let you know that I've met somebody else and we're going to get married. I know it's all happened very quickly but we're sure of each other and Denny – that's her name – is four months pregnant. So I'm going to be a daddy as well which is awesome. Suddenly I feel all grown up.

Anyway, I hope we can stay in touch and still remain friends. It would be great to speak to you again or we can email if you prefer.

I hope everything works out for you JJ and that you meet someone who suits you much better than I did.

All the best and thinking about you,

Tim x

I re-read the letter a couple of times trying to digest the staggering news of him getting married and about to become a dad. My emotions range from anger at his comments about not being able to cope with the new me – well tough matey, I'm the one with the injured brain and the problem – to shock that he could just jump straight into a new relationship. And as for getting married and becoming a dad, I can't imagine Tim being sorted enough to be good at either.

I make my mind up that I don't want to keep in touch and I'll reply to him saying as much. We were just not meant to be a couple and now I can see why we didn't move in together. Even without my injury, things wouldn't have worked out in the long run. I scrunch up the letter and throw it in the wastepaper bin where it belongs.

Meeting with Micky and Callum takes my mind off the letter. The Hoggy Poggy pub resembles an old style east London drinking den without the sticky carpet and smell of spilt beer. There is dark wood everywhere with a sit down restaurant at the front and the bar stretching along the back. When I arrive Micky and Callum are sitting in the far corner of the bar and are chatting animatedly. I already know that Josie is working late so won't be turning up.

Micky sees me first and raises his hand in a half hearted 'hi' gesture. Callum turns around and immediately gives up his bar stool. I'm dressed casually tonight in T- shirt and jeans. Micky and Callum are in their usual loose shirts and shorts. Micky looks tired and is sporting a nasty looking scratch at the side of his left eye.

"Evening JJ" he says sheepishly as I sit down on the bar stool next him. Callum goes to look for another stool and Micky asks me what I'd like to drink. I have my usual diet coke and this time he orders it without any of his sarcastic banter. He looks a bit subdued and has lost his cheeky swagger - this isn't the same Micky I met and wrote about just a few days ago.

"I expect you'll want to know where I've been?" he asks after ordering my drink.

"Everyone was worried about you" I reply. "Josie even rang the police"

Micky winces at the mention of police and touches the scratch above his eye.

"Got this during my little frigging adventure but it looks worse than it is"

Callum arrives back with a spare stool and pulls it up alongside us.

"This one gave us all a fright didn't he JJ?" he says putting his hand on Micky's shoulder in a reassuring way. "Still at least he's back now and as pug ugly as ever"

Micky doesn't rise to the bait and clears his throat before speaking.

"Look JJ I'll cut to the chase" he says "I'm in a shit load of trouble and that's putting it in the nicest way"

I look around instinctively to see if anyone at the bar has picked up on Micky's swearing. The middle aged group just behind us are too preoccupied with the drinks menu to notice.

"What sort of trouble?" I ask lowering my voice.

"Well let's put it like this - enough for me to have been snatched for the past couple of days"

"Snatched?"

"Yeh, or kidnapped more like. Bastards"

Callum spots a table being vacated and he dives across to claim it. Micky and me follow and I notice a few people looking across at his uneven gait.

Micky spends the next twenty minutes telling me about what happened to him. It seems like something out of a Tarantino film but I can see that Micky is still frightened by what has happened. He tells me that after he finished his shift at Finnegans, he was on his way to meet a friend when he was bundled into a car "a sort of small dark hatchback". He was then driven out to what he describes as some sort of disused workshop or garage which smelt strongly of petrol. He couldn't see where he was going because he had a scarf wrapped tightly across his eyes but guessed the drive took about 40 minutes.

He thinks there were three men and he thought he recognised one of the voices but couldn't be sure. Once at the workshop, he was left on his own with his hands tied behind his back and told that if he made an effort to move or take off the blindfold, then he'd be attacked by their guard dog. He knew the dog was for real because he could hear it panting and pacing around in the background.

After what seemed like hours the men returned. He was untied, given some water to drink and allowed to go to the toilet. When he tried to push down the side of the scarf to get a glimpse of where he was, one of the men lashed out. That explains the deep scratch on the side of the eye.

I can barely believe what I'm hearing. Here I am sitting in a tourist packed pub in Bermuda with attentive waiters serving meals and exchanging pleasantries with diners. There is laughter, joy and excitement about being on vacation. Then there is Micky's tale of kidnap and terror.

"So who are these people and why did they pick on you?" I ask glancing across at Callum who is staring vacantly into his pint of beer.

Micky pauses for a few seconds as if he is reluctant to say anything.

"You'll have to put JJ in the picture if our plan is to work" Callum says looking up at us both. Micky moves his bar stool closer to mine.

"Ok JJ. I've got to trust you on this one right? You've not to tell anyone or even write anything down in that diary of yours. Can you promise me that?"

I nod and get this surreal feeling that I'm back in the hospital and this is all part of some weird post injury dream.

Micky dips his voice and glances across to the next table to check that nobody is listening. The young couple dining are too engrossed in their meal and chat to even notice us. They look like besotted honeymooners with no interest in anyone else.

"I'm being chased by some gang members here – the P Crew – who are one of the biggest gangs on the island. They want $250,000 from me which I haven't got"

My eyes widen at the figure mentioned. Quarter of a million dollars is a hell of a lot of money for anyone, let alone Micky whose only income is from bartending.

"But why do they want that sort of money from you? You only work in a bar and you can't be making that much."

Micky takes a quick swig of beer looking around again to see if anyone is listening. The honeymoon couple are sharing a dessert and still oblivious to the goings on around them.

"A few months ago before my accident I got to know one of the P Crew – a guy called Wes. Nice guy – or so I thought – and always smartly turned out. Then, out of the blue, he offered me a well paid job. All I had to do was pass over a parcel once a week to one of his 'associates'. He said it was high end American clothing and the associate wanted to avoid paying duty on it. I got $200 a time and his associate would turn up to collect the package from me at the little alleyway just up from Finnegans"

"And was it really high end clothing?" I ask.

"Never looked inside it. It felt like clothing – all squishy and padded – but at $200 a time I wasn't bothered"

"Ok but what has it got to do with this $250,000 they are asking from you?"

"It was all going great until one night an outbuilding behind Finnegans was burgled. I'd stashed the parcel in there so I could pass it over the following morning like I usually did. The associate would always turn up when I was on my way to work. I'd grab hold of my parcel and then walk down to meet him. Later I'd get my 'tip' from Wes"

Micky is momentarily distracted as the honeymoon couple get up to leave. Once they've gone he continues, still in a hushed voice.

"Anyway, this day I get into work and the outbuilding has been broken into. And my fecking parcel is missing. The police are all over the place like a rash but I can't tell them anything about the package"

Micky then tells me how Wes quickly turned from Mr nice guy to Mr not-so-nice.

He didn't believe that Micky hadn't stolen the parcel and demanded to know what he'd done with it. Micky says it was only then that he realised the 'high end clothing' was something much more valuable. And it explained why the police sniffer dog kept going back to the place where he had stored it. But nothing was found and there was no proof.

"I must have been stupid not to realise it was drugs but the guy seemed genuine enough and the money came in handy. I wish to God I hadn't ever taken it but can't turn round the fecking clock now"

I feel sorry for Micky and a bit taken aback that he could be so naïve. Callum is still staring into his beer, deep in thought.

"Are you going to tell the police?" I ask, knowing that this is unlikely.

"Feck no" Micky replies "that's the last thing I want to do. When they finally dumped me back in Hamilton this afternoon they made it clear what would happen if I involve anyone else. You don't mess with this lot. They are the ones who forced me off the road"

"What – you are kidding me yes?" This is getting worse by the minute.

"No I'm not. It's what they told me when I was stuck in that hell hole for nearly two whole days. And it makes sense. The accident happened just a few days after the parcel went missing"

"But that's pure evil" I say staring across at Callum for back up. He doesn't look me in the eye and flips over his beer mat distractedly.

Micky laughs but it's that scared nervous sort of laugh which usually comes before you do something frightening.

"Yeh well these are evil bastards JJ and you don't want to get on the wrong side of them believe me"

"But you're already on the wrong side of them" I say glaring across at Callum who is now flicking the beer mat over and over. He notices my irritation and stops.

"Yes and that's why I've asked you here tonight JJ. There might be a way you can help. Me and Cal have been talking it through all afternoon"

"Me? But how?" I am beginning to believe that this really is a weird side effect of my brain injury and I'll wake up any minute to find myself back in the hospital or brain rehab centre.

As it is, I'm about to hear how they'd like me to help.

And it means keeping a big secret from my new friend and namesake Tralee Josie.

Chapter 11

A Man With A Plan

After I get home I'm at a loss what to do. Micky has made me swear that I won't write anything down about this evening but how am I supposed to remember what we discussed if I don't? And having re-read my previous diary notes on Micky, I also realise that I didn't say a thing this evening about spotting him in the street with the young guy sporting the snake tattoo.

Just before I left them at Hoggy Poggy, Micky had reassured me that he and Callum will go back over everything when we meet up again tomorrow. I've got an appointment with Dr Silver first and then afterwards I'm due to meet them in Hamilton's Par La Ville park. At least that bit I'm allowed to record.

I'm tempted to have done with it and just write it all down anyway. But then a promise is a promise. So I just jot down "discussed plan" in the hope that it will somehow jog my memory tomorrow. I keep this brief note separate from Dr Silver's detailed diary page, so that he doesn't start quizzing me about what it means.

When I get into bed, I start to go over what I've

been asked to do while the details are still intact. Micky kept telling me this evening that I'd be doing him a huge favour and it would help to get the P Crew gang leader, Wes, off his back.

It seems that Tralee Josie's employer keeps a separate charity account with another bank and she is one of people who can sign the cheques, pay in and withdraw money. She doesn't go in there very often, so the staff don't recognise her as a regular customer.

Micky says he wants me to go into this bank as Josie James – it's only a 'white lie' he says because that's my real name anyway – and to put some money into the charity account from him. He says he is trying to get some sort of down payment together for the P Crew to get them off his back. By putting it into the charity account, it means he won't be able to spend it. When he's got a few thousand dollars together he'll hand it over to Wes. So all I need to do is go into the bank and pay in the money for him. Then at the right time he'll ask me to withdraw his money. Callum chips in that Josie mustn't know as she'd "hit the roof."

I have a few questions. Why doesn't Micky just open another bank account or put the money directly into Callum's or Josie's account? Callum tells me that he can't open his own separate bank account here because he doesn't have a job. He's in the same position as me - I don't have a Bermuda bank account either and have had to pay my landlady in advance from my UK one.

And Callum adds that Josie would not be happy about Micky putting payments into her personal account. Besides Josie knows nothing about the P Crew and Micky's problem with them. If she did find out she'd just want to go straight to the police and Micky has made it clear that his life is on the line if she does.

Micky insists that he "wouldn't trust himself" not to spend the money and the charity account would be best bet because he couldn't access it.

I'm not happy about keeping this from Josie or about them asking me to effectively impersonate her at the bank. But Micky looks so forlorn and worried that I don't really have a lot of choice. He is relieved when I agree reluctantly to the plan on the strict condition that they tell Josie that it was all their idea if she ever finds out. Callum promises that he'll make sure "she never knows a thing about it."

Still I feel troubled by it all. I hardly know these people and here I am in a strange country offering to pose as Tralee Josie James and pay money into a charity account so Micky can save up for his first gang down payment. I drift off into a fitful sleep having completed a partly edited version of my day for Dr Silver.

Waking up to the sound of rain makes me think for a moment that I'm back in England. The rain is heavy but here it feels like you are standing under a warm shower. As I head off to see Dr Silver, Pauletta tells me to "stay safe" and adds that she's glad it's raining because the island has had a drought for the past three months. After exchanging pleasantries with Pauletta I catch the bus by the skin of my teeth and have to stand up all the way to Point Finger Road. I get off with various health workers wearing their hospital uniforms and I'm surprised how quickly the rain has turned the outside world into a swamp.

By the time I get to Dr Silver's place my thin blouse is sticking to my back and I can feel beads of sweat on my face. Dr Silver greets me in person today and I notice he's wearing a loose fitting shirt and the classic Bermuda shorts. He still manages to look quite dapper despite his casual dress – a trick that not many people can pull off.

"Hi JJ – humid today isn't it?" he says as I step into the blissfully cool hallway.

"Just a bit" I reply wiping my face with a tissue "any chance of a glass of water before we start?"

He laughs and tells me that I haven't seen anything yet as far as humidity is concerned.

"Wait till you get to August – it's like living in a jungle" he says handing me a large glass of ice cold water. I gulp it down gratefully as we make our way into his consulting room. I'm not quite sure why but the office seems different today. Dr Silver turns around and looks at me for a few seconds.

"Notice anything?" he asks.

I take another look around but I'm still unsure about what has changed.

He points to his desk.

"A clue? Do you remember where you sat last time?"

Something isn't right but I'm still flummoxed.

"I think I sat here" I say pointing to the small chair to my right hand side.

"Well you're correct about the chair but it's not where you sat. I've moved my desk to the other side of the office so that it isn't the first thing people see when they come in. But it's good you noticed that there was something different"

We then get straight down to the contents of my diary. Dr Silver spends a few minutes reading my entries while I study a consultation form he has given to me. Apparently I'll need to sign this before I can take part in his research project.

I'm still immersed in the form when he comes back across from his desk and settles himself into his creaky brown leather chair.

"I must say JJ that I've found your diary entries absolutely fascinating" he says pouring himself some water. He asks if I'd like my glass topped up but I tell him I'm fine. I also feel absurdly pleased that he has enjoyed reading my diary.

He's keen to know if my new way of keeping a record of each day is helping my memory. To be honest I'm not really sure yet.

"It is much more detailed than my old system" I reply "so there is loads to write down and more to read up the next morning. There's a lot to take in and I have to work harder at remembering. But I did have one interesting memory which came out of the blue the other day"

I then tell him about seeing some men in the street with Micky and how some time later I recalled a tattoo image on the neck of one of them. Amazingly I was able to draw it in some detail.

"Yes, I noticed you mentioned something about drawing a snake tattoo" he replies making a note on his memo pad. "Have you got the drawing with you?"

I don't, but I say that I'll show him next time. He tells me that short term memory jolts like this are quite common with brain injured patients and that it is a good sign for my recovery. He also likes the idea of me painting or drawing and is impressed that I've used the idea of contacting my namesakes on the island to make friends.

"That's a clever idea JJ. Meeting more new people can be a great stimulus for the injured brain"

We then spend the next few minutes going through the consent form he's given me and what I'll need to do if I take part in his study.

"At first we'll just use the deep hypnosis and see how that goes" he says "then if I think you'll benefit from the drug we'll introduce that as well. Do you want to discuss it first with your family or anyone else?"

I'm not sure I do. I don't really want the complication of asking other people's opinions and especially not my mom who is the world's worst worrier. I may mention it to St George's Josephine at some point because she seems like a sort of surrogate mom type. But I don't know her well enough yet and I tell Dr Silver that I'm happy to go ahead. He makes some more notes and then insists that I take the consent form away and read it properly before signing it.

Mercifully the bus back into Hamilton is quiet and I can sit in peace for a few minutes. I use the time to try to recall any small detail of my chat with Micky and Callum last night. But all I can remember is that there is some sort of game plan and without that all important note of it in my diary I've got no clear idea of what it is.

I make my way to Par La Ville Park which is just off the main Front Street. For someone with a dodgy brain like me, Hamilton is a straightforward city to navigate as all the streets lead back down to Front Street and the harbour area. Par La Ville Park is popular with lunch time office workers who sit on the benches and grass munching on their sandwiches or sushi. Micky and Callum are waiting for me by the wrought iron gate entrance and they are both looking worried.

"JJ" Callum says giving me a perfunctory hug "We were thinking you weren't going to show"

It's only then that I realise that I'm half an hour late because my appointment with Dr Silver over ran.

"Oh sorry, I should have texted to say I'd be late. I must be getting into Bermuda time" I smile apologetically and Micky tells me not to worry and to take no notice "of that uptight git Callum".

I like the way they rib each other and it reminds me of my little brother when we were kids. I was always winding him up and unlike Callum, he usually rose to the bait.

We go into the park and head towards a hot dog stand. There are a few tables available for customers so Micky and I sit down while Callum goes to order our food. I go for the vegetarian option which turns out to be a selection of sautéed peppers and onions in a bun. Still it's tasty enough and for the first ten minutes we munch on our dogs and make idle talk.

"Heh, I've got some tickets for a jazz evening next week" Callum says out of the blue "do you fancy coming along?"

Micky snorts at the mention of jazz and calls its "boring fecking old man's music" Callum ignores him and looks to me for a response.

"I'd love to" I reply "what evening is it?"

"Next Tuesday at a place called Hoagies. Not been there myself but I hear it is good"

"Count me in then" I say fishing out my note book to write down the date.

"You've not put anything in there about what we spoke about last night have you?" Micky asks staring at the little black note book I always carry around with me.

I assure him I have not and he looks like he believes me.

"Right we need to get down to business" Callum says swallowing the last bit of his hot dog.

We go over last night's agreement and as I'm reminded of the details, my main concern is that I don't do anything to upset Tralee Josie. Callum assures me that they have a water tight scheme to make sure she doesn't find out anything.

"Trust me" he adds "none of us want to upset Josie, least of all me."

Micky then says that he'd like me to put the first of his down payments into the charity account today. Did I hear that right? What today? I'm surprised at the speed of things but Micky says that the sooner he gets the money together the better.

I must say I'm starting to get nervous now. Just talking about it is one thing but actually going ahead and doing it is quite another. But I don't have much time to dwell on it because within minutes we're standing outside the bank. Micky hands me a white envelope which he says has $2,000 inside.

"Here's the paying in book and the slip is already made out. You just need to sign it at the bottom" Callum says passing it over to me. "Don't look so worried JJ – it'll only take a few minutes and we'll be right outside. You'll be fine"

I certainly don't feel fine as I enter into the air conditioned interior of the bank. There aren't any queues so I go straight up to the counter.

"Good afternoon" The young woman behind the counter greets me with a big smile and warm Bermudian accent. Immediately I feel more reassured.

"I'd like to pay this in please" I say returning her smile.

She takes the notes and counts them quickly. She removes the paying in slip which I sign and then stamps a piece of paper.

"Can I do anything else for you?" she asks beaming again at me.

"No that will be fine" I reply relieved that she hasn't asked any potentially awkward questions.

And so I exit the bank clutching a receipt for the payment. It has all happened in a blur.

"That was quick" Micky says as I emerge into the steamy afternoon heat.

Then out of the corner of my eye, I see a young man staring across at us from the other side of the road and I notice that he's got the very same neck tattoo that I've been drawing at home.

And despite the heat of the afternoon I feel myself breaking out in the coldest of sweats.

Chapter 12

Getting in deeper

I've just got off the bus from Hamilton and my head is buzzing. I still feel that I'm having some bizarre dream and that at any moment I'll wake up with mom standing over me with a cup of tea. The afternoon sun isn't helping either and the thing I most want now is a long cool shower.

The steep driveway up to my apartment is a killer in the heat and my clothes are literally sticking to me by the time I reach my front door. Pauletta is probably taking an afternoon nap which is just as well because I'm in no mood to talk to her.

I'm just stepping out of a much needed and leisurely shower when I hear my cell phone ringing out. I ignore it while I wrap myself in the lightest towel I can find and then it rings out a second time. I just about manage to grab it with wet hands before it clicks into answer mode.

The number isn't one with a name id, so I finish drying myself and throw on a loose cotton dress shirt. Guessing that the call might be something to do with Dr Silver I press the redial button. Tralee Josie answers the phone straight away which takes me by surprise.

"JJ – how are you? I'm just on a break at work and thought I'd give you a call"

"I've just stepped out off the shower" I reply trying to sound far more nonchalant than I feel. "The heat is a killer today"

"Can't say I've noticed JJ. I've been stuck in meetings all day and the air conditioning has been on at full pelt. So what have you been up to then?"

I'd like to be truthful and say that I've been impersonating her at a bank and paying in money to her company charity account on behalf of Micky. But I stop myself and tell her instead about my latest visit to Dr Silver.

"Wow – are you going to take part in his study then?" she asks and wants to know more about what it will involve. Inevitably she then turns the conversation to Micky.

"What did you think when you saw him last night?" she asks unaware that I've just spent part of this afternoon in his company along with her fiancé.

"Well he looked tired and that scratch on his eye didn't help" I reply still trying to sound casual. I wonder whether she can pick up the stress in my voice as I hate lying.

"I know you won't remember everything JJ but did he mention much about what happened to him? Only Callum thinks he met up with someone and for some reason doesn't want even his friends to know about it"

This is getting complicated and I'm scared about putting my foot in it. So I just tell Josie that Micky seemed a bit more cagey than normal and was reluctant to say much about his two day adventure.

I'm convinced that she knows I'm lying through my teeth and she does pick up that something isn't right.

"Are you OK JJ? Only you sound a bit, er, tense if you don't mind me saying so. Have I rung you at a bad time?"

"No, not at all" I reply unconvincingly "just a bit tired that's all"

Josie seems to accept this, adding that she'll try to get a bit more information out of Micky.

"It's not like Micky just to go off for days at a time and not let anyone know where he is. To be honest I don't think he's telling the truth but Callum says I should just drop it and let him tell us in his own time"

I tell Josie that it's probably not a bad idea and that Micky must have a good reason not to want to talk. At least that bit is true and I can feel my voice relaxing.

To get the conversation away from Micky, I mention that Callum has invited me to go to Hoagies jazz club with him.

"Why don't you come as well?" I ask hoping that she'll say yes. I'm still not comfortable about being with Callum on his own, although I like him a lot more than I did when I first met him.

"Nah – not my sort of music. Can't stand it really. In fact I suggested to Callum that he take you along. You'll enjoy it JJ"

After I finish the phone call I decide that I'll go back to my snake drawing. Having seen the young man earlier today staring at us from across the street, I can now recall more details about the tattoo.

It has a predominantly red and green coloured head while the main body is more of a mix of yellow and black markings. I'll look up some snake examples later on and see if it is a particular type.

I become absorbed in the drawing trying to recall every last detail. The young man's face is also clearer and I start to outline some features. He has wide almond shaped eyes and quite a girly looking full cupid bow lips. When I look at the finished product I'm quite pleased and I email St George's Josephine to let her know that I've been making good use of her present. Losing myself in drawing is actually a lot more enjoyable than I thought it would be and I'm glad now that Josephine suggested that I take it up.

I'm just taking another look at Dr Silver's consent form when my cell phone rings out again. This time it's Micky and I can hear loud voices in the background.

"Hi JJ. Sorry about the noise. I'm in Hoggy Poggy and there's some guys have just come in who are celebrating big time. Hang on while I move outside"

The background voices recede and I can hear Micky's uneven walk as he makes his way to the exit.

"Sorry about that. Now listen up, there's a couple of things I need to mention. But first thanks for your help earlier. I really appreciate it"

I don't answer but wait for him to continue.

"Anyway I've just had a call from Josie asking me all sorts of frigging awkward questions about where I've been and then she mentioned this Dr Silver guy you're seeing. She said something about hypnosis and maybe special memory drugs?"

"Yes" I reply "he's going to use hypnosis first of all to see how I get on"

Micky pauses for a few moments.

"Hmm – that's exactly what I'm worried about"

I'm not sure where he's coming from. Worried? Why should he be worried?

"Well look at it this way JJ. What if you start talking about my asking you to pay money into the charity bank account while this Silver guy has you under his spell?"

The thought hadn't even crossed my mind and I don't know how to respond.

Micky fills in the gap.

"Trouble is you don't know what you're likely to say once this guy has got you in his clutches. Anyway it all sounds a bit hocus pocus to me. I mean, who does he think he is?" Micky laughs nervously and I can feel myself getting angry. He knows nothing about Dr Silver and his worldwide medical reputation.

"You should read up a bit about Dr Silver before jumping to judgements" I say unable to keep the irritation out of my voice. Micky realises immediately that he's over stepped tye mark.

"Oh hell – that came out all wrong JJ. I didn't mean to diss your Dr. But we do need to keep this bank paying in business to ourselves until I get this gang lot off my back"

This is now getting even more messy. First of all I'm having to deceive Josie which I don't like one little bit and now Micky is questioning whether I should take part in Dr Silver's research experiment.

How the hell did I manage to get myself into this?

He suggests that I hold off filling out Dr Silver's consent form for now until we can discuss it more. Before ending the call, I agree to do what Micky suggests but make it clear that I'm not too pleased. I'm really beginning to wish that I hadn't said yes to going along with this little scheme because it is just complicating everything. And complication is something I don't need in my life right now.

A note on my desk catches my eye and reminds me that I have to reply to Tim's letter. It's a good time to do it because I'm feeling miffed and retrieving his scrunched up self absorbed letter from my wastepaper bin just makes me feel worse. I decide to follow his example and hand write my reply. The words come easily and I make it short and sweet.

"Hello Tim,

Thanks for your letter and first of all congratulations on the news about your plans to marry and the baby. You must be thrilled although it has all happened so quickly. Who would have thought it this time last year?

I'm loving it here in Bermuda and I've made lots of new friends. My treatment is going well too and I might be taking part in a research study for Dr Silver.

Look there's no nice way of saying this, but I'd rather we didn't keep in touch. I've got my new life now and you've got yours. I think it's for the best and we can both move on with a clean slate. Thanks for the apology about your attitude towards me at the hospital and rehab centre but you have to realise how selfish you were – it was me who needed the reassurance and sympathy and not you. Still, as you say, it was probably all for the good and I can see that from how things have turned out. Bye Tim and please do not try to contact me again either by letter or email as I will not open them. Have a good life and do try to be the best dad and husband you can. JJ"

I feel strangely elated and relieved after writing the letter. I don't feel sad at all which is surprising because before all this happened to me, I did think that Tim was the man I was going to marry and start a family with. I put the letter in an envelope to post later and check my emails. There is a reply from St George's Josephine who is delighted that I have started drawing again and she is suggesting that we meet in Hamilton at the weekend for "proper afternoon tea" as she puts it. I haven't had a high tea since I was a little girl when my nan took me to a posh London hotel and we had delicate little cucumber sandwiches and lots of cream cakes. That's another one of my lovely childhood memories filed away, even though I was sick when I got home from eating too much. My mom said it served me right for stuffing myself and for not saving any for her and Jeff.

I tell Josephine that I'd love to meet her again and then I hear a text popping into my cell phone inbox. It's Micky again.

"Hey JJ. Really need to talk to you more but let's keep it between ourselves this time. Can you see me tonight when I finish my shift at Finnegans? Will be clocking off at 7pm. Let me know asap Micky."

Wonder what he wants now? I can feel the butterflies building in my stomach and it's not because I'm excited about seeing Micky on his own. Quite the opposite in fact – these so called butterflies are much more about being scared.

I look up to see my drawing of the young man with the snake tattoo staring back at me with a fixed hard gaze which the perfectly formed cupid bow lips do little to soften.

And for the second time today I feel an overwhelming sense of dread.

Chapter 13

Mind Games

I'm on my way to meet Micky as arranged. This time I've made a bit of an effort taking a leaf out of Tralee Josie's 'power dressing' book. There's no doubt about it, smart clothes make you feel more confident and I need to be in the right frame of mind. I want him to know that I'm no push over and that I'm not going to agree to do anything more unless I'm comfortable with it.

I've chosen a deep blue silk blouse and a cream pencil skirt with a wide shiny black belt. Unusually for me I'm wearing high heels similar to the ones Josie likes to wear. They add several inches to my height but are a killer to walk in and by the time I get to Finnegan's I'm beginning to regret that I'm wearing them.

Micky is just finishing off behind the bar and the place is unusually quiet. There are just a few off duty police officers standing by the bar – I know this because I overhear them talking about their shift duties and a recent spate of house burglaries – and an elderly couple sipping beers and leafing through guide books.

Without asking, Micky pours me a diet coke and

a Guinness for himself. We head to a seat away from the main bar and he compliments me on my outfit.

"Thanks Micky. Just felt like dressing up a bit tonight. Mind you these heels are killing me" I kick off my shoes under the table and push them to one side.

"You women are fecking sadists when it comes to shoes" Micky says taking a deep slurp of his Guinness. "Aah – that's good. Here at Finnegans we know how to pour the old liquid velvet"

And that's it as far as the small talk goes. Now it's straight down to business.

"Look JJ I need to be upfront with you and you must keep this between you and me. Is that ok?"

"Depends what it is" I reply smoothing my skirt across my knees.

"Well don't worry I'm not going to ask you to go back into the bank – not yet anyhow. You did a good job today so thanks for that. No I just want to give you a bit more background about what's going on with this gang lot – just to put you properly in the picture."

I look across at him noticing how the bruising around his eye has already started to change colour. It's now got a distinct yellowish hue and the scratch is turning into a deep brown raised line.

"You see JJ, this is really fecking serious for me. Even Callum doesn't realise just how bad it is. If I don't start paying these guys back soon I'll be a frigging gonner"

"But why don't you just come clean and go to the police? Surely they can protect you?" Call me naïve but I really don't understand why Micky just doesn't ask for help.

"If I do that these guys will track me down. Between you and me, they've already told me how they bumped off someone who made the mistake of talking. Even if I got off the island I'd be living in fear. I've already lost my fecking leg over this"

Part of me still thinks Micky is exaggerating their power over him but then I can see how scared he is – you can't fake genuine fear that's for sure.

"Ok, so you can't go to the police. But how are you going to get this $250,000 dollars together? It's going to take a mighty long time to get that amount on a bar wage" I look him straight in the eye and he breaks my stare by taking another large gulp of his drink.

"Well, I expect I'll have to do some more favours for them but they want some dollars upfront as well. As long as I give them something they'll stay off my back for a while. That's what I'm hoping anyway."

"What do you mean you'll have to do them some favours? I hope you're not talking about drug dealing Micky. That's madness and what if you're caught?"

"I don't know what they'll ask me to do but they've made it clear that I owe them big time and that they'll call in the debt pretty soon. I'll get the message one way or another. But I still have to give them some readies"

"Come on Micky, tell me something new. We went through this earlier today and believe it or not I can still remember what we talked about though I can't guarantee that I will tomorrow – unless I write it all down of course." I give him another long fixed stare to underline my point.

"My, we are feisty this evening" Micky laughs and pulls a face. I don't react but just carry on staring him out.

"All right JJ, I take your point. Do you want another drink before I get on to the real reason I've asked you here tonight?"

I shake my head but offer to buy him a drink if he wants one.

"Nah, need to keep a clear head for now. Listen I'll come straight out with it - I need to know if I can borrow some money from you? If you could help me out I'll pay you back as soon as I can"

This is unbelievable and for a minute I'm dumb struck.

"Micky I haven't got anywhere near that kind of money. I'll get some accident compensation at some point but for now I'm living off my redundancy money. And a lot of that is going to pay for my treatment over here"

Micky puts his head down and when he looks up I think I can see tears in his eyes. He makes a quick excuse to go off to "the loo" before things become more embarrassing. I'm left sitting there wondering whether I should just make an exit and be done with it. But of course being the well brought up girl that I am, I stay put.

When Micky comes back he's holding another pint of Guinness and he sits back down awkwardly.

"Sorry about having to ask you that JJ but when you are desperate, needs must"

"Are you ok? Only you looked a bit upset just

now"

He runs his hand along the raised scab at the side of his eye.

"Oh I'm fine – I think this eye is a bit sensitive after that fecker decked me. Keeps going all watery like"

I feel like asking why the other eye is watering as well but think better of it.

Now it's clear that I can't lend him any money, Micky turns the subject to Dr Silver.

"You do realise it would be fecking awkward if you did that experiment Josie's been telling me about. What if you were to blurt something out about the bank payment?"

I deliberately wait a few seconds before answering to make him stew.

"Well Micky I hate to say it but this was all sorted out with Dr Silver before you guys came along with this stupid idea of yours. I know you're in trouble but none of this is my making and if I want to walk away from all of this I bloody well will" I'm surprised that I've sworn as I rarely do it and I can't stand it when others do either.

Micky looks a bit taken aback as well and trails his finger across the froth of his Guinness distractedly.

" Look JJ I'm really grateful that you helped us out earlier and I hope you won't change your mind. I'm relying on you"

I can see that his eyes are starting to well up again and this time it is me who makes an excuse to leave the table on the pretext of wanting another drink. Pete, the Aussie barman, is serving a customer and waves to me from behind the counter. Throwing caution to the wind I order a glass of white wine as I feel I really need it and grab a bowl of complimentary mixed nuts from the side of the bar.

When I get back Micky is texting and seems to have regained his composure. I take a few sips of wine while he finishes sending his message.

Micky then suggests that "we just change the fecking subject" and he starts asking me questions about my family back in England. It's a relief to talk about other things rather than gangs and threats and I slowly begin to relax. The wine tastes good as well which comes as a bit of a surprise. Could this be another sign of my brain recovering I wonder?

Micky is due to back at work behind the bar and makes me promise yet again that I won't write down the details of our chat anywhere. After a couple of hours in his company I do feel even sorrier for him than I did earlier. I can see that he doesn't want to panic Callum too much and in some ways I'm flattered that he has confided more in me than his best friend.

Just as Micky gets up to say goodbye, I decide to put him out of his misery.

"Look, just to put your mind at rest I will hold off taking part in Dr Silver's research project - at least for now"

Micky looks like a weight has been lifted from his shoulders and thanks me before planting a big kiss on my cheek. I can feel myself blushing and in some ways I quite like this bit of power I've now got over him. But it doesn't stop me feeling bad about letting

Dr Silver down over his memory experiment and for deliberately omitting information from my diary.

When I get back I take another look at my snake drawing. I'm pleased with it and will it to show St George's Josephine when I see her in a few days time. I feel strangely excited about meeting Josephine again and I re-read all my previous diary entries about her. As I do so, I find myself smiling and can recall instantly the beautiful floral smells from her garden.

I've been putting off doing the rest of today's memory diary but however tired I feel it's got to be done before I fall asleep. I decide to choose Josephine's invite to high tea in Hamilton as one of my favourite memories of the day. The other is my snake tattoo drawing and the third is being able to conjure up the fragrances from Josephine's garden.

Nowhere do I mention going into a bank and depositing a $2000 cheque. And nowhere do I mention the meeting in Par La Ville Park or joining Micky on his own at Finnegans.

So you see I'm already beginning to erase key events in my daily life just like an editor does with a film. Except I've no way of knowing whether I'll ever recover the deleted parts and I just have to hope that some nuggets will stay with me.

Just as I'm about to fall asleep, I remember with vivid clarity another thing about the tattoo – the markings on the snake's body seem to spell out two interlinking letters. P and C.

And with heavy eyes I feel compelled to get straight back to my drawing.

Chapter 14

The law man beckons

I'm so elated about meeting St George's Josephine today. She has chosen Hamilton's main hotel for our afternoon tea, a sprawling pale pink coloured building on the edge of the main town. It is a beautiful day, bright sunshine but with a little less humidity than of late. The main town harbour is shown off at its best on a day like this, with the glistening still water acting like a mirror to the yachts and boats moored up. Two Dutch tourists on the bus into town keep 'oohing' and 'aahing' at the sights out of their window. Inwardly I'm doing exactly the same.

As I'm running a little early, I decide to get off a few stops before the one by the hotel and take a leisurely stroll along Front Street. It's that quiet bit of the afternoon between the shopping period and the start of the main evening out. I spot a gorgeous pair of red suede shoes with towering heels in a shop window and I'm tempted to go in to try them on. But the blister on my heel from last night's ill advised stilettos stops me from doing so.

Apart from the prospect of meeting Josephine again, I'm excited about something else. When I woke up this morning I had a definite flashback to my meeting with Micky at Finnegans yesterday. I deliberately tried to recall as much as I could before looking at my diary. I could see his tearful eyes and I remember that he asked me to lend him some money. Why he asked me this I have no idea and there is nothing in my notes to say what we discussed. I have a vague inkling that it connects to 'the plan', those two little words that I've written down in separate note to myself but otherwise that's it. Nothing more. It's like when you wake up and know that you've had some sort of dream but can't remember what it is. But in my case that un-remembered dream is what I did yesterday.

Still, it's yet another flash memory and according to Dr Silver this is all good. He'll be pleased when I tell him - I'll do it later on when I email him my diary notes. Now that I'm keeping a separate note to myself, I see that there is another line in big bold letters saying that I need to hold off taking part in Dr Silver's research until 'the plan' is finished. But the detailed content of 'the plan' has now been erased from my brain. So it will be back to square one next time I see Micky or Callum and I'm certainly not looking forward to telling Dr Silver that I'll need a bit more time to think about taking part in his study.

The sight of the imposing pink hotel building as I walk up the sweeping driveway takes my mind off things. The reception is spacious and elegant with a cool marble floor and a myriad of tropical plants placed around the squishy pastel sofa style seating. I can't see Josephine so I take a seat near the reception point and watch as a harassed looking young couple jostle suitcases while trying to keep a boy of around three years old from sliding across the shiny floor. The man nearly goes flying as he tries to catch the youngster while wearing a flimsy pair of flip flops and I try not to laugh. The young woman, presumably the boy's mom, raises her eyes to the ceiling and mumbles an apology to a passing smartly uniformed hotel worker who smiles and shrugs.

"Ah, boys will be boys" the hotel worker replies graciously and heads towards the reception with a business like stride. By now the boy is being carried back on the man's shoulders and is laughing uncontrollably. Then just behind him a smiling Josephine appears carrying a large bouquet of flowers.

"These are for you my dear" she says giving me a peck on the cheek "I picked them myself from my garden this morning"

It is a huge mixed bunch of lilies and freesias with some other tropical flowers which I don't know the names of yet. I say 'yet' because Josephine says that she'll teach me the names and it will be good practice for my memory. She's wearing a pale green linen trouser suit and a crisp white blouse. I can see that she's made an effort with her hair and make up and I wish I had done the same.

"You look very cool and summery" she says looking at my light blue checked shirt and matching shorts. I've tied my hair back into loose bun which she says "suits my face" and compliments me on my glowing tanned skin. It seems that it's impossible to spend a few minutes in Josephine's company without her making you feel good about yourself. She's just that sort of person and I can see exactly why my diary tells me that she is so popular with the people living in St George's.

We head straight out to the terrace where Josephine orders afternoon tea for two. The view out to sea view is stunning and Josephine tells me that the author, Mark Twain, used to sit in this very spot when he lived in Bermuda.

The tea arrives in dainty white china pots and is served with a mound of tiny sandwiches, English scones and a towering batch of exquisitely decorated cakes which look far too good to eat.

"Come on, dig in JJ. Don't hold back" Josephine says passing over the plate of sandwiches. I choose some cucumber ones and tell Josephine about the time I went for high tea with my nan. She laughs loudly saying that she much prefers the salmon ones to the cucumber.

"I can't understand why anyone would want to just serve cucumber sandwiches – it feels like there's something missing, like there's no real filling"

And with that she pops a whole salmon sandwich triangle into her mouth while still managing to look elegant. I decide after several attempts at nibbling on the edges to take a leaf out of Josephine's book and just go for the whole thing. Except I can't quite manage Josephine's lady like precision and end up with several stray bits of cucumber on my lap.

Out of the blue, Josephine waves to someone across the terrace.

"Hey Graham! How the hell are you?" Josephine is already on her feet as a tall slim man with neatly cropped black hair strides into view. He hugs Josephine and says that it has been ages since he's seen her.

"Graham – this is my new friend JJ who is visiting the island from England"

Graham smiles and shakes my hand. I notice that he has dark but freckled skin and earnest looking blue eyes. He's wearing an expensive looking navy suit with an open necked cream shirt and looks like he's been to work or some sort of business meeting.

"Graham's a lawyer JJ. The best criminal lawyer in Bermuda or so I'm told" He smiles and tells Josephine that she should do his PR work. His voice is soft Bermudian which I wasn't expecting. I'm not sure why – maybe it's because he looks so Latino but then I should know by now that Bermuda has a sizeable mixed race population who were born or brought up here.

Josephine suggests that Graham joins us for tea.

"I'd love to but I haven't got long though" he says taking a seat alongside me. He throws his jacket across the back of the chair between Josephine and me and I can't help noticing his long muscular arms. He's also got meticulously manicured nails which in my experience is unusual for a man. Close up he has a striking angular sort of face, not exactly handsome in the conventional sense but attractive nonetheless.

"So JJ, are you enjoying being here in Bermuda?" he asks politely declining Josephine's offer for him to help himself to some cakes.

119

"It's great, fantastic in fact" I reply suddenly feeling quite shy. Why I have no idea. The waiter comes over asking if we would like any more tea. Josephine orders another pot and Graham opts for lemon tea.

"Good, I'm glad" Graham says with another smile that instantly makes his face even more attractive. I can feel my face turning red which I find ridiculous at my age. After all, I've lived in the big city and have travelled thousands of miles across the world on my own. Yet here I am feeling like a clumsy dumb struck teenager.

Graham tells me that he was born in Bermuda and has lived here all his life, aside from a few years away in Canada where he went to study law. He is now a partner in a large Hamilton law firm and he specialises in criminal law.

"And before you ask, yes there is enough work here to keep me busy. In fact I'm in the middle of a murder case at the moment. It's a tit for tat gang land thing, bloody stupid but there you are. The family I'm representing had their son shot down in broad daylight only a few miles up the road from here"

Josephine sighs and shakes her head.

"So tragic that you're having to deal with stuff like that Graham. I don't know how you do it. Still somebody has to I suppose. But poor JJ doesn't want to be hearing about things like that now do you?"

Inevitably the conversation comes around to the reason I'm here in Bermuda. Josephine fills in Graham who then has a barrage of questions. Like most people he is fascinated and wants to know how I cope with such a major "disability" as he puts it.

I tell him that I don't really see myself as disabled as such but yes, it is hard work and it is no good pretending otherwise. He nods and looks serious, like the lawyer that he is.

"Hmm, you'd be an interesting challenge in a court" he says "a really interesting challenge. I expect you'd have to be seen as 'unfit to plead' as it would be difficult for you to follow the proceedings from one day to the next"

Josephine laughs and tells Graham that she's sure I have no intentions of ending up in court.

"Actually I could probably follow things if I kept a detailed diary" I reply "I mean that's how I get by day to day as it is. That's why I'm here this afternoon with Josephine. I'm still capable of doing a lot, it's just that I have to make a much more effort than I did before"

Graham nods and I can see that he is listening intently. When I mention Dr Silver he tells me that he already knows him.

"Ah Ray Silver. Now there's a coincidence. Would you believe that I played tennis with him only last night?"

I shouldn't be surprised, as Pauletta is always telling me what a small island this is. But I am still taken aback to be sitting next to Dr Silver's tennis buddy.

"Look I'm going to have to dash" Graham says suddenly glancing at his watch. "But it's been great meeting you JJ and hopefully we'll bump into each other again. I'm sure we will"

He shakes my hand and Josephine says she'll walk back with him to the reception.

"You ok to stay here for now JJ? Why don't you order some more tea while you're at it?"

I watch them disappear back towards the hotel reception area deep in conversation. I notice again how tall Graham is – well over six foot I reckon and it doesn't surprise me that he plays tennis. He has that outdoor sporty look which I find incredibly appealing. And I like the way he looks after himself, making an effort with his appearance. My mind flits back to my scruffy ex Tim and I now wonder how the hell I found him attractive in the first place.

When Josephine comes back I can't help asking her a few more questions about Graham. Josephine's eyes twinkle and she tells me that "Graham Tucker is a great guy. One of the best. And good looking too don't you think?"

So his surname is Tucker then. Apparently an old Bermudian family name. Josephine winks at me adding that she thinks I've caught Graham's eye.

"It's not surprising, a good looking girl like you JJ. In fact he's given me a copy of his card for you to have and asked me for your phone number. Don't worry, I haven't given it to him – unless you want me to? Oh and he's free and single just in case you were wondering" She winks at me again and helps herself to another cake.

"You're not trying to fix me up with a date are you?" I reply trying to make light of the situation. But yes, truth be known, I'd like to get to know Mr Graham Tucker a bit more.

Josephine gives me one of her raucous laughs and asks me what she should do. Text Graham with my number?

I give a nod and with another one of her big grins she pulls out her mobile and sends the text. So that's it. The signal has gone to say that I'm interested in another meeting with Mr Tucker, lawyer extraordinaire. Let's see what happens then.

"So you say you've got your drawing to show me? Come on then let's see it" Josephine looks down at my bag expectantly and I dig out my snake tattoo drawing.

She spends a few minutes looking at it from different angles.

"Hey JJ this is really good. How did you come up with the idea of a snake design on a young man's neck? I must say I don't recognise the species but perhaps I'm not meant to?"

"Oh I just saw this young guy on the street and the amazing thing is that I've done all this from visual memory – not from a photograph or anything. I thought you might be able to tell me the species"

Josephine has another close look at the drawing and shakes her head.

"From memory you say? Wow, that is incredible. Have you told your Dr Silver? This might mean you are starting to recover some powers of recall. Wouldn't that be great?"

I'm pleased that Josephine likes the drawing but on a closer inspection she says that she really doesn't recognise the snake type.

"I've just noticed that there's two overlapping

letters - P and C. So it's obviously a made up type of snake. Wonder if that's the initials of the young man?"

I nod, somehow sensing that P and C stands for something quite different and a much more threatening message than the young man's name. I also know instinctively that I can't share this thought with Josephine.

And not for the first time today, those two little words 'the plan' suddenly loom large in my mind.

Chapter 15

Deeper and deeper

My mom has just rung and has spent the whole time quizzing me about who I'm seeing in Bermuda – "have you got a boyfriend yet?" – and doesn't sound surprised when I tell her my ex Tim's news.

"Yes I've heard he is getting married" she says sniffing disapprovingly. I know that sniff and somewhere from my hard wired childhood memories I recall it means disapproval.

"I didn't want to tell you because he asked if I'd wait for him to send a letter first. So you've had the letter then?" she asks giving a second sniff.

"Yes and I've written back asking him not to contact me again, not even by email." I wait for her response which takes a few seconds.

"Well, I suppose that's that then. Shame though because I do like Tim. I just think he couldn't cope with your injury and all that. Still, he didn't take long to get hitched to someone else – and her pregnant as well." Another sniff.

"Look mom I don't want to waste time on talking about him. What's done is done. How is Jeff getting on with his new girlfriend?"

Obviously not a great question to ask. Yet

another even louder sniff.

"Oh he's smitten with her. Out every night they are and he's not been doing his homework. I keep telling him he'll fail his exams but he won't listen."

"She looks very pretty in the photos Jeff emailed me" I say sensing that mom does not approve of her.

"I suppose so if you like that tarty over made up sort of look." I wait for another tell tale sniff but it doesn't come this time. Best to change the subject I think.

I tell mom about meeting Graham Tucker and about afternoon tea with St George's Josephine. I also tell her that I've taken up drawing again on Josephine's advice.

"Oh that's good – it sounds as though you are meeting some nice people then. And how's the treatment going?"

Just as well I haven't told her anything about Dr Silver's research project.

"Oh it's going well. I'm getting more flashback memories than I did and he's got me keeping a much more detailed memory diary. I think it's doing the trick."

"What do you mean 'flashback' memory?'" mom asks sounding confused.

"I mean that I sometimes remember bits from the day before now. Not everything, just bits, but it's a start. Dr Silver thinks it's a good thing."

As it is, I've been talking to Dr Silver this morning. He wants to know why I've changed my mind about taking part in his experiment. I tell him that I haven't had a change of heart but just need a little longer to think about things. He seems to understand but I can hear the puzzlement in his voice. Still, he is delighted about my news of more short term memory recall and he tells me to make sure I bring my drawing in with me for our next appointment.

"Now write that down before you forget!" he quips before hanging up.

Part of me is still really pleased about the increasing memory flashbacks but I don't want to get my hopes up too much. I've been told that it could take years before my brain recovers and that it might never approach anywhere near normal. I understand this but it doesn't stop me from hoping and sometimes praying.

After I finish my phone call with mom, I decide to head down to Elbow Beach for a swim and a relaxing sunbathe. When I get there it is already packed but I manage to find a sheltered spot behind some rocks away from the main crowd. It is a great place to people watch and provides a bit of shade from the early afternoon sun.

The sand in Bermuda is famous for its coral pink shade and powder fine texture. Just before I set off, Pauletta tells me about a 'natural pedicure' made by mixing some sand with a little sun cream and massaging it into the feet. I decide to give it a go and I'm concentrating on rubbing the mix onto my heels when I get a text message which startles me. It's from Callum confirming the Hoagie's jazz concert for tonight and suggesting that we meet outside first. I get back to say that I'm looking forward to it and ask him if there is any kind of dress code.

He replies sarcastically "as if" and says that smart casual usually does for Bermuda. That's fine by me but I'll still make a bit of an effort because I have the time to do so. Apart from a few hours on the beach I have nothing else planned for today – it's the sort of lifestyle I could only dream about when I was in London. So aside from the little matter of the damaged brain, I'm living the life only seen in glossy magazines and I still have to pinch myself sometimes that I'm actually here.

And talking about being thousands of miles from home, my little brother Jeff keeps telling me that I should get into Facebook or another social networking site and at least give a nod to 21st century fast communications. He says I'm the only person he knows who isn't into the social networking scene. But I really don't want the complication of socialising online. It's enough having to deal with emails, texts and my daily diary without having to log on to all those other sites as well. Anyway, it would just be another means for Tim to get in touch and I definitely don't want that.

Although I've had the occasional emails from old college friends and workmates, I've tried to distance myself from people back in London as much as possible. If truth be told, I'm not really hankering after my old life all that much although I do miss Jeff and of course mom's home made treats. Just thinking about mom's culinary skills makes my mouth water and I realise that I'm actually feeling quite hungry.

I make my way across to the bar at Elbow Beach before the main lunchtime rush and I order a tuna sandwich. As I'm eating my lunch I can't help wondering about Tralee Josie - I've made a note in my diary to call her after tonight's jazz concert. For some reason I'm starting to feel uneasy about her without really understanding why.

After a leisurely gap spent amusing myself by making up stories about the people sitting around the bar – "she's bound to be a top model, he runs a gym" that sort of thing - I decide to head back home as the afternoon heat is starting to become oppressive. I put the air conditioning up onto the highest level and sit directly underneath it as I check my emails. St George's Josephine has sent one asking if I've heard anything from Graham yet. I'm about to reply 'no' when I spot another email from 'Tucker Associates' so I open it.

"Hey JJ. Enjoyed our chat the other day. So much so that I'd like to do it again. Do you fancy a spot of lunch in town sometime? Let me know and we'll fix something up. Have a great day. Graham."

So has Josephine set this up I wonder? Even if she has I don't mind. I've re-read my diary entry about Graham and my words bring back an image of a man who is definitely worth meeting again. Before replying to Graham I send Josephine a message.

"Hi Josephine. Funny but just after I opened your email, I noticed that there was one from Tucker Associates. And guess what? Graham has asked me to lunch. Of course I'll say yes! Thanks again for the introducing me to high tea Bermuda style and hope to see you again soon. JJ xx"

Then I reply to Graham saying that I'd be

delighted to have lunch and that I'll leave it to him to suggest a time and place. Hey. My social life is certainly getting better out here that's for sure and I still have this evening to look forward to.

Hoagie's jazz club is located on the outer edges of Hamilton and the front of the building is made up of a mix of blackened wood and dark tinted glass. The name is etched on the front door in large gold coloured letters. Over the years it has seen many famous jazz players and Callum tells me that John Lennon probably came here when he spent his last summer on the island back in 1980.

Callum is waiting outside and is wearing his regular uniform of shorts and a T-shirt. Despite my earlier thoughts of making an effort, I've also opted for the casual look – linen trousers and a thin blouse.

Despite the air conditioning, the inside of Hoagies is hot and sticky from the sheer number of people crammed in there. You can hardly move or hear yourself speak as the noisy and excited crowd waits for the first act to come on. Callum fights his way to the bar and comes back with a tray of drinks – my usual cola and his two glasses of lager.

"Best to get them in now before the acts are on" he says balancing the tray precariously on the end of a small table. My first drink barely touches the side and after a few minutes we give up trying to have any sort of decent conversation. We edge our way towards the small stage hanging on to our drinks and trying unsuccessfully not to bump into anyone. Already an argument has erupted at the other side of the room and in an instant two huge bouncers are marching the men towards the club door. There is an overwhelming smell of sickly clashing perfumes and aftershaves mixed with sweat and spilled drinks. It's a claustrophobic's nightmare and I try not to think too hard about how little air there seems to be.

All this is forgotten though when the first band appears. It's a mix of Blues and Jazz with the odd reggae number thrown in. 'Pearl' is the lead singer and her voice is tremendous – a mix of Aretha Franklin and Dusty Springfield if you can imagine such a combination. The crowd are loud and appreciative and the band is only allowed to leave the stage after a twenty minute encore. Callum looks entranced and in a world of his own. When Pearl and her band leave the stage we make another attempt at conversation.

"So what do you think JJ? Great eh?" Callum takes a swig from his second beer and I nod in agreement.

"Yes, fantastic. Pearl has an amazing voice, really versatile too" I say trying to side step a large man as he stumbles across the room with his skinny lollipop head girlfriend trailing behind him.

Within minutes the next band is on and the crowd grows wild. It's boogie woogie piano style this time and a small group by the side of me is attempting to dance despite the obvious lack of room.

Out of the blue there's a loud cracking sound like a massive firework going off. The band stops playing and the two burly bouncers are hurtling towards the door. There is a piercing scream followed by another crack.

An eerie silence falls on the crowd as a young woman comes into view her white dress splattered with red.

She lets out an anguished yell.

"He's been shot – my Dwayne's been shot."

As the crowd part to let her through, I can see one of the bouncers pressing down on the chest of a man slumped on the floor a pool of blood. The other is on the phone and gesticulating wildly.

I look across at Callum and his face has turned a deathly white. More screams, this time from the crowd as they begin to take in what is happening.

I glance back at the stage and the band are standing perfectly still, like ornaments on a mantelpiece, while a single piece of sheet music wafts gently down onto the floor.

And then the blaring sound of sirens transporting me straight back to the day everything changed.

Chapter 16

After Shocks

We're hanging around outside Hoagies watching the white suited police forensics team come and go. Word has it that the guy who has been shot has survived but it is touch and go. There's a large crowd milling, despite the police appeals for everyone to keep out of the way.

Callum has already been on the phone to Josie who is on her way down to meet us. I notice that Callum is still looking pale and if I'm not mistaken, is shaking. I feel surprisingly calm, disconnected even. Yes, the sounds of sirens did momentarily send me back to that hot day in London over a year ago when I stepped out into the road. But now I'm feeling quite serene and feel as though I'm on some sort of film set. Any moment now I expect someone from the TV series CSI to spring into view with those funny torch style lights they seem to carry around all the time.

Tralee Josie runs over and gives Callum a big hug.

"Thank god you're ok". They stay in an embrace for a few minutes and I feel a bit like a spare part.

Josie then spots me and puts her hand on my

arm.

"JJ I'm so sorry. How are you? Are you all right?"

We hug for a few moments and then we stand staring at each other not quite knowing what to say. Despite the crowds there is a hushed atmosphere, a bit like a funeral. Those who are speaking are doing so in whispers.

Callum breaks the silence saying that he wants to "get out of this hole" and we follow him back up towards town. None of us are in the mood for talking and we barely say a word as we make our way along the crowded street towards the centre of Hamilton.

We head into Finnegans where the talk is all about the shooting that took place just a few hours ago. Micky is behind the bar tonight and says he'll join us once he gets a spare minute. He winks at me and I give a perfunctory smile in return.

Josie orders Callum a double brandy which she says is good for shock. Again I actually feel like a glass of wine so I join Josie in ordering a Pinot Grigio. No soda water this time to dilute it - tonight I'm in the mood for the real deal.

"So come on, spill you two - I want to know all about what happened in there" Josie says after we find a table.

"Nothing much to tell really" Callum replies "It all kicked off so quickly. One minute we were listening to the boogie woogie piano guy and then we heard this almighty cracking sound. Next thing a girl runs in covered in blood."

Josie shakes her head in disbelief.

"Did you see anything JJ?" she asks sounding

disappointed that Callum has offered so few details.

"Not really" I say truthfully. "Like Callum says it all happened in a flash. I thought somebody had let off a firework or flare outside. It was only after the young woman starting talking about her Dwayne being shot that it began to sink in what had happened."

Josie stares across at Callum looking concerned.

"Are you sure you're all right Cal?" she asks him touching his shoulder.

He shrugs and looks away from us both staring vacantly into space.

"Is it all right if I tell JJ about what happened in Belfast?" she asks Callum taking hold of his hand. He shifts slightly and then nods before taking a sip of his brandy.

"You see JJ" she says turning back towards me "Callum nearly lost his dad in a shooting in Belfast about ten years ago. A guy burst into a church social club and fired into the crowd. It wasn't meant for him but Callum's dad took a bullet to the chest and was in intensive care for weeks"

No wonder Callum has been so shaken up tonight.

"That's why we moved to Tralee to be near my dad's family" Callum adds his colour starting to return.

"How awful" I say not quite knowing how to react. Just as the earlier sound of emergency sirens had hurtled me back to the day of my accident, so too had the sight of a blood splattered dress catapulted Callum back to the nightmare evening of his dad's shooting.

"Fortunately Cal had just left the club with his mom so didn't see it all but still the shock of this brings it all back. You should see the size of the scar on his dad's chest" Josie takes a large swig of her wine and puts her arm through Callum's and kisses him affectionately on the cheek. He looks a bit embarrassed about this public display of affection and blushes slightly. His awkwardness is interrupted by Micky who looms into view.

"You lot want more drinks?" He's carrying a plate of pizza slices which he plonks down in front of us.

"These are a present from the kitchen" he says "someone just ordered them and then disappeared. So free to you lot"

"Ah thanks Micky" Josie says taking a slice and handing the plate to Callum. For once he refuses food and says he'll stick to the brandy for now.

Micky tells us that the guy who has been shot is a regular Finnegans customer.

"Yeh, know him well. Nice guy too. Hope he pulls through" He stretches out his dummy leg and stares down at it. I wonder if he's thinking how lucky he was to escape with own life after the incident with his bike.

It seems from what Micky has heard, that the shooting has something to do with two rival gangs on the island – what the police call a tit for tat attack.

"Looks like it could be mistaken identity, someone mistook this Dwayne guy for a rival gang member who had walked into the other gang's territory" he adds taking a furtive glance around the pub.

This is a new part of Bermuda I'm learning about – the underbelly of paradise. And from what I understand from my landlady Pauletta, these gang attacks are a recent thing. According to her, there were hardly any killings on the island until a few years ago but the emerging gang culture has put paid to that. It's nowhere near as bad as some of the neighbouring Caribbean islands like Jamaica or Trinidad but for a tiny socially conservative island it has still come as a seismic cultural shock.

Despite the circumstances we've found ourselves in this evening, it's good to have Josie around. The conversation seems easier when she's there and after we move on from the subject of shootings, she tells us all about her bank company's plans for their annual charity ball.

"It's all going great. Hard work but exciting. We're expecting to raise over $500,000 dollars and there will be a big presentation to the charities with press photographers and TV cameras there."

Yet again Josie tries to persuade me to come along and I say that I'll think about it.

"Ah go on JJ. It's for a good cause. And an excuse to splash out on a posh frock"

"Look she says she'll think about it so just let it go" Callum snaps adding that he wants to go home. I can see that Josie is annoyed by his comment but she ignores it and picks up her jacket. Micky and I avoid eye contact as I decide it is best that I head off too. We leave Micky in the bar and after saying my goodbyes to Callum and Josie I flag down a passing taxi.

When I finally get home, Pauletta is waiting up

for me. She's heard all about the shooting on the news and says that she couldn't get to sleep thinking about me being out there on the streets. I laugh telling her it's Bermuda, not the Bronx, but she pulls a stern face and reminds me that there are still some "bad apples" out there even on this idyllic island.

"Did you see what happened?" she inquires following me up the stairs that lead to my apartment. Clearly I'm not going to get to bed any time soon and I still have my diary to write.

It's a full half hour before Pauletta finally stops quizzing me and by now I'm bone tired. It's tempting not to bother with the diary but I know the consequences if I don't do it – a virtual blackout of today's events however momentous.

So there's no choice but to get to it. I go through the last part of the day using Dr Silver's template and there is no doubt about the choice of my three key memories of the day. Hoagie's music, Hoagie's shooting and Callum's troubled past. No need to make up a creative narrative to stimulate my recall – there is enough real drama for today's diary without having to embellish it.

With everything else going on this evening, I realise that haven't checked my phone for messages. When I do get around to it, there is a voice message waiting and it's from Graham Tucker.

"Hi JJ. Graham Tucker here. You know I mentioned lunch? Well how about tomorrow if it's not too short notice? A court case has been cancelled and I've got a free afternoon. Call me back when you can."

I glance at the clock and it's just gone 12.30am. It's too late to call so I send a text instead.

"Hello Graham, just got back from town. Yes lunch would be great. I'll call you back tomorrow morning. JJ."

I've now reached that infuriating point where you go beyond tiredness, so I decide to get out my drawing materials. The girl in the white blood splattered dress seems as good a subject as any, so I start to draw her. Her eyes are wide with fear and her mouth is opened into a scream. The marks on her dress look like some macabre tie-dye pattern, with most of the blood centred on the middle of her dress and fanning out towards the edges. Her arms are outstretched with her long red finger nails pointing out towards the crowd who are just a blur in my drawing.

Then a small black blob appears on the edge of the paper. It's no bigger than a thumb nail and I flinch as I see it move across the page. It's the tiniest of tree frogs and I watch fascinated as it jumps across my drawing before leaping down onto the floor.

As hard as I try, I can't find out where it's gone. And probably by this time tomorrow, I won't even remember it has called by.

Chapter 17

Raising The Stakes

It's been a week since the shooting at Hoagie's and even after re-reading everything about that night it still seems surreal. As does my lunch with Graham Tucker the following afternoon.

Graham Tucker, law man Mr Tucker. Just seeing his name in my diary brings me out in goose pimples and silly as it seems, I can feel those butterflies starting up in my stomach. His photo is already staring out at me from a small gold frame at the side of my bed, his broad smile, black hair and dark freckled skin contrasting with the bright orange backdrop of the restaurant where it was taken. As clichéd as it may sound, in my eyes Graham Tucker really is drop dead gorgeous.

I can't tire of reading about that first lunch that went on long into the evening. It was Graham's suggestion that we meet at the Onion Patch, a trendy restaurant and bar with a view to die for across Hamilton Harbour. When I arrived he was already waiting at the bar dressed in a cool cream linen suit and open necked dark blue silk shirt. He was propped on a stool and was busy scrutinising the drinks menu when I walked in.

After the events of the night before, I'd slept in late so didn't have a lot of time to deliberate over what to wear. So I opted for a simple turquoise cotton dress and wore Josephine's hand crafted beaded bracelet which matched perfectly. I wore my hair down loose and added a touch of bronzer to enhance my tan. I probably looked better than I felt - a mix of nerves and shyness. When I tapped him on the shoulder he nearly toppled off the stool which made us both laugh and got rid of my own feelings of awkwardness.

Unlike Micky, Graham didn't go for over the top compliments about how well he thought I looked. He was far too sophisticated for all that and we made our way outside where he had already reserved a discreet table at the far end of the terrace.

As it turned out Graham was easy to talk to and before we knew it, lunchtime had drifted into early evening with the after work drinkers making their way in. But rather than move on we decided to stay put and I finally got back to my apartment just before 11.00pm. It seemed hard to believe that we had spent so many hours just chatting but yet we had managed to. I learned all about his extended family with their links to the military, his job and his love of the island where he grew up. He wanted to know everything about my life in England and more about how I was coping with the effects of my accident. It all felt so simple, so enjoyable and above all totally relaxed.

A week on and I've now had two more dinner dates with Graham. The latest was last night and that's when we finally had our first proper kiss. A long lingering slow one, right at the end of the evening just before my taxi arrived. I think we both know that this is the start of something special and I feel oddly that I've known Graham all my life. And for somebody with a memory problem like mine, that's saying something.

I haven't told Tralee Josie, Callum or Micky about Graham yet. I've not seen any of them since the shooting incident and I know Josie has been busy organising her bank's annual charity ball. As for my other namesake, St George's Josephine, she knows only too well about my growing closeness to Graham and I can sense she is doing her best to encourage it.

Today I've got another appointment with Dr Silver. He too knows about Graham and last time I saw him he gushed about what a great guy 'Tucky' – his nickname for Graham - is. I feel a bit awkward that they already know each other, especially as Dr Silver is reading my daily memory diary. I will need to be careful about what I write even though Dr Silver has assured me time and time again that everything he reads will be treated in strict confidence.

I'm on the bus heading to Dr Silver's place when I receive a text from Graham.

"Morning JJ loved yesterday evening – especially the last bit which I hope will be continued! Got two complimentary tickets for the Bermuda Child Welfare Charity Ball on Friday. Do you want to come along? Please say yes – it will make the whole thing worth going to. Graham x"

Hey ho. Little does Graham know that I've

already got a complimentary ticket from Tralee Josie. It sounds as though Graham finds these fundraising shindigs as challenging as I do - still it would be much more fun with him there. And besides, it will be a chance to introduce him to Josie and Callum, assuming that he'll be dragged along as well. I know that Micky won't be there because Friday is his evening shift at Finnegans and posh charity balls are definitely not his scene.

Decision time then.

"Hi Graham. Yes enjoyed last night and even remembered the last bit this morning without prompting! I've already had an invite to the charity do and wasn't going to go....until you changed my mind. You do realise I've now got to find myself a posh frock?! Catch up later. JJ xxx to be continued...."

I smile at the last bit as I hope Graham will. He responds with two happy face icons and I'm so distracted that I nearly miss my stop for Dr Silver.

"Well you look cheerful today" he says as I walk into his office apologising for being a few minutes late.

"I feel cheerful" I reply "and who wouldn't be here in this lovely place on such a gorgeous day?"

"Hmm I wish all my patients were as bright and breezy as you JJ. Now about these drawings you've done – they are quite magnificent"

Dr Silver is looking at my snake tattoo drawing and the one of the young woman with the blood splattered dress.

"This one of the girl – you say you did that from visual memory after the shooting last week?"

I nod and glance again across at the drawing. I

haven't seen it since I left it with Dr Silver a few days ago. He spends what feels like several minutes staring at the drawings and seems transfixed.

"This is all very promising JJ. Your purely visual memory seems to be strong – probably much stronger than most peoples. And you say you are still getting more brief flashback memories when you first wake up?"

"Yes Dr Silver I am. I've noticed that most mornings there are some images or snippets in my head from the day before. Nothing complete, just bits and pieces jumbled up"

"But you think these are getting more frequent – I mean that you are getting a bigger number of these 'snippets' as you call them?"

"I think so. I usually lie awake and try to make sense of them before looking at my diary. You know, just to see what is there without any reminders. Then when I look at the diary things start to fall into place"

I'm relieved that Dr Silver doesn't mention my 'delay' in taking part in his memory study. Instead he talks me through my diary and winks when he gets to the latest mention of Graham Tucker.

"So you and Tucky are getting along well then?" he laughs as he notices me blush and I find it hard to look him in the eye.

I change the subject by mentioning the charity ball.

"Are you going?" I ask him as I pick up my drawings from the side of his desk.

"No not this time" he answers still scanning down my diary entries. "But you are I guess?"

"Yes and I'll be going with Graham" I feel myself blushing again which is maddening.

"Well I hope you both have a good time" he says smiling and putting my diary notes back in his file. "Now let's put you down for your next appointment"

After finishing my consultation with Dr Silver, I head into Hamilton to buy a dress fit for a ball. It doesn't take me long to find a red silk gown which the shop owner says "is absolutely made for me" and has fifty per cent knocked off the asking price. Not that it's saying much because the price is extortionate but the dress is divine and fits perfectly. Ah well – 'in for a penny in for a pound' as my mom would say.

Of course I then have to get the shoes, bag, necklace and make a hair appointment for an "up do" as the hairdresser puts it. At this rate I won't have much money left to donate to the charity, which is supposed to be the whole point of the evening.

Two days later and here I am waiting for Graham to pick me up which he has insisted on doing. Pauletta has already told me how glamorous I look and I must say that a few hours of effort has paid off. I virtually jump out of my skin when I get a call from Graham to say that he's waiting on the driveway.

As I approach the car Graham gives out a low whistle which isn't like him.

"My you look a picture – absolutely beautiful" he says helping me into the waiting car. It's a sleek black Mercedes with a smartly dressed driver at the wheel who greets me with a small wave. Graham is dressed in a formal tuxedo 'penguin' suit yet still manages to look cool.

When we get to the main Hamilton hotel, Graham reminds me that this was the first place where we met - as if even with my dicky brain I was going to forget. Tralee Josie is standing in reception and looks her usual stunning self in a shimmery aquamarine dress, while Callum stands at her side looking hot and uncomfortable in his evening suit.

"JJ red really suits you – wow you look amazing." I tell her that she looks superb too before she spots Graham standing behind me.

"Er this is my friend Graham" I say as he extends his hand out to Josie.

"Hi Graham" Josie says shaking his hand before introducing him to Callum. Josie has to stay at the reception area to greet the guests so Graham and me make our way into the main ball room. The tables are crammed closely together so it takes a few minutes for us to find where we are supposed to be sitting. Tucker Associates has taken out a table for twelve people and I'm relieved to be sitting right next Graham as I don't know anyone else at company.

There isn't much time for introductions before the main event kicks off with a live band while dinner is served. As usual with these sorts of events, the food is a tad overcooked and with the band playing in the background it's hard to make conversation. Graham's colleagues are pleasant enough but I'm happy to spend the time talking to my new boyfriend. Can I say he's a boyfriend yet? I think so, especially the way he is looking at me this evening with his arm draped loosely across the back of my chair.

After dinner the raffle starts and I'm astonished at the high level of the bids. One of Graham's colleagues bids $500 for a white teddy bear for his young son who he says "will love it".

"Well he should do at that price" I whisper to Graham who shrugs and smiles. Next there is a bid for a dinner for two at one of Hamilton's top restaurants. Graham makes an opening bid of $200 dollars but the price carries on rising. I keep telling him to stop but he says that it's "all in a good cause" and he finally wins the bid at $1,000.

"So that's us sorted for a slap up meal" he laughs after he collects the ticket and sees the gobsmacked look on my face. I can see Tralee Josie glancing across at our table and she winks at me as I catch her eye.

I make a half hearted bid for a garnet necklace but back off when the bid goes above $300. It's all good fun but I can't help feeling that it's really about showing off and it makes me feel uncomfortable. Whereas Graham's view is "heck what the hell?" if lots of well paid people are prepared to part with their cash for a good cause and a night out.

At the end of the raffle it's announced that a staggering $550,000 has been raised for the children's charities. And Tralee Josie's boss, a Mr Michael Mountfield, announces that there will be the usual annual presentation of cash with a photo opportunity for TV and the press.

"They do that every year" Graham tells me "it's

done with real dollars too. Last year they gave out $300,000 at the press conference in great wads. It's an awesome sight and a much better photo opportunity than a cheque although everyone does have to sign receipts"

"I expect the security is tight" I reply trying to imagine what so much money looks like.

Graham laughs and says that in the ten years it has been happening nothing has gone wrong.

After the raffle everyone is invited into the main ballroom for more live music and dancing. I can see Josie in the background trying to entice Callum onto the dance floor and if I'm not mistaken, he looks a bit unsteady on his feet. Poor Callum, I'm sure he'd rather be down at Finnegans with his mate Micky.

Next thing I can feel Graham's arm on my shoulder.

"Shall we skip the dancing bit and just sneak off?" He has a cheeky grin on his face and I'm left in no doubt what sneaking off will mean.

I make a quick call to Pauletta to say that I've decided to spend the night at a friend's place and then make my way back to Graham who is waiting by the main reception door.

"It's a lovely evening so let's walk back to my place. It's not too far" he says "and I make a mean coffee"

I laugh and say that I'll still have to remember to fill in my diary.

"I'll remind you about everything in the morning" he replies putting his arm around my waist "and by the way, I make a mean breakfast as well"

We both laugh, me a little nervously. Is this all happening a bit too quickly? But then as I know only too well, life is too short for procrastination and for the second time in a few days my mom's favourite expression "in for a penny in for a pound" comes to mind.

Chapter 18

Getting into murky waters

Graham has left for work and I'm padding around his swanky uber modern waterfront apartment wearing one of his old shirts. Two weeks have passed since the night of the charity ball when Graham and me became a 'proper couple' as I put in my diary the following day. I can't help but laugh at my own twee expression here but that's typical of me.

Since then I've hardly been back to my rented flat, a fact not unnoticed by my landlady Pauletta. Going over my diary, I can see that yesterday she phoned me to check that I was ok "because I've not seen you around for a few days." I decided then and there to tell her that I've got a new boyfriend and note that this seemed to appease her. I know I'll get the third degree when I go back to my flat later on today but I don't really mind. It's really not difficult to find an excuse to talk about Graham and I'm sure Pauletta will approve.

I haven't told my mom or little brother Jeff yet but I can't put it off for long. Mom will have a million questions and will want to know everything about him from the off. I can hear her now demanding details about his family, his looks and whether he is 'minted'. She'll love the fact he's a lawyer and that he's a good five years older than me.

I haven't yet met Graham's parents but already feel that I know them from the pictures dotted around the apartment. His mom, Evelyn, is elegantly slim, dark skinned with short silver hair and has an enigmatic smile. She exudes a certain reserve and has intelligent deep brown eyes like Graham's. His dad, William, or Bill as he likes to be known, is tall with a lightly freckled complexion and sandy coloured hair. Bill is a lighter coloured version of his son and I can see how Graham is going to look in twenty five years time.

Graham has regaled me with tales of his idyllic childhood in Bermuda, with Evelyn combining her time as a stay at home mom and charity worker. Dad Bill used to be a senior officer in the island regiment but retired about ten years ago and now spends a lot of his time playing golf. Graham is an only child because doctors advised his mother not to have any more children after she nearly died of a haemorrhage giving birth to him. So Graham grew up cosseted and adored although he assures me that he isn't "one of those only child spoilt brats"

I need to go back to my flat get some more clothes and later on I'm due to meet Callum and Micky to go through the next phase of 'the plan' whatever that is. I've not heard from either of them since before the charity ball and I've only managed to have a few snatched phone conversations with Tralee Josie. There hasn't been much contact from St

George's Josephine either, though we have been in touch by email. She knows that Graham and me are now an item and from what I can gather she is delighted for us. I make a note to go and visit her soon and to show her my latest drawing of the young woman caught up in the recent shooting.

Talking of that incident, it seems that the victim has pulled through although his injuries are still life threatening. The early rumour that it was a case of mistaken identity seems to be true if you can believe what the newspapers are saying. And this latest shooting has been the talk of the TV and radio stations with most of the locals barely able to believe this has happened in their generally low crime and peaceful idyllic island. Despite everything, I feel incredibly safe here and much more so than I did back in London. Still, I can understand why the politicians, police and community workers want to nip this gang activity in the bud. They don't want Bermuda turning into another Jamaica or Trinidad where the murder rates have already gone through the roof.

When I finally arrive back at my flat it doesn't take long for Pauletta to knock on my door asking if I'd like to join her for coffee. It's a thinly veiled excuse for her to hear all about Graham and I don't disappoint her.

"Well you've certainly done well for yourself there" she says pouring me another cup of her deliciously strong coffee "and good for you. You deserve a bit of luck after what you've been through"

I smile, adding that I feel very lucky to have such

an intelligent and charismatic man interested in me.

"He's lucky to have you too" Pauletta replies "and I hope he knows it"

I'm not quite so sure about that, as he has a lot to put up with at the moment. The constant diary writing and my lack of coherent short term memories must get to him sometimes. But if that is true he doesn't show it and he has been incredibly patient with me. He also has a great sense of humour about everything and makes me laugh – I think that's much better than being all po-faced and overly concerned about my predicament. We're having lots of fun and every day with him is a new adventure. I can't remember when I was last so happy and so head over heels in love. And I know Graham feels the same which is all that matters to me right now.

I make my excuses to Pauletta and then set off carrying my compact overnight bag to meet Callum and Micky, or the 'gruesome twosome' as I've now nicknamed them. We are meeting up again at Par La Ville Park in the centre of Hamilton and this time I arrive ahead of them.

They turn up fifteen minutes late and Micky is the first to apologise.

"Fecking hell JJ – hope you haven't been waiting too long. We got talking and lost track of the time so sorry about that"

Callum hangs back awkwardly and gives me a nod. We find a bench in the park to go through what Callum says is another "huge favour" they need me to do at the bank.

As a reminder, they go back over my original

agreement to pay regular money into Josie's employer's charity account on behalf of Micky. In other words "the plan" as I've been referring to it cryptically. Micky tells me that this is to build up a ring fenced fund that he can't get at easily. He will use the saved money to pay off the P Crew gang members who are still on his back over the disappearance of their 'parcel'. So far so good.

Callum then adds the killer extra request, the big 'but.'

"Only today JJ we need you to do something a bit different and this time it isn't just about putting money in. It's taking some money out as well"

Now I'm really confused.

"What do you mean?"

Callum now has a concerned look on his face, while Micky stays quiet for the moment.

"JJ you don't know this yet but Josie had to dash back to Ireland yesterday because her little sister has been taken seriously ill with meningitis. She didn't have time to ring you last night because it was all such a panic booking flights and getting her to the airport"

I stare at Callum for a few moments while I take in this bombshell news. Poor Josie must be frantic with worry and I know how close she is to her "little sis".

"I'm sorry to hear that. How bad is it?"

"Pretty bad" Callum replies "that's why Josie just had to jump on the first plane out. I'd have gone with her but there was only the one spare seat. Besides, she said she wanted to go on her own and that she'd ring me as soon as she has more news"

Momentarily distracted by Josie's bad news, my mind returns back to the bank transaction. As if reading my thoughts, Callum goes straight back to the subject.

"You're probably wondering what all this has got to do with needing you to go into the bank today?" I nod and he adds "It's a favour for Josie this time. You probably don't remember about the photo shoot planned for the children's charity do you?"

I look suitably bemused so he continues.

"Well, every year there is a photo shoot for the children's charity which involves a lot of money raised by the annual ball. I've got a signed withdrawal slip here for $300,000 and the photo shoot is due to take place tomorrow. Josie suggested last night that you collect the money on her behalf because you have the same name. You'd be doing her a big favour and I'll deliver everything to the charity afterwards"

To say that I'm staggered is putting it mildly.

"What are you serious? You expect me to go into the bank impersonating Josie and pick up $300,000 dollars just like that? And why can't Josie's boss do it himself anyway?"

"He's in Boston for some medical treatment and won't be back until tomorrow afternoon just in time for the photo shoot. He thinks Josie is doing it before heading back to Ireland – only the thing is she left last night. She doesn't want to get into trouble with her boss so you'd be doing her a really big favour by stepping in" Callum looks desperate but I still can't understand why no one else from the bank can do it.

"There are only two people able to withdraw and

put in money to the charity account and that's Josie and her boss. Honestly JJ this really isn't such a big deal as you think. You just need to collect the money – it's all bagged up in tight $50 dollar batches and ready to go – then I'll take it straight in a taxi to the charity venue. They'll then put it in a safe until tomorrow's publicity shoot and nobody will be any the wiser"

He makes it sound really simple. Yeh right. I just walk into the bank and with the same name as Josie James I take out a cool $300,000. I look across at Micky who has a strange expression on his face which I can't work out.

"And what's this got to do with you Micky?"

Micky takes out a cheque for $1,000 dollars and hands it to me.

"Yeh, I still want you to pay this in for me anyway - after you collect Josie's charity money. That part of our deal still stands"

"But I'm not Josie, I look nothing like her" I say getting increasingly exasperated.

Callum puts his hand on my arm reassuring me that everything will be fine.

"Look Josie doesn't go in there all that much and it was only a few weeks ago that they saw you in there as a genuine 'Josie James' paying in a cheque to the charity account. Trust me, they'll just get you to counter sign for everything and this is something they've been doing for years dealing with different people. It will all be fine"

I am far from convinced but Callum reminds me that I'd be stopping Josie from getting into trouble for jumping on an earlier flight. The Josie sympathy card wins despite my misgivings.

And so it is that I head off for the bank, with Micky and Callum reassuring me that they'll meet me at a nearby taxi rank after I've collected the money and paid in Micky's cheque. My heart is hammering as I walk into the imposing concourse of the bank and straight up to the main desk, as just as Callum has told me to.

The young woman behind the desk smiles when I introduce myself and tell her why I am here.

"Ah yes, we're expecting you Josie. Will you need an escort to your vehicle?"

As Callum has already instructed me to say, I turn down the offer of a bank escort. The package she hands over is quite heavy but doesn't look nearly as large as I was expecting.

"It's great that you guys raise all this money every year for charities" she says smiling before getting me to sign at the bottom of a cash release form.

"Anything else you'd like to do while you are here?" she asks after I've given my signature.

"Yes can I pay this in as well?" She nods as I pass over Micky's cheque for $1,000 and I quickly sign the paying in slip.

"Have a great day and I'll look out for the photos in the paper tomorrow" the bank teller says.

And with that I head out into the heat of the early afternoon my heart still pounding and I make my way up towards the taxi rank, where Callum and Micky are waiting with my small overnight bag in tow.

As I head towards them carrying my bulky

parcel containing a fortune in money, I make up my mind that this will be my last ever visit to that bank as my namesake Josie James.

Yes, absolutely my last visit.

Chapter 19

Stepping into a nightmare

Up until this point, I thought my biggest nightmare was steeping into the path of a motorcycle on a busy London street. How wrong was I.

No, as it is I'm now slap bang in the middle of my worst ever nightmare and here in beautiful Bermuda, a tropical paradise. If it wasn't for Graham and St Georges Josephine, I think I would be asking to be sectioned at the nearest psychiatric hospital. Instead I'm confined to Graham's apartment with an electronic bracelet around my ankle.

I'd like to know exactly how I got to this point but I've only got a few fragmented images and none of them make much sense. Graham keeps telling me that I'll be ok and justice will prevail in the end. He's a lawyer so he should know. But I'm just confused and bewildered – it's as though someone has thrown me in a room with a huge jigsaw puzzle and keeps asking me to put the disjointed pieces together.

Anyway, here's what I understand to have happened so far. I know I saw Micky and Callum on

Wednesday afternoon because I made a note in my other private book – the one I don't show to Dr Silver – that I'd met the 'gruesome twosome' to discuss 'the plan'. As things now stand, I still have no idea what that it refers to.

I know from my 'proper' detailed diary, that I also called into my flat to collect some clothes and that I told Pauletta all about me and Graham. I also know that I arrived back at Graham's place around 4pm and later that evening we went out into Hamilton for a meal at a swanky restaurant called Chicos. As my diary tells me, Graham used the restaurant vouchers he bid for at the children's charity ball a few weeks ago. So far so good and understood.

The next bit is where the confusion really starts and I keep re-reading my diary entries to check for any clues as to what may have led up to it. So here goes.

The very next morning, Thursday, Pauletta rings me to say that two police officers are at her house and they want to speak to me urgently. Could they talk to me right now?

A man then comes on the phone and introduces himself as Detective Inspector Andrew Robinson. He says that he needs to see me as soon as possible but not to worry – they just need to check something out and I might be able to assist them. He asks if he can come over straight away and I give him the written down address to Graham's apartment. He is reluctant to discuss details over the phone but reassures me that it's nothing to do with my family in England. He tells me to stay put and they'll be with me in ten minutes.

I get dressed hastily throwing on a T-shirt and shorts and pull a comb through my hair. I wonder what it's all about? At least it's nothing to do with my mom or Jeff which was my first concern.

I'm just putting on the kettle to make some coffee, when DI Robinson and his colleague Laura Barton arrive. As it turns out, they are both from England which I find reassuring. But not for long as it turns out.

As soon as they get into the house they announce that I'm being arrested on suspicion of theft and that they have a warrant to search the property.

"But I don't understand – what do you mean theft? And you can't search here because it's not my place. It belongs to Graham Tucker"

They both exchange glances when I mention his name and DI Robinson tells me that I'm being arrested on suspicion of taking $300,000 from a Hamilton bank yesterday which was meant to be delivered to the premises of the Bermuda Child Welfare charity. Apparently I've been caught on CCTV cameras entering the bank and exiting with the money bound up in a large package. A bank teller has identified me as the person who collected the money around 2pm yesterday afternoon.

"Look I don't understand any of this" I say truthfully. "And before you start searching this place I need to call Graham – he's my boyfriend"

The officers glance across at each other again and then agree that I should call him. I can barely speak when I get him on the phone and pass him over to DI Robinson. They talk for several minutes before

DI Robinson puts Graham back on to me.

"Look just stay calm JJ, I'm on my way over. This is probably some really bad misunderstanding but try not to get yourself into too much of a state. I'll be with you in a few minutes"

There is an awkward pause while we wait for Graham to arrive, with none of us wanting to say too much or even to exchange glances. I ask if I can get changed into something more formal and they agree as long as Laura is allowed to stand outside the bedroom door while I do so. There is a surreal scene as I hurriedly throw on a dress with Laura standing guard immediately outside. What exactly did they expect me to get up to in here I wonder?

When Graham arrives he gives me a comforting hug before disappearing into the kitchen with DI Robinson. Laura and me are left standing in the living room still trying hard not to look each other in the eye. Meantime I'm left puzzled about this $300,000 and exactly what it has to do with me.

After several minutes, Graham and DI Robinson come in from the kitchen and I can see straight away that Graham is agitated.

"Look JJ you're going to have to go to the police station. Don't worry though I'll come with you and I'll get someone from Tuckers onto the case straightaway"

" But why can't you sort it out yourself?" I ask suddenly feeling very scared.

Graham puts his arms around me and tells me that he can't represent me because we are in a relationship.

"Will she need an appropriate adult as a

vulnerable person?" DI Robinson asks looking across at me with a pitying look.

"What do you mean vulnerable person?" I ask annoyed that he's speaking as though I'm not in the room.

"It's all right JJ" Graham reassures me. "He's just doing his job. He means you're vulnerable because of your memory problems – I've already told him all about it"

I glare across at DI Robinson while he reads out the sort of arrest statement that I recognise from the old TV episodes of 'The Bill' I used to watch all the time in London. Strange how these words have stayed lodged in my long term memory hard drive.

Later on at the police station I'm introduced to solicitor, Clare Thompson, from Tuckers and she says that she has met me before at the children's charity ball. I believe her but I can't say that I recognise her.

The next few hours are a blur with the police quizzing me about something I know nothing about. Yes, it is definitely me on the bank CCTV pictures – I have seen the still grabs from the camera – but I have no memory of going into the bank or taking away the package of money. Looking at the pictures I'm not even getting a flashback image of being there.

And why would I do that anyway? DI Robinson has taken away my computer and phone, passing them over to his "digital forensic investigators" as he calls them. He keeps asking me about this 'plan' I keep referring to in my separate diary and also wants to know about this 'gruesome twosome.' I tell him that they are friends of mine, Micky and Callum, and that it is just an affectionate name for them. DI Robinson says that he is going to have to interview all of my friends and associates in Bermuda including Pauletta and my two namesakes.

"Tell me more about how you met this 'Tralee Josie' as you call her."

I'm getting tired now and I'm desperate for a cup of coffee. I also tell DI Robinson that I need my computer back because I have to write and back up my daily memory diary.

"Sorry JJ but that's not going to be possible for a few days at least" he says looking across at my solicitor Clare. "You'll just have to record things manually or use your boyfriend's computer"

This is all I need. I'm starting to feel sick with anxiety and Clare interrupts to say that she will insist that I get my computer back as quickly as possible and that the interview should now end because "my client is clearly exhausted and needs to be given some rest." She says that I should be allowed to return home for tonight under the care of Graham Tucker and adds that they will request bail while police carry out their inquiries.

However the police have other ideas and insist that I remain at their station overnight until the question of bail is resolved. So I spend a sleepless night in a police cell, listening to the shouts and cries from other prisoners and trying to write down as much as possible about my memories of this horrific day. I must have fallen asleep at some point because I'm sharply awoken by the sound of heavy doors slamming and for a few minutes I'm totally disoriented. Until my new notebook brings everything back and I realise what a mess I'm actually in.

Graham arrives early and we spend several minutes just holding each other. He keeps telling me that he'll sort this out and that I'll be back home with him by this afternoon.

"You haven't said anything to my mom and Jeff have you?" I ask, panicking at the thought of their reaction to the news of my arrest.

"Good lord, of course I haven't" Graham says looking surprised that I'm asking such a question

"Sorry, I didn't mean to accuse you of going behind my back. It's just that my mom is such a worrier and Jeff won't understand why his big sister has been arrested like this"

Clare then arrives clutching a large sheaf of papers and three coffees balanced on a small tray. Never has a coffee tasted so good.

"Right then JJ" she announces. "We're off to court to sort out your bail. And just to warn you, if they agree to you staying at Graham's place you'll probably be fitted with an electronic ankle bracelet to monitor your movements."

"What?" I look across at her and Graham wanting to scream.

Graham puts his arm across my shoulders and tells me that it's not as bad as it sounds,

"They are very discreet JJ – if you wear trousers no one will be any the wiser. But you'll be restricted to certain areas – you won't be able to go near the bank or to see any possible witnesses like Micky,

Callum or Tralee Josie"

Electronic tags? Witnesses? Already I'm beginning to feel like a criminal and yet I know deep down that I haven't done anything wrong. The CCTV pictures might say differently but I still know that I'm not a thief.

Then Clare delivers the bombshell that makes me feel lightheaded like I'm going to pass out.

"Listen JJ we're working on the assumption that you have been set up by someone taking advantage of your disabilities. Can you think of anyone who might do that?"

I slump on the cell bed unable to move. Graham looks concerned and asks me if I'm ok.

"Of course I'm not ok – I'm in a bloody cell accused of stealing thousands of dollars and now she's telling me that I might have been set up by god knows who. Yeh I'm absolutely great, never felt better"

Graham looks shattered and immediately I regret snapping at him. Then DI Robinson appears saying that we need to make a move for the court appearance.

I grab Graham's hand and whisper sorry. He squeezes my hand in return and tells me to try to relax.

From the back of a police patrol car, I can see people going about their morning business on the sunny Hamilton streets. People heading off to work and tourists peering at street maps. The stuff of everyday, ordinary lives. Only yesterday I was one of them. But today I'm JJ, the woman accused of a despicable theft from a children's charity. And however hard I try, I already feel like a criminal caught in a forensic web. After all, as the saying goes, the camera never lies and I'm right there in the thick of the frame.

Snapped and trapped for posterity.

Chapter 20

To Catch A Thief

It's now been three days since my arrest and although I'm not locked up, I feel like a prisoner. Admittedly my 'prison' is a beautiful penthouse apartment with amazing views across Hamilton harbour. But with this ankle tag and restrictions on where I can go and at what times, I already feel like someone who is tried and sentenced.

Graham has attempted to pull me out of the deep depression that has taken hold in the way he knows best – by joking about it. Only last night he quipped that people pay "good money" to buy ankle jewellery and here I am getting mine for free. I pretended to laugh but then went into the bathroom and sobbed my heart out. I know he doesn't mean to be insensitive, but this is about as far from a joke as anyone can get.

My mood hasn't been helped by having to tell mom and Jeff about my arrest. Predictably mom's first response was that she was on her way over here and nothing was going to stop her. Fortunately Graham was able to talk her out of it, saying that he was sure it wouldn't take long to catch the 'real' culprits and that I was in the best legal hands. That seems to have done the trick – for now at least.

So here I am today, left on my own in a gilded cage. Thank God I've finally got my computer, cell phone and notebooks back so I can keep some sort of grip on reality. Since my arrest I've heard nothing from Tralee Josie, Callum or Micky. My solicitor, Clare, has advised me not to contact them as they are going to be quizzed formally themselves by the police. At least I've got a visit later today from my other namesake, St George's Josephine, who has already been a pillar of support and I can't wait to see her again.

I know it's only a matter of time before I bump into Josie, Callum and Micky in town and I'm dreading it. It's surprising that I haven't done so already, although I suspect Josie is still over in Ireland visiting her sick sister. Actually I've now developed a real fear of going out on my own, as if I can't trust myself. The only time I've been out since my arrest has been with Graham in tow and even then I feel like everyone is staring disapprovingly. So far there has only been a brief piece in the newspapers about the arrest of an "unnamed female ex-pat" accused of the theft of $300,000 destined for children's charities. Still, I feel I've got a big sign on my forehead saying dirty rotten thief. Silly I know, but true.

So to take my mind off things I decide to make some fresh lemonade for St Georges Josephine's visit using one of Graham's tried and tested recipes. As a distraction it works well and for a blissful hour I manage to put the arrest to the back of my mind. I'm just putting the final swirls of lemon zest into my mix when my phone rings out. The caller id shows that it is Micky, so I'm not sure whether I should answer it. I let it ring off and there is no message. When it rings again a few minutes later, I decide to pick it up.

Micky sounds weird, as if he is speaking through a piece of thick cloth.

"Hi JJ. You ok? Shouldn't be ringing you because the police have just been round and told me not to. But I'm so shocked about what I've heard. Er, you still there?"

I take a deep breath.

"No Micky I'm not ok. Far from it and yes, you shouldn't be ringing me. It's a bloody nightmare and I've no idea or memory of how I got into it in the first place"

Micky stays quiet for a few seconds.

"Sorry JJ, I'm really sorry for you. I hope it all gets sorted. Stay strong"

And then the phone goes dead. I feel uneasy about the call and wonder whether I should tell Clare straightaway. But I don't want to get him into trouble and it's not as though we've actually really discussed anything. He's probably just wanting to check that I'm all right, which is quite nice of him really. No, I'll just ignore it and get back to my lemonade.

Josephine arrives with another huge bouquet of flowers from her garden and a book about painting and drawing techniques "to get my mind off all this silliness". She gives me a long hug and immediately I burst into tears, apologising through my sobs. Josephine insists that I sit down while she pours our drinks.

"You ok over there?" she asks pouring the drinks and treating me to one of her gorgeous trademark big grins. You can't stay miserable for long in her company, so I nod and return the smile.

"Hey JJ this tastes divine and lemon as well – my favourite."

I sip my lemonade gratefully while Josephine congratulates me again on my culinary achievement.

"Now then" she says after wiping her lips and pouring a second glass "I want to hear properly what all this nonsense is about"

I can barely decide where to begin but I go through the little of what I do know. Josephine has already heard the headlines from myself and Graham but she still looks as though she is listening for the first time, her mouth slightly agape.

"And you say that there are photos of you with the money at the bank? And leaving the bank too?"

I nod glancing down at my ankle bracelet which is just about visible beneath my loose cotton trousers.

"And you can't remember anything of this? Not even the smallest bit?"

I nod again adding that I have written something about meeting Callum and Micky to go through 'the plan' which the police think is suspicious.

"But surely they don't think you did it? Are they mad?" Josephine says looking angry "It's obvious that someone has set you up knowing that you have these memory problems"

"That's what my solicitor Clare thinks" I reply "but the police say they are keeping an open mind.

The trouble is that I'm caught on camera so I that puts me at the bank and I did leave with the money"

Josephine frowns and takes another sip of her lemonade.

"Tell me about this Callum and Micky. If I remember right, Callum is the fiancé of Tralee Josie as you call her?"

I go over everything I know about Callum and Micky. She is interested that their names seem to be connected to this 'plan' and that I've previously written about Micky being threatened in the street.

"Are the police going to investigate all of this?" she asks tapping her long red varnished finger nails on her drink glass.

"They've taken copies of all my diaries so yes, they will do. They've also taken my drawing of the young man with the snake neck tattoo and the drawing of the girl in the blood splattered dress I did after the shooting at Hoagies"

Josephine eyes my jug of lemonade as if deliberating whether to have yet another one. She decides not to and pushes it out of her line of vision.

"Well JJ it's good that they have all this background and I'm sure I'll be getting a call anytime now. When they do get in touch I'll tell them that there's no way this is down to you. No way"

I thank her for all her support and she leans across to give me another hug. I can feel my eyes welling up again but manage, just about, to hold it together.

Josephine is still here when Graham arrives home and she rushes over to greet him.

"Graham sweetie, you're looking as handsome as ever!" she says throwing her arms around him. Graham laughs and smiles across at me. Just seeing him makes me feel happier and safer.

I leave Graham and Josephine chatting in the sitting room, while I go into the kitchen to make some coffee. They are speaking in hushed voices so I guess they must be talking about what's happened to me. When I get back with the coffee, Graham is on the phone and from what I can gather he's talking to Clare. Josephine says she'll head off now because she needs to call in and see her dad on the way home.

"You really must meet him sometime JJ, you'd like him. Now say goodbye to Graham for me and remember we're all rooting for you"

She kisses me on the cheek and waves across to Graham as she heads for the door. Graham waves back but carries on talking to Clare with a preoccupied look on his face.

I follow Josephine outside to her small navy blue car which is laden at the back with boxes of her home made jewellery. She reaches over and takes out a pair of earrings which she says are made from something called Bermuda lucky stone. The colours are a stunning mix of pink, lilac and pale green.

"They're absolutely beautiful" I say holding them up to inspect the colours against the bright afternoon sunshine.

"They're for you JJ and I hope they bring you the luck you deserve"

"But you must let me pay for them. You've already given me loads of presents" I reply wanting to go back into the apartment to get my purse.

"Absolutely not. You just make sure you wear them every day until this mess is over with"

And before I can argue she is inside the car and starting the engine.

"Bye JJ and you give me a call anytime if you need to chat. Now go back in to that great boyfriend of yours"

With that she is off and I watch her car disappear out of the communal gates. A neighbour sitting on his terrace looks across and gives me a friendly wave. I wave back, but then dash back into the apartment not wanting to engage in a neighbourly chat. I still think that everyone here really knows about my arrest and are just trying to be polite. Paranoia really is starting to take hold but then who can blame me in the circumstances?

Graham is sitting on the sofa when I get in and looks deep in thought.

"Josephine had to dash off" I say sitting down beside him and planting a kiss on his cheek. He puts his arm around me.

"Listen I have some interesting news" he says "really interesting news"

"What's that then?" I say snuggling up closer.

"That was Clare on the phone just now and it seems that a police officer recognises that young guy you drew with the snake marking. Seems he's involved with one of the biggest gangs on the island"

I sit upright to look him in the face.

"Really? But why is that so interesting?"

Graham leans across to pick up his mug of coffee

which by now must be going cold.

"Well this guy has form for extorting money from people and for serious assault. As he was one of the men you saw threatening Micky, the police think it's worth getting him in for questioning"

"But what's that got to do with my case?" I ask not understanding where this is going.

"They're not sure either but I get the impression that the police think Micky is being threatened and is running scared. So it's worth them checking out this young guy just to see if he knows anything "

"So they think this guy and Micky might have set me up?"

Graham shrugs and grimaces as he drinks the now tepid coffee.

"Urgh – think I'll pour myself something stronger. But yes, they could have something to do with what has happened to you. It's certainly a good line of inquiry"

Graham gets up and takes a beer from the mini fridge perched at the side of his computer desk and asks if I want anything. I opt for cold ginger beer which I'm starting to get hooked on in this summer heat.

Graham raises his beer glass in a toast and then spots my Bermuda lucky stone earrings which I've put down on the glass coffee table.

"Josephine made those" I say handing them across for him to look at. "She insisted that I have them and she said it will bring me good luck"

"Well let's see them on then"

Graham smiles as I put on the earrings and flick back my hair for him to see.

"They look great" he says "the colours really suit you"

I go across to look at myself in the large mirror and the sparkling stones glint back at me reflecting the light perfectly. I'm going to do what Josephine suggests and wear these every day.

A police siren goes off suddenly in the background which makes me flinch. At the same time a Kisskadee bird lets out a loud squawk as if it has also been surprised by the siren sound.

Graham is now standing behind me and puts his arms around my shoulders.

"Well you and Josephine and can believe in lucky stones but me? I count on good old fashioned legal investigation. And my gut tells me we're already on to something"

I'd like to believe him but my own instinct tells me that the answer to this nightmare won't come easily either through the law or Bermuda lucky stone.

The phone rings out again and this time it is Dr Silver. I haven't seen him since my arrest but he already knows all about it.

"I've suggested something to the police that might help" he says "but I'll need you to agree first. I'll come over to see you at your place tomorrow if you like"

He hasn't yet told me what the suggestion is but I've arranged for him to call in at 10am tomorrow morning and I put the appointment straight in my diary.

Another piercing cry of a Kisskadee bird resounds across the room and looking out of the window I can see it perched on the overhead cable outside. It seems to be staring straight at me, its beady eyes homing in as if hunting for prey. Then it swoops down on the grass below scooping up a small greenish red lizard in its beak before taking off into the warm evening sky.

The lizard is clamped and stuck unable to move freely. It's a feeling I know only too well.

Chapter 21

The Camera Never Lies

I've woken up in a lighter mood this morning and I'm looking forward to seeing Dr Silver. I'm going to talk to him about my increasing feelings of anger and frustration over the position I now find myself in. Strangely enough, I quite like the angry bit. It's as if my old personality – or the bits I remember of it - is resurfacing again. I quite like this feisty and opinionated JJ and as the saying goes, some good things can come out of adversity.

Graham has left for work but will call by at lunch time to hear how the Dr Silver session has gone. And I've already had a phone call from the UK Foreign and Commonwealth office inquiring about my recent arrest and asking if I need any further advice. I reply that I'm not sure at the moment but will call them if things change. The politely spoken man on the end of the phone seems relieved at my response and wishes me well. Hopefully he won't be called up again by my mom who is still panicking back at home - even suggesting that I should get a UK newspaper involved. Once more, Graham has come to the rescue, telling mom that involving a newspaper at this early stage wouldn't be helpful. As he's a lawyer she takes his word for it, although I know she's not happy about "doing nothing, diddly squat" as she fumes.

Dr Silver arrives politely early and I ask if he'd be happy to sit out on the terrace as it's such a lovely day.

"Good idea JJ" he says "I expect you're keen to get out from this apartment, as attractive as it is"

"Yes, it's good to get some fresh air" I reply as he follows me out to the large terracotta tiled terrace with its views straight across Hamilton harbour. There are a lot of boats out today and we watch them for a few minutes before getting down to business.

"Right JJ. Just to put you in the picture, I do know about everything that has happened. The police have visited me but of course I won't talk in detail about your medical condition without your permission"

"It's fine as far as I'm concerned Dr Silver. I've already told them everything anyway. They've had my computer, my mobile phone and my diaries"

Dr Silver pauses for a few minutes and gives a small cough.

"Er, yes I wanted to talk to you about that. They tell me that you have your main diary – the one I've seen – but there's another notebook too?"

I blush recognising full well that I've been keeping some details back from him. I'm not quite sure why I've done this but I guess from how I've worded things that it has something to do with Callum and Micky.

"Never mind" Dr Silver says "it sounds like there

isn't much in there anyway. Just some vague mention meetings and a plan? I suppose that's what is getting the police going, wondering what it's about. And you don't know what it means?"

"Absolutely not" I reply looking Dr Silver straight in the eye. "I know it must appear bad but I really haven't got a clue what it refers to. But I've written it down so I suppose it must mean something"

Dr Silver looks thoughtful and then takes a piece of paper out of his soft leather briefcase.

"I've brought this for you to read" he says passing it across to me. "It's another magazine article from a few years ago when I helped a young woman to recall what happened to her after she was attacked and left for dead. She'd been hit on the head and ended up with brain injuries and loss of short term memory"

I look at the article and a smiling pretty blonde haired woman stares out at me. There is a picture of her with Dr Silver standing outside what looks like a court.

"By using my deep hypnosis technique and a particular drug, I managed to get her to recall key details of what happened to her and she was even able to remember what her attacker looked like. In the end they caught the guy and he was sent to prison for attempted murder"

I stare again at the face looking out from the magazine, which shows no sign of the terrible attack she has suffered. I guess that's how I look to other people. A normal young woman with no outward signs of what I've gone through.

"So are you saying that I should do the same thing?" I ask unable to take my eyes off the woman in the magazine.

"Well, it's really only what we talked about doing earlier – you know, when I mentioned you taking part in my memory study?"

I do remember but only because this morning I've gone over all my notes about past visits to Dr Silver. I also realise that for some reason I've told him that I want more time to think about taking part.

"Yes Dr Silver but I don't understand why I've written down that I need more time to think it over. That's just plain odd"

Dr Silver peers over at me, his intelligent brown eyes trying to make some sense of what I'm telling him. If he's confused, imagine how I'm feeling. This whole secondary note I've been keeping is a complete mystery now.

"So JJ - are you saying you are ok about me trying the same techniques to see if I can get you to remember anything about this bank and money business?"

I can't see why not and if it can help get me out of this nightmare then the quicker we get started on it the better. I tell Dr Silver as much.

"You'll need to sign that consent form I gave you – I've brought another copy just in case you need it - and I'd strongly advise you to talk it through with someone close to you. Tucky, er I mean Graham, might not be a bad starting point"

He smiles reassuringly and for a few moments we are distracted by a small boat full of excited tourists snapping away with their cameras and pointing to local landmarks.

"Graham is due home in a few hours" I reply pouring myself and Dr Silver a glass of water. "I'll talk it through with him but the way I see it, let's get going on this hypnotism thing as quickly as possible"

After Dr Silver has gone, I notice that I've received an email from Tralee Josie. It's the first time I've heard anything from her since my arrest but my initial excitement in seeing her name pop into my mailbox soon disappears when I open it.

"JJ how could you do this to me? And here's me thinking you were a good friend, someone I could trust. Don't bother replying to this because I never want to see or hear from you again."

For a few minutes I'm frozen to the spot as her vitriolic words dance across the screen. My uplifted mood, helped by Dr Silver's visit, is instantly wiped away and I click off the email so that I don't keep re-reading it. I know that if I erase it and don't mention it in my diary, the memory will be gone by tomorrow. But something tells me to hang on to it and to make a note. So I describe the contents, the time and date it arrived and how upset I now feel. Surely Tralee Josie, my namesake and new found friend, can't believe I'm guilty of this? But her email suggests otherwise and that means Callum must think the same.

I'm sorely tempted to contact Micky to see what he thinks of it all. But then I can see a note in large red letters by my computer telling me not to contact Josie, Callum or Micky, as instructed by my solicitor

Clare. So best to resist that temptation and just try to rationalise Josie's email as an angry response triggered by shock. Once she's calmed down, she'll realise that she has been too quick to take things at face value. Then again, given the stack of evidence piled up against me, who can blame her?

Graham arrives home with a seafood salad from the local deli and a bottle of Lili Bermuda perfume to "cheer me up" as he puts it.

He can see that I'm upset and I show him the email from Tralee Josie.

"Well you've done right not to delete it and to make a note of it" he says giving me a quick hug and ruffling the top of my hair. I make a weak attempt to smile and then distract myself my sorting out plates and cutlery for the salad. Over lunch I tell him about Dr Silver's suggestion that I undergo deep hypnosis to see if I can remember any details, however minor, about the bank incident. I show him the article that Dr Silver has given to me, which I still haven't got around to reading.

"Looks interesting" Graham says giving the piece a quick scan. It amazes me how quickly he can read and take in the main points. I guess that's years of practice as a lawyer and having to get up to speed on things quickly.

"And what do you think?" he asks looking up from the magazine and scooping up a forkful of salad.

"I'm all for it. Anything to try to get to the bottom of this mess. Dr Silver says there are no guarantees but it must be worth a try?" I look across at Graham for approval and he nods in agreement.

So that's it then. I sign the consent form in front of Graham and he says that he'll drop it over to Dr Silver's place for me.

I'm starting to clear up the plates when Graham grabs me around the waist and tells me that he has a quiet afternoon at work so there is no rush back.

"How about we find some way to take your mind off all of this?" he whispers kissing the back of my neck and pulling me towards him.

And for a couple of blissful hours I put the arrest ordeal back of my mind and focus on being the girlfriend, one lucky girlfriend, of lawman Graham Tucker.

Afterwards we are dozing in each others arms when we are jolted by the loud buzzing of the doorbell. Graham jumps out of bed throwing on his dressing gown and almost slipping on the wooden floor as he goes to answer the door.

I get up and pull on the long shirt dress I discarded earlier on the floor. I can hear voices in the hallway and then Graham pops his head around the door raising his eyes to the ceiling.

"Hell, it's DI Robinson" he whispers "you ok to see him now? He says it's important"

I nod and say that I'll just need a few minutes to look more presentable. Graham winks and disappears while I hurriedly pull a comb through my hair and splash some cold water on my face.

When I walk into the sitting room, Graham is still in his dressing gown and making some coffee. I can sense that DI Robinson guesses what we've been up to but he is far too polite to make any quips.

I sit down opposite him trying not to look too

embarrassed about my slightly dishevelled appearance.

"So JJ" he says giving me a stare that seems to go straight through me. "Tell me again about this young man with the snake tattoo that you've drawn". He pulls out my drawing, remarking on how good it is.

"Can I get my diaries so that I can remind myself of things?" I say and he nods, looking across at Graham who is pouring out three cups of strong smelling coffee. Graham says that he'll disappear out of the way while we talk and after handing us the coffees, he goes off to the bedroom to get dressed.

Glancing back over the diaries, I answer DI Robinson's questions as best I can. Every so often he nods, makes notes and peers again at my drawing. Then he says something that completely throws me off guard and I just about manage to stop myself spilling my coffee on the pristine cream chair that I'm now perched right on the edge of.

"You should know JJ that we're about to bring this guy in for questioning and I'd like you to come into the station and take a good look at him. Don't worry, you'll be behind a screen and he won't see you". His piercing stare continues to cut through me like a knife.

I can feel my heart start to race at the thought of entering that police station again and DI Robinson can see that I'm not exactly pleased with the prospect. But the he makes it clear that I have no choice.

"JJ you're facing very serious charges here and

you need to co-operate with us in every way you can. Understand?"

I nod silently while inwardly I let out a long loud scream.

A scream that if it were for real, would be heard right across Hamilton harbour.

Chapter 22

Twists and Turns

In the middle of all this turmoil I've been asking myself "how would the old JJ deal with it?" I do still have a strong memory of the old me, the JJ who worked hard, liked to party, to stand her corner in any argument and who was fiercely loyal to her friends and family.

That's still me I think and fundamentally my personality hasn't changed. Perhaps I've become a little more introspective but that's only to be expected after what has happened. At times though, I feel like I'm looking at myself in a disconnected way like a stranger would. Who is this JJ character? What makes her tick? How does she define herself?

I thought that I was starting to find answers to these questions. Moving to Bermuda, meeting new friends and starting a new relationship with Graham have all been fantastic experiences. And after months of feeling numb and dead inside, I was starting to feel alive again. Gloriously alive.

Then all this happened. And here I am once more at Hamilton police station with DI Robinson standing by and waiting for my solicitor Clare to arrive. I wish Graham was here but he's had to get back to work to deal with a new case that has just come in. DI Robinson has already showed me the screen where I will be allowed to view the young man with the tattoo. He's called Vernall apparently and is a junior member of the P Crew gang. He's only 20 years old but has already been to prison for a vicious attack on a rival gang member.

"Clare shouldn't be long now" DI Robinson remarks giving me a look which is a strange mix of pity and suspicion.

I nod, just wanting to get this over with. I can see the afternoon sun glinting through the glass bricks of the station waiting room and I long to be outside, to feel its warmth on my skin.

"Sorry I'm running late" Clare says as she arrives carrying a stack of files and red faced from rushing in the heat of the day.

DI Robinson leaves us alone, while Clare tells me what to expect.

"You just need to look through the screen. You can see him but he definitely can't see you. We just need you to confirm that he is the same young man in your drawing but judging from what I've seen, there seems little doubt"

I know she's a colleague of Graham and that she means well, but I can't help feeling that Clare can be a bit patronising. It's as if she thinks that I've also lost my intelligence as well as my short term memory. I have to bite my tongue though, because the last thing I need is to get on the wrong side of Clare.

After a few minutes, DI Robinson comes in and asks if we are ready. We both follow him along the long narrow corridor to the viewing room. We take our seats in front of the large screen and behind it I can see two police officers standing alongside a wide smoked glass desk. DI Robinson tells them through the linked microphone that we are ready. I take in a deep breath as the handcuffed young man is led into the room and is immediately flanked by the two officers.

It's the eyes that I notice first. The same dark eyes and long lashes I recreated in my drawing. Then the bow shaped lips which are now curled in defiance and that tattoo literally snaked across his neck. I suddenly get a fleeting memory of him standing in a road and staring at me. It's over in a blink but it is there.

"So do you recognise him in the flesh?" DI Robinson asks giving me another one of his piercing looks.

"Yes, that's the same guy I saw" I reply looking back again through the screen. "Definitely the one in my drawing"

DI Robinson makes a note and then presses the connecting microphone switch to tell the police officers that we have finished. Vernall stares back at the screen his lip still curled into a disdainful snarl and I instinctively look away.

Afterwards I tell Clare and DI Robinson about my flickering memory of him staring over at me in the street.

"Can you remember which street it was?" DI Robinson asks, while Clare gives him what appears like a warning glance.

I try to conjure up the vision again but there isn't

much there. Just a hint, a passing image and certainly nothing in the way of a specific street.

DI Robinson gives out a loud sigh making me feel uncomfortable.

"Ah well. If you do remember anything more you must let us know" He glances across at Clare who seems to be making a note of our conversation. Clearly there is no love lost between these two.

When we get outside, Clare asks me if I'd like to be dropped off anywhere in town. The truth is, I'd love to go to Marco's café for a cup of cappuccino but I decide that it is best if I just get dropped back home.

"Are you sure?" Clare asks "You don't want to go to the shops or anything?"

I don't want to tell her that I'm scared of going out into Hamilton on my own after what has happened. So I just make out that I'm a bit tired and need to go home for a rest. She shrugs and we make the short drive back in virtual silence.

When I arrive back at the apartment, Pauletta and her husband Dave are standing outside looking flustered.

"Ah Josie" she says still refusing to use my assumed name JJ "there you are. We were just about to set off back home. How are you?"

She throws her arms around me while Dave hangs back shyly. Just seeing them makes me feel tearful again but I just about manage to hold back.

Once inside, Pauletta demands a tour of the apartment and coos about how beautiful it is while Dave goes straight out onto the terrace to check out the view. They have brought a large case full of my remaining bits and pieces left at their place and a dish of Portuguese casserole.

"That's for you and Graham to try later" Pauletta says placing the ceramic dish on the kitchen worktop. "Made it myself last night and as usual I did far too much"

I thank her before putting the dish into the fridge and we both head out to the terrace to join Dave. He seems besotted by the harbour view and barely joins in the conversation.

I tell them all about my latest visit to the police station and because I'm still upset about it, I also mention the email I've received from Tralee Josie.

"You poor thing" Pauletta says being her usual sympathetic self. "First the accident and now all this. How has your family taken it?"

"Not well, especially not my mom" I reply biting my lip "but I don't want them coming over here. I can't deal with them at the moment and it will just make things worse"

"Well I told the policeman who came to interview us that you are a nice young woman and that something definitely isn't right about all this. They took ages searching your room even though I told them there was nothing in there apart from a few of your spare clothes. But they wouldn't listen, would they Dave?"

Dave nods and then continues staring out across the harbour. After all these years together, I think he's decided that it's best to let Pauletta do most of the talking and to react only when invited to.

Just before they leave, Pauletta tells me to keep in touch and to contact them anytime if I need help.

"We won't let your flat out just yet in case you want to come back" she adds giving a parting glance around Graham's apartment. "But now I've seen this place I can't imagine you'll want to come back to our place in a hurry"

I smile and tell her that I've loved staying at their house and that they are like a second family to me.

"Well don't be a stranger and make sure you bring that boyfriend of yours over for a meal soon. And don't forget the casserole I brought – it's delicious isn't it Dave?"

Another cursory nod from Dave and then they are off, Pauletta still waving from the car as it makes it way down the road.

Even though I've promised myself not to, I log back onto my emails and re-read Tralee Josie's missive. I can't help wondering whether Callum was with her when she wrote it. And if so, does he go along with it? Given that he'll do anything for Josie, I think I have just answered my own question. Of course he will.

I don't know whether it's because Callum has come to mind but I suddenly get the urge to put on some jazz music. I find the Nina Simone compilation he gave to me at Hoagies jazz club and after just a few tracks I begin to feel calmer. There's something about her rich voice that is soothing, despite the lyrics which often speak of despair and disappointment.

I'm jolted out of my musical escapism by Graham phoning to say that he is going to be late because the new case he's just landed is a complicated one.

"How did it go with the police?" he asks

sounding distracted.

I give him the quick low down and tell him that I'll fill in the details later.

"My landlady Pauletta and her husband came around this afternoon so dinner is sorted – she brought some Portuguese food with her" I can sense that Graham is only half listening, so I suggest that he gets back to work and to ring me when he's setting off. He pauses for a moment and I make out someone in the background asking if he can get to a meeting in five minutes.

"Ok sweetheart, I have to dash. Now are you sure you're all right? You don't want to come down to the office and hang around here? Clare is about"

I'm reluctant to tell Graham that the last person I need to be with right now is Clare. So I tell him that I'm fine and having one of my Nina Simone sessions. He laughs and says "enjoy", before dashing off to his meeting.

It's only six o'clock and potentially I've got most of the evening on my own. I decide that it's a good time to read the article Dr Silver has left with me, while keeping Nina on in the background. As it turns out, the story is quite fascinating and there are a few similarities between the young woman featured and myself.

She's called Cassie, is American and lives in California. The article describes how she was attacked while out on a beach jogging one night, hit on the head with some sort of blunt instrument, probably a hammer. Like me she has been left with short term memory problems but her longer term memory has stayed pretty much intact. And just like me she keeps a daily diary and at the time the article was written, about two years back, she had started to get occasional flashback memories.

The piece goes on to explain how Dr Silver becomes involved in her case by offering hypnosis treatment to see if she can relive anything about her attack. It seems that the first few sessions don't come up with anything but by the third and fourth session, Cassie starts to recall some details about her ordeal.

Dr Silver suggests that they return to the stretch of beach where the attack took place and that seems to trigger even more residual memories. In the end, Cassie describes seeing a man running up quickly behind her. At first she thinks it is just another jogger, but then he runs alongside her and she remembers him raising his arm and feeling a sharp pain at the side of her head.

The magazine shows a photo kit image of the man as drawn by a police artist. He has long straggly blonde hair and a pock marked complexion. He's wearing a red shirt with a distinctive white cross pattern on the front and it turns out that he's a known drug addict who has been living rough on the beach. As well as leaving Cassie for dead, he made off with her purse and cell phone.

Within days of releasing the image and description of the man, he is arrested and he stands trial for attempted murder. He's now serving a long prison sentence and the article quotes Cassie as wanting to "get on with her life as best I can" although she has had to give up her teaching job. Dr

Silver is quoted as saying that he hopes to continue with a controlled study into short term memory problems caused by brain injuries and to use his hypnosis techniques on other patients.

The piece inspires me to fire off an email to Dr Silver.

"Just read the magazine article about Cassie. I found it fascinating and this is just to confirm that I'd like to get things moving quickly. I've signed the consent form and Graham should have already dropped it over to you. Look forward to getting started! Have a good evening. JJ"

So let's see where this experiment takes me. Whatever happens, it can't be worse than the situation I'm now in. Suddenly I feel there is some light at the end of a very long tunnel. And Cassie's smiling face looks out of the magazine giving me hope and strength.

Yes, the old feisty JJ is definitely still alive and kicking.

Chapter 23

One step forward, two steps back

Sooner or later I'm going to have to bite the bullet and go out on my own again. As lovely as Graham's apartment is, I can't stay cooped up all day while he's at work. I'll start with some short walks around the apartment complex and down to the nearby beach. Then, when I begin to feel brave enough, I'll walk into Hamilton by myself. I know from my numerous notes on the matter that I mustn't go close to where the theft took place. So I'll need to keep reminding myself of that before going 'walkies' solo.

I'll also need to prepare myself not to speak to Tralee Josie, Callum or Micky if I bump into them. And that's the problem. How will I react if I do see them? And more importantly, how will they behave towards me? So far, when I've been into Hamilton with Graham, I've managed to avoid them. That's probably because we haven't been anywhere near Finnegans or the Oggy Poggy pub where they like to hang out.

I've noticed in the newspaper that there's another jazz performance at Hoagies over the coming weekend but even if I manage to persuade Graham to take me, there's a good chance that Callum could be there. So even though I'd love to go, it's probably best to give it a miss.

Amazingly, I've been keeping up with my complex daily diary despite the distractions of living here with Graham. But I haven't done much drawing lately, even though I've received plenty of compliments about my artistic abilities. I know I'll return to it sometime but for now I need to focus all my energies on getting out of this mess.

My next appointment with Dr Silver is in two days time and it's going to be an important one. As I've never had hypnosis before, I'm not really sure what to expect. Will it be like going into a deep, deep sleep? I note Dr Silver's description of it being like a form of total relaxation, a sort of halfway between sleep and being awake. It seems that we'll focus on the parts of my diary the police are interested in, like the various meetings I've had with Tralee Josie, Callum and Micky. He will also try to get me to recall anything about the day of the bank theft. In some ways I'm looking forward to it because it might trigger something significant and could answer the question everyone is asking.

Just why did I walk into a bank and take away a huge amount of charity money?

Talking of the money, the police's economic crime team are keen to know where it has all gone. It's clear that I haven't got it – my bank accounts have been trawled over and my flat has been searched. Graham has even allowed them to look over this place and unsurprisingly nothing has been found.

The police have also quizzed me again about two odd transactions of $2,000 and $1,000 paid into the charity account by me, one on the day of the theft and another a few weeks before. Again, CCTV puts me in the bank on the day of the first deposit. As I keep telling them, I have no recollection of making either payment and I'm as bemused as they are. I note in my diary that sometimes I think they believe me and other times I'm not so sure. Perhaps they suspect my memory problem is just a big ruse to get away with a crime? But then again, Dr Silver has already made it clear to them that I have genuine and continuing short term recall problems. I know the police are only doing their job but I resent being seen as a criminal, guilty before being proven innocent.

I also hate wearing this ankle tag or 'bracelet' as they call it. It means that I have to be at home between 10pm at night and 8am in the morning, so going out for a late meal or to a later movie is impossible. Also I'm responsible for making sure that the ankle tag battery doesn't run down, so I have to keep reminder notes to check it.

Anyway, I've really got to get over this recent 'not going out on my own' phase. So starting from now, I'm going to take a walk down to the small beach just a short distance from here. It's late morning and the temperature is already in the high 70s although the humidity isn't too bad. There is also a light breeze which will make walking a lot more pleasant. I'd really like to wear shorts but with the awkward ankle bracelet that's out of the question, so it's my trusty linen trousers which are just about long enough to cover the tag.

The apartment is part of a large complex with a communal swimming pool, bar and gym. The old JJ would have been in the gym like a shot and I can remember going several times a week in London. But after my long spell in hospital I have no desire to get back into working out, although I do love walking even in this searing Bermuda summer heat. As for the pool, well there's no chance with that tag on display. I already feel paranoid enough about the neighbours without risking the chance of someone spotting my unusual leg 'jewellery.'

Several people say a cheery hello as I make my way through the complex towards the large ornamental wrought iron gates that separate us from the outside world. The gardeners are out tending the grounds and one of them is in the mood for a chat.

"Hi there sweetie, how are you today?" He smiles at me putting down his shovel and wiping away the beads of sweat running down his face.

"Oh fine thank you" I say even though I'm not really.

"You off to the beach?" he asks spotting my portable rolled up beach mat.

"I'll come with you if you like – better than working in this heat"

I laugh hoping that he's joking. He laughs back and shrugs.

"Listen to me - I wish! Well enjoy your day. I'd better get back to the digging before the boss sees me chatting to a beautiful young lady"

It amazes me how readily people pass

compliments in Bermuda. The words gorgeous, sweetie and beautiful are used routinely as casual greetings and there is genuine warmth to them. No wonder the island has some of the happiest people on earth, with these uplifting little words being bandied about every day.

The beach is actually less crowded than I expect and I manage to find a shady place to sit. I've brought Dr Silver's article on Cassie's story to re-read and also my laptop so I can go over all of my diary entries since I've arrived. I have a feeling that if I keep going back over everything, a little bit more will stay with me each time. Drip, drip to make it stick.

When I get to the bit about my first meeting with Tralee Josie and Callum, I can feel my eyes welling up. Immediately I can recall how excited I was at meeting them and how much I liked Josie. If only I knew back then how things were going to turn out. It seems such a long time ago but in reality it is less than two months and the past few weeks have been one terrifying roller coaster ride.

I'm immersed in the diaries when I hear my phone ringing out and I'm not too pleased to see DI Robinson's name pop up on the screen. His voice sounds tense.

"JJ where are you now? I need to speak to you urgently"

"I'm down on my local beach"

"Well I'm going to have to pick you up. Can you walk back towards the apartment and I'll meet you at the gates?" I hear what sounds like car keys jangling in the background.

"Any chance of telling me what it's about?" I ask already getting up from the mat and shaking the powdery pink sand off my feet.

"I'll explain in the car. If you set off now I'll be with you in ten minutes" He then rings off and I quickly gather up my things before heading back along the beach road which leads to the apartment. I pass a young couple who are playing Frisbee without a care in the world and I'm consumed with envy of their freedom. Let's hope I don't have to go back to the police station to answer yet more questions about something I know nothing about.

When I get back DI Robinson is already waiting, so I clamber into the car apologising about my beach mat which is still covered in a fine dusting of sand.

"Don't worry about that, it's the least of your worries. I'm taking you straight to the station and Clare's on her way"

Oh no, here we go again. As we pass the front of the gates, I can see the gardener who chatted to me earlier. He's laughing and joking with the other workers and they seem to be on their break with bottles of water and lunch bags scattered about. He spots me looking out of the car, mercifully an unmarked one, and waves. I give a small one back and DI Robinson glares across to see who I'm waving at but doesn't say anything.

After a few minutes he breaks our silence.

"That lad with the tattoo you drew, he's been talking to us and telling a fascinating tale if it's to be believed. If it's true we'll have to get him off the island for his own safety" He reaches across the dashboard and grabs a pack of fruit pastilles. He pops one in his mouth before offering me one. But I'm in no mood for eating.

"And has this anything to do with what has happened to me?" I ask feeling a headache coming on. It's probably dehydration and I fumble in my bag for a bottle of water.

DI Robinson sucks loudly on his pastille before popping in a second one.

"Possibly JJ. Possibly. I'm going to take you through his interview at the station and I think you'll find it interesting. By the way, my colleague Laura is on her way to Ireland tonight to interview those mates of yours, Josie and Callum"

What? Josie and Callum are both over in Ireland? That comes as a shock and I take a few seconds to digest this jaw dropping piece of news.

"Has something happened to Josie's sister?" I ask trying to keep the surprise from my voice.

DI Robinson swerves sideways as a scooter cuts up on the inside lane narrowly missing his car.

"Bloody idiot. If I had the time I'd pull him over. Er, the sister? I'm not sure what the score is there. Josie and that fiancé of hers have been off the island since all this happened and we need to know what's going on" He pauses to give the offending scooter rider an angry stare as we stop at the traffic lights.

"We've already had a chat with both of them on the telephone but Laura will turn up unannounced to double check on their story"

We spend the rest of the short journey to the police station in silence as DI Robinson expertly navigates Hamilton's busy traffic. When we get there, Clare is waiting in reception reading a copy of the Gazette newspaper. She seems relieved to see us.

"That was quick" she says putting down the paper and standing up. I'm not sure if it's because she is wearing higher heels but she definitely looks taller today and more immaculately made up, as if she's made an extra effort.

It turns out that she is due at a cocktail party to celebrate a friend's exam success and is keen for us to get started as quickly as possible. DI Robinson leads us into a small interview room and then disappears for a few minutes telling us to help ourselves to water from the cooler. I pour myself a large glass while Clare sorts out a note book and checks messages on her cell phone.

"Right then let's get started" DI Robinson says as he arrives back with several sheets of paper. He sits down opposite Clare and me, grabbing himself a ballpoint pen from a pile scattered on the table.

"Just for the record, I've got a statement here from Vernall Smythe, known as VS, who we know is a junior associate of the P Crew gang"

We listen intently as he goes through the statement. It seems that Vernall is involved with the P Crew through a cousin who is a more senior member of the gang. He's been linked to them for the past seven years, three of which he has spent in prison for an assault on an opposing gang member. And then DI Robinson reveals the killer information which has got him so excited. It's written in a sort of street patois but DI Robinson gives us the gist.

"Basically he's saying that he's been asked to lean heavily on Micky Doyle. He say's that the P Crew think he's stolen something valuable from them and recently they held Micky for a couple of days to put the frighteners on him. Seems like it has worked and he's scared witless. And it looks like this supposed accident Micky had a few months ago may well have been a deliberate shunting off the road"

Something tells me that I may have heard parts of this story before but I can't be sure. It's a bit like déjà vu when you get that vague feeling of familiarity without quite knowing why.

Clare interrupts DI Robinson to "clarify something" as she puts it.

"Can I just check – what has Micky Doyle supposed to have stolen exactly?" She looks up from her note taking, while DI Robinson shifts across his chair so that he can stretch out his long legs.

"We haven't got that information yet and I'm not sure if Vernall knows. The younger gang members tend to be kept in the dark a bit. If I had to guess I'd say it is something to do with drugs "

Clare nods and makes a note. DI Robinson then turns his attention to me.

"Ok JJ, I know we're not taping this and it isn't a formal interview. But does any of this ring any bells? We notice in your diary that you mention that Micky is in some sort of trouble and that he went missing for a while. Does that trigger anything at all from you?"

I pause for a few moments before answering.

"Well I had this feeling when you were going through the statement that a couple of things seem sort of familiar. Things like Micky being pushed off the road - sounds as though I've heard something like that before. And the bit about the stolen thing, that is vaguely triggering something as well"

It's frustrating because I'm trying to be as truthful as I can but all I have at the moment is a load of disconnected signals.

"And what do you think about this idea your Dr Silver has about hypnosis to help you remember?" DI Robinson asks looking across at Clare who is still jotting down notes.

"I'm all for it" I reply "Anything that might help"

DI Robinson nods and Clare looks up from her note taking .

"You know that we've got to clear everything with both Dr Silver and JJ before you can use anything from the hypnosis sessions as potential evidence?" She stares hard at DI Robinson who returns her gaze with an equally deadpan look.

"Yes, yes. Understood. I'm just trying to find out what JJ thinks of it ok?" He reddens slightly and Clare folds her arms defensively across her chest.

"Good. Just checking because that's my job as a lawyer. Now is there anything else?" I can sense she is keen to wrap things up to get to her party.

There's a slight pause before DI Robinson answers.

"Yes there is actually. JJ, do you know if Micky Doyle has been in touch with you since all this happened?"

I shift awkwardly on my seat. Reading back over my diaries earlier, I noticed a small mention about Micky calling me a few days ago.

It's no good trying to pretend, I'll have to come

out with it.

"Yes, I have a record that he called me briefly a few days ago to check if I was ok. But I also note that I didn't really speak to him as such"

DI Robinson looks interested and sits more upright.

"Ok - did you write down anything else about what he said?"

I shake my head and DI Robinson makes another quick note. Clare gives me a dagger-like look that would slice through thick metal and also starts writing something down.

DI Robinson then says he'll need to take my phone back for his digital forensics team to look at, assuring me that they won't have it for long.

"But why?" I ask, irritated that yet again I'll be without my cell phone for a few hours at least.

"Because JJ, you might be the last person to have heard from Micky. He's disappeared again and from what we've heard from Vernall today we're concerned for his safety"

I feel the colour drain from my face and suddenly the small interview room feels cold.

Deathly and bone chillingly cold.

Chapter 24

Remember, Remember

It's the day of my first hypnosis session with Dr Silver and I have to admit that I'm feeling nervous. It's that stomach churning kind of nervousness, the sort you get before doing an exam or taking a driving test. I've been advised to have a light breakfast so I'm now picking at a mixed fresh fruit salad topped with some Greek yoghurt. Graham is in the bedroom getting ready for work and I can hear him jabbering away on his cell phone.

"Any coffee left sweetheart?" he says emerging from the bedroom his hair still damp from the shower he's just had.

I reach over to pour him a coffee and he gives me a peck on the cheek.

"Still feeling jittery?" he asks putting a small brown sugar cube into his black coffee.

"Sort of - but excited as well" I reply trying to sound upbeat.

"Well give me a call when you've finished. I'll make sure I'm free by mid day so I can hear all about it" He gulps down his coffee, grabs an apple from the fruit bowl and gives me another kiss.

"Ok I'm out of here. I hope it all goes well, love

you loads" I watch from the window as he makes his way down the road, cell phone clamped to his ear. Poor Graham, he has a lot to put up with me at the moment.

I see that I've written a reminder about Dr Silver's offer to give me a lift home afterwards because he says that I might feel a bit out of sorts, like you sometimes do when you wake from a really deep sleep.

Today's newspapers are reporting that Micky Doyle has disappeared and there's a telephone number for people to ring if they have any information. There's also a photo of Micky staring out with a cheeky grin and wearing an Ireland rugby shirt. He hasn't been seen now for over a week and the reports say that there is real concern for his safety. There are still a couple of old texts from him on my cell phone which the police have copied and I feel incredibly sad looking at them now. No use trying to make contact even if I could because the police tell me that the phone signal is dead. And the clear implication is that Micky could be too.

When I finally arrive at Dr Silver's, his wife and young sons are there and it's the first time I've seen the boys other than in the photographs dotted around the house. They are delightful, lively and lovely looking kids. I joke with Dr Silver's wife that they will be real heart breakers one day. She laughs and tells me that they already have a number of 'girlfriends' lined up even though they are only five years old. We watch as they charge along the hallway to greet Dr Silver as he emerges from his office.

"Hey you two, enough now. I've got work to do" He brushes them off affectionately as he heads towards his office. He then nods over in my direction.

"Just give me a couple of minutes JJ. Just got to send a few emails and then we can get started. And don't look so worried, it'll all be fine"

With that he closes the office door while his wife and sons prepare to set off for their trip to a bowling alley. Mrs Silver wishes me good luck and says that she's sorry to hear all about my 'troubles' as she puts it. I feel like quipping "Which trouble – the brain or the accusation of stealing thousands of dollars?" but I stop myself from doing so. Instead I just smile and say thank you.

The treatment room is cool and is decorated in soothing pastel blue shades. There is a couch, like the sort you get when you go for beauty treatments and a couple of solid looking cream leather arm chairs. There is also a pervading scent which I think I recognise but I'm not quite sure where from.

"What's that smell?" I ask Dr Silver as he pulls one of the chairs towards the couch.

"Mainly Lavender" he replies adjusting the couch to a slightly lower position. "Do you like it? It's known for its relaxing properties"

Ah, that explains things then. My nan used to use a lavender polish and my mom would moan about the "disgusting smell". Whereas I associated it with seeing nan and getting all those sweets not allowed at home because mom thought they were unhealthy.

"Yes I like it" I reply removing my shoes as Dr

Silver has suggested. "It reminds me of my nan's house"

"Well make yourself comfortable" Dr Silver says "By the way is the couch at a comfortable height for you?"

"Yes it seems fine" I reply "Just a shame I'm not here for a relaxing facial and eyelash tint"

Dr Silver laughs and starts to get his small recording device set up. This time he also has a video camera and while I'm settling myself down, he checks the lens and wipes it with a tissue.

He then puts on some low level music which sounds like sea waves. It's very soothing and already I'm starting to feel more relaxed.

"Right JJ if you're ready I'm going to first take you through a few muscle relaxing and deep breathing exercises. Then I'll get you to count with me from 100 backwards. Ok let's get started"

He asks me to concentrate on relaxing each part of the body starting with my feet. Then I have to inhale and exhale slowly and with each breath imagine myself sinking further down into the couch. By the time we start the number count it seems like I'm floating and I can barely feel my limbs. I can hear Dr Silver all right but it is as if I'm in a bubble disconnected from the outside world.

"So JJ you'll be able to hear me speak. You're in a deep state of relaxation but still awake. Now I'll start by taking you back to the first time you met Tralee Josie and her fiancé Callum. I'll read out what you've put in your diary first"

As Dr Silver reads extracts from my diary about that day, I'm instantly transported back to the

Elbow Beach bar and my first vision of Josie and Callum as they wait for me to arrive.

"Now JJ, try to remember if you spent any time telling them about your brain injury. No rush, just say if anything comes back to you"

Although I can visualise the scene, I can't recall exactly what we talked about that day. I have lots of pictorial images floating through my mind but it's like a silent movie with no words.

"I think we must have spoken about it but I'm not getting any sense of exactly what was said and for how long we chatted about it"

Dr Silver pauses for a moment and I still feel like I'm disembodied, here in the same room but at the same time somewhere else. It's not an unpleasant feeling but quite surreal.

Dr Silver then takes me back to my first meeting with Micky at Finnegans. Again I'm able to visualise the pub and Micky but can recall little about what we spoke about. Though I do have this nagging sense that we spoke about my accident as well as his one.

I'm asked to go back to my other meetings with Josie, Callum and Micky and again I can recall virtually nothing of what we talked about. But when Dr Silver reads out my diary entry about going to Hoagies jazz club with Callum, I can remember vividly the shooting that took place that night. I can hear two shots ring out and I can see a young woman standing there in a white dress splattered with blood. Although the image is distressing, I still feel completely calm as I relive the scene.

Next, Dr Silver takes me back to the very first

day I go into the bank. There is nothing about this in my diary to help, so he asks me to visualise the exterior of the bank. I try to do so but all I get is a vague impression of a grand building with its huge doorway.

"Can you see the inside JJ? Just see if you can mentally walk through the door"

I attempt this but get no images. Dr Silver waits for a little longer but still there is nothing there. It's the same when he asks me about the day of the theft. It's as if I've never set foot in the place even though the security camera says differently.

"Ok JJ I'm going to stop things now. I'll count to ten and when I stop you'll open your eyes slowly. 1, 2, 3....."

When I do open my eyes it takes a few minutes to adjust and I focus on the ornate crystal light fitting on the ceiling which is sparkling in the bright sunshine. Beads of light bounce off the ceiling like animated droplets of water.

"Take your time sitting up JJ, there's no rush. How are you feeling?"

"Sort of fuzzy – like you do when you've dozed off and get a rude awakening"

I rub my eyes to reinforce the point and then realise that I'm probably looking like a panda because I put some mascara on this morning.

Dr Silver smiles and tells me that I've done well for a first session. Personally I'm not convinced because I haven't really come up with any new details.

"If you say so Dr Silver but I'm sorry not to have given you more to go on. I feel a bit deflated to be honest"

"Well JJ it took several goes with Cassie before she recalled anything significant. The T-shirt logo was the clincher and she only remembered that after three sessions. So not to worry. The main thing is that you have reacted well to the hypnosis and not everyone does"

After Dr Silver drops me home, I get a call from St George's Josephine asking how I got on.

"Not wonderfully but Dr Silver says it can take several goes"

Josephine tells me that she once considered hypnosis to help her give up smoking.

"What? You used to smoke?" Josephine is the last person I'd imagine to be a smoker. I can't even conjure up a vision of her with a cigarette in her hand.

"Yes, back in the day mind. In the end I decided to do it by willpower but it was hard. I kept getting these cravings and it was like withdrawing from a powerful drug – come to think of it, I suppose that's what tobacco is"

We chat about the goings on over the last few days and she says that she has read about Micky's disappearance in the papers.

I'm trying to focus on our conversation but I suddenly feel very tired. Josephine senses this saying that I "sound sleepy" and she'll call me back tomorrow.

"You go and have a lie down JJ and make sure that Graham looks after you"

I laugh and tell her that he's been brilliant and much more than I deserve. And it's true because I don't know how I would have coped without him over the past horrendous few weeks.

Although tired, I don't feel like going to sleep just yet. Instead I pour myself a ginger beer and head out onto the sunny terrace. There are lots of boats out and about and I watch as one colourful yacht moors up with a good number of people on board. I can see two women setting up what appears to be a picnic table, while a stocky man in fluorescent orange shorts is lugging a cardboard box full of bottled drinks. There is some music playing in the background but from where I'm sitting I can't quite make out what it is. It looks like they are having fun and I wonder what they are celebrating. Birthday? Anniversary? Or perhaps just life.

I'm still transfixed by the goings on in the yacht when Graham calls.

"Hi sweetheart, how did it go then?"

I tell him what I've just told St George's Josephine. In a nutshell, not much to write home about.

"Well you shouldn't expect too much from the first session and it sounds as though Ray is pleased which is good"

It seems funny to hear Dr Silver described as Ray but then again Graham's relationship with him is different from mine.

"Yes, he told me that I'd reacted well to hypnosis and I'm going to have another session in a few days time" I can hear a text message coming in on Graham's phone and it distracts him momentarily.

"Sorry about that – I'm going to have to go sweetie because I'm being called back into court. But put your glad rags on because we're going out somewhere nice for dinner tonight"

Well at least I don't have to worry about bumping into Tralee Josie, Callum or Micky in town now. Graham hasn't said where we are going but I know if he tells me to dress up it must be somewhere swish.

The yacht crowd are now tucking into lunch and several of the men are swigging from beer bottles. They must have turned the music up because I can hear a Tina Turner song being played in the background and one of the women is dancing along to it. She's wearing a bright pink swimming costume, lots of gold jewellery and is attracting a good deal of attention from some of the men. She's blonde, tall and willowy, the sort of classic model type. Now she's gyrating playfully along the yacht mast and gets a cheer from the same group of men. The other women are looking on and even from this distance I can sense their disapproval of this pink clad siren in their midst.

I could watch the yacht celebrations all afternoon but I need to crack on with my diary and to get ready for my surprise dinner out. I wonder if this is the evening I'm going to meet Graham's parents properly? There's only one entry in my diary about them and this was after they called in on their way to a friend's party. At the time I observed that it was a bit awkward because by then they knew all about my arrest and I guess they were wondering just who their beloved son had struck up a relationship with. The word I put down to describe our first brief meeting was "stilted"

But looking again at the photos of Mr and Mrs Tucker senior staring out from their silver frames, they seem like a really nice couple and I know they've brought up a fantastic son. I would love to meet them again in more relaxed circumstances but perhaps it is best to wait until this unholy mess is cleared up. And for everybody's sake, let's hope it is soon.

I notice out of the corner of my eye that my computer is flagging up a new message. It's from Clare with a curt 'For Your Information' heading and it is a forwarded email from DI Robinson. My heart sinks and I hope it isn't going to ruin my day.

"Good afternoon,

Just to update you. Our digital forensics team have retrieved material from several CCTV cameras around Hamilton on the days before the theft and on the day itself. They are now analysing this material and we will keep you informed if anything significant emerges. Regards, DI Robinson"

I stare at the email several times my feelings swinging between optimism and trepidation. While I hope that these other cameras will tell a story that can end this nightmare, at the same time I fear that they will do exactly the opposite. That they will only make things look at lot worse and put me even further into the frame.

The old JJ would never resort to prayer and would have laughed out loud at the very idea. But hell, this is the new JJ and right now I'm praying hard, with all my heart.

Chapter 25

A Wonderful Distraction

I'm not disappointed by Graham's choice of restaurant. It's out on the edge of town and has a gorgeous beach side view. Even in the fading light, the scene takes your breath away with the twinkling lights from the restaurant terrace dancing on the gentle ocean waves.

I'm in the same red dress that I wore on the night of the charity ball although I've customised it with a white shimmery throw. I'm also wearing my lucky Bermuda stone earrings which I've had on constantly since St George's Josephine gave them to me.

Graham has made an extra effort too and looks handsome in his cream linen suit and pale blue shirt. We must look like a typical young couple out for a romantic meal and our waiter asks if we are on vacation. Graham laughs.

"No, we're fortunate enough to be living here" He winks across at me and I'm thrilled that he's used the 'we' word.

I order sword fish with salad and Graham opts for a medium rare steak. He also orders a bottle of champagne.

"What are we celebrating?" I ask expecting that Graham has had a good day in court.

Graham leans across the table and takes my hand. He kisses it and stares at me for a few moments keeping hold of my hand.

"JJ, the past seven weeks have been the happiest of my life. You are beautiful, funny and my soul mate. So, the celebration is all about us and I'd like you to move in permanently with me – what I mean is, you don't need to keep that Paget flat on of yours. What do you think?"

I can't quite believe what I'm hearing especially after everything that has happened as well. To put it mildly, it's hardly been the best start to a relationship. I can feel my eyes welling up.

"What's this about then?" he says dabbing my face playfully with a paper napkin. "I hope these waterworks are a good sign"

I laugh and nod trying not to cry even more.

Graham gestures to our waiter to bring over the bottle of champagne and I can sense that the other diners know we are celebrating something.

"Are you toasting something good tonight?" the waiter asks as he carefully pours our champagne.

"You could say that" Graham replies smiling across at me but not giving anything else away. Sensing our need for privacy the waiter says "enjoy" and retreats back into the restaurant.

I can barely taste the champagne as I keep my eyes fixed on Graham and try to take in what this really means. We're not just a boyfriend and girlfriend anymore but a live-in couple, partners in a serious relationship. I tell Graham that I love him and that despite the horrors of the past few weeks, my relationship with him has been the best thing to happen to me.

"Of course you do realise that this means we're sort of engaged? No ring just yet but still pretty much there" Graham says taking my hand across the table.

"But you haven't asked me yet!" I reply already feeling the champagne bubbles going to my head.

Graham laughs and clinks his glass against mine.

"Hey first things first JJ, I'm that old fashioned sort of guy. A proper bit of time living together and we'll take everything from there. How does that sound?"

Well, well it's a proposal – at least a sort of one – and so soon after meeting up. The former JJ would have been more wary, wanting a bit more time to get to know someone before taking the plunge and living together. Not anymore though and the prospect sounds wonderful, amazing. While I wouldn't wish a car accident, head injury and wrongful arrest on anyone, finding Graham has been incredible. And to think how things might have turned out if I'd moved in with Tim. Would I turn the clock back? Right here, right now, I'd have to say no.

The question of properly meeting Graham's parents has been on my mind from earlier today but I'm not sure this is the best time to raise it. After all, what's the rush? As things turn out, it is Graham who brings up the subject of meeting his mom and dad.

"Of course I'm going to have to tell the folks

about this" he says pouring us another glass of champagne. "We can invite them over to lunch next week and you can meet them for real"

I can't resist asking him if he has spoken much to his parents about me. And what do they think about this arrest business and accusation of theft?

"Well I can't deny that they're worried about it. My mom has dealings with a number of the child care charities affected by this. But I've assured them that it's all been a horrible mistake and I think they accept that now"

I pause for a few moments before asking the next big question, perhaps a more important one than the first.

"And what do they think about my brain injury? They can't be too happy about that either"

The waiter arrives with our food so a few minutes go by before Graham answers my question.

"Truthfully? Yes they are concerned about that. I've tried to explain things but I'm not sure that they really understand. I think they'll be more reassured when they meet you in a more relaxed situation and talk to you about it"

I nod not feeling totally convinced. Looking at it from their point of view, they have a potential daughter-in-law with a bad head injury, a shot to pieces short term memory and an accusation of major theft hanging over her. It's hardly the sort of woman anyone would want for their son, let alone their only child.

Sensing my concern, Graham changes the subject and wants to know all about my first hypnosis session today. It was only a few hours back but it seems like a long time ago. I've already put a detailed description in my diary but I tell Graham that it is difficult to explain what it feels like.

"You know when you are just about to fall asleep? That bit between still being awake but you can hardly keep your eyes open? Well, it's a bit like that except you stay that way instead of falling off to sleep. It's a sort of awareness 'limbo' – floating between being conscious and unconscious. Weird really but quite nice"

Graham nods and we spend the next few minutes chatting about Dr Silver's questions and my frustration at not being able to recall details of the conversations I've had with Tralee Josie, Callum and Micky.

"Hmm – sounds as if it all went quite well" Graham says slicing a chunk of his steak. "You'll have to be patient with this sort of thing and Ray knows what he's doing. If he says things have gone ok then I'd take that as a given"

Yes, he's right of course but it doesn't stop me from feeling annoyed that I can't retrieve any additional verbal memories. And yes, I do have to be more accepting that these things take time, damn it.

So here I am the following morning, pouring over my diary notes from last night and still hardly able to believe that to all intents and purposes I'm now engaged to Graham Tucker. On the way back to our apartment – yes I can now truly say 'our' place – Graham explained to me that our more stable relationship means I can stay in Bermuda. As my notes reveal, there are few things to sort out first with immigration but that has to wait until this infernal criminal investigation is over.

The mere thought of the police investigation casts a shadow over my happiness about last night. And almost on cue my cell phone rings out and I can see that it's Clare.

"Morning JJ" she says briskly "Are you all right to talk for a few minutes?"

I say 'yes' less than enthusiastically and it crosses my mind whether Graham has said anything to her about our plans for the future. If he has done so, Clare isn't giving anything away.

"Well JJ, first things first. The police have recovered some CCTV of you in and around Hamilton on the day of the theft. It tracks you heading up towards Par La Ville Park and Callum and Micky waiting at the entrance for you. You all then disappear into the park and after about 40 minutes you all head back out of the main entrance. Unfortunately the CCTV camera nearest the bank wasn't working that day but there is a call out to various businesses in the area to see if anyone has any useful CCTV"

I listen carefully waiting for Clare to continue. After a brief pause she asks if I'm still there and I tell her that yes, I'm just taking it all in.

"Good. Now this CCTV find is important because it clearly puts you with both Callum and Micky just a short time before the theft and that fits with your own brief note about the meeting. We just now need to get more footage about what happened next"

She pauses for me to say something but I can't

really think of anything to add. So Clare ploughs on with the next bit of news.

"Now you also need to know that DI Robinson's colleague, Laura, flew back from Ireland yesterday. She's interviewed Josie and Callum and they've both made statements. The sick sister story is partly true but not as dramatic as Josie has made out. There's no serious illness, just a case of chicken pox"

Clare is briefly interrupted by someone in the background and I can hear them discussing court dates. It gives me a few minutes to digest the news about Josie's little sister and I wonder why they both still feel the need to remain in Ireland.

"Hi JJ, sorry about that" Clare continues. "Now, where was I? Yes, the sister story seems to be a bit exaggerated but at least there's a grain of truth. As for their statements, they are both denying anything to do with the theft. No surprise there but Josie is also insisting that she knew nothing about this arrangement for Micky to pay money into her company charity account. Callum backs this up, saying that the idea came out of a private discussion between the two friends over some gang threats Micky was getting. According to Callum it was Micky's idea to put some cash into an account he definitely couldn't access"

I make a 'hmm, hmm' noise to show I'm still all ears. Clare takes this as her cue to carry on.

"And that's where the idea of getting hold of Josie's employer's charity bank details came in and for you to impersonate her"

"And how did Josie take the news that her fiancé had been plotting this with Micky behind her back?" I ask, imagining how angry Josie would be.

"Surprisingly well actually by all accounts. She says she realises that Callum must have felt under pressure to help out his friend. But to put it mildly, she's not too pleased with you for going along with it"

I don't react to this but feel stung. Surely Tralee Josie must realise that I too must have been trying to help out Micky?

"Anyway, they both seem to be pointing the finger towards Micky, saying that he must have got the idea for the charity money theft when he found out how easy it was for you to impersonate Josie at the bank. In other words, if you could pay money into the account then you could take it out as well. And he was also privy to the fact that Josie was due to withdraw a large amount of money for the children's charity press photo shoot"

I'm trying to digest all of this but something – and I don't know exactly what – doesn't ring true.

A voice calls out in the background telling Clare that she'll have to get going soon if she wants to make court for 10.30am. She tuts and tells the person that she needs to finish this call first.

"Look JJ you've just heard that – I need to get off. There are a few more things to discuss so it would be good if we could meet up later. How are you fixed for this afternoon?"

There are no appointments in my diary so I tell Clare I'm fine.

"Well, I'll pop over to your place about 3pm then – I'll ring you if there's a problem. Right, I'd better get going then. Oh just one more thing"

I'm writing down the time of Clare's appointment but her next comment stops me dead.

"You should know that Josie and Callum are saying that you and Micky were getting close - if you know what I mean? They both say that they suspect you were having a romantic liaison. I just thought you ought to know this"

She finishes by saying something about giving me more information later today but I can hardly hear her words.

After Clare has gone off the line I notice that my hands have started to shake, so much so that I can't write anything down.

Half an hour later, I'm still sitting in the same place when I hear a rustling sound by the door and notice that today's newspaper has just been delivered. The headline catches my breath.

"Police Find Body Washed Up"

Chapter 26

Meetings and Revelations

The sight of the newspaper headline is a distraction from the shocking revelation that Tralee Josie and Callum have pretty much accused me of having an affair with Micky. I can't understand why they would say such a thing and yet another trawl of my diaries shows no hints of this. I do mention Micky's mesmerising green eyes and infectious personality, but it's hardly a declaration of undying love or even a sign that I fancy him. The whole idea is just too ridiculous for words.

Yet I still feel unsettled and thrown by their comments. Until, that is, I spot the lurid headline and I grab hold of the paper to read the main story.

"Police are investigating the macabre discovery of a body by a fishing boat at Admiralty Bay. Few details have emerged but police say the remains are of a white male aged around 20-30 years. A man out fishing discovered the body, badly decomposed and missing some limbs, after he saw what he thought was a large bag floating alongside his boat. According to police the bag gave way to reveal the horrific find and the man immediately called in the police. The area has been sealed off for forensic investigation and police spokesperson said he could not

comment on whether the remains could be those of missing bar tender, Micky Doyle, adding that detailed forensic examinations are still ongoing"

I re-read the story several times and each time I'm more convinced that this has got to be Micky. The estimated age fits and no one has seen him for over 10 days now. I desperately need to talk to someone and I know Graham is in court this morning because he took off in what he calls his 'Judge Judy Garb' – in other words, an even sharper than usual pin striped suit.

So I turn to my other namesake, the lovely St Georges Josephine. The phone rings out a long time and I'm just about to hang up when she finally answers it with her distinctive exaggerated Bermudian 'o' sound.

"Hellooo?"

"Hi Josephine it's me – are you all right to talk?"

"Ah JJ. Sorry about that I was down in the studio and didn't have my hands free phone with me. How are you anyway?"

I say – untruthfully – that I'm fine but Josephine instantly picks up that I'm not.

"What's up JJ? You sound really stressed"

I tell her about the newspaper headline which she hasn't seen yet.

"Oh 'nooo'. How awful. And you think it's that Micky Doyle guy?" She sounds as shell shocked as I am by the news.

I reply that yes, I do think it has to be Micky.

"I mean who else could it be? He's the only person I know about who fits the age profile and who has been reported missing"

Josephine agrees but adds that we shouldn't jump to conclusions before the police have carried out their investigations. After all, sometimes people go missing and the police know nothing about it. On that basis it could well be someone else.

So should I tell Josie about the statements that Tralee Josie and Callum have made? As if reading my mind, she asks me if there is anything else bothering me.

"Well yes there is and it's connected to Micky"

I then go over what Clare has told me about their police interviews.

Josephine stays quiet for a few moments while she ponders what I've said.

"And what does Graham think about this?" she asks sounding as troubled as I feel.

"I haven't had a chance to tell him yet – he's in court this morning" I reply, suddenly wondering how on earth I'm going to raise it with him. Unless, of course, Clare has got to him first.

"Hmm, I'm sure he'll agree that this is all stuff and nonsense" Josephine coughs as if to underline her point. "To tell you the truth JJ, the more I hear about this Tralee Josie and her fiancé the more I dislike them"

I don't respond to this but I understand what she means. I've still kept Josie's last email where she has condemned me without even trying to hear my side of the story. And then this.

Now that I've shared things with Josephine, I feel a bit calmer and decide to go for a stroll through the apartment grounds to take my mind off things. It isn't long though before my cell phone shows a text message from DI Robinson.

"Morning JJ. Could you give me a call as soon as? Regards DI Robinson"

I suppose I might as well do it here and now. DI Robinson answers straight away and unusually for him, sounds quite cheery.

"Hi JJ, thanks for ringing back so quickly. How are you today?"

Thrown by his matey tone, I reply that I'm fine in the circumstances. He laughs before getting on to the real reason he has asked me to call.

"This is just an update and I'm sure Clare will fill you in later. Listen, this young gang associate, Vernall, has started to sing like a bird now that we've given him assurances about getting him off the island. Having told us that the P Crew were responsible for kidnapping Micky Doyle first time around, he's going to show us where they took him"

This information suddenly feels familiar but again I've no clear idea why. It's as if I've been told this somewhere before but can't recall where or when. I decide not to say anything and let him continue.

"Anyway, I thought you should be aware of this development as we're now looking at the possibility that Micky could have cooked up the whole idea of sending you into the bank to withdraw the charity money. I suppose you've seen today's headlines as well?"

I reply that I certainly have and ask outright if they think the remains are of Micky Doyle. DI Robinson refuses to be drawn and just tells me that they are keeping an open mind. He sounds shifty though and I'm convinced he isn't telling the truth.

When I get back Graham is there – he's seen the newspaper reports and has popped home to check that I'm ok. I quickly go over what Clare and DI Robinson have told me and just as St Georges Josephine has predicted, Graham laughs off the suggestion that I've been having some sort of romantic liaison with Micky.

"But why do you think they'd say such a ridiculous thing in their police statements?" I ask, relieved that he isn't taking it seriously.

"People say all sorts of stupid things when they are under pressure JJ. It's just how things are. I expect they were spooked by the police suddenly turning up unannounced in Tralee. Anyway, from what I can gather from Clare they seem to be pointing the finger firmly at Micky"

Graham has to dash back to court but tells me to try not to worry.

"Oh and by the way" he says as he's heading towards the door. "I'm thinking of inviting mom and dad over tomorrow evening. Are you ok with that?"

A proper meeting with them has to happen sooner rather than later, especially after our momentous decision on our future together.

"That's fine by me" I reply adding that I'm more than a bit nervous about it.

Graham hugs me and says that they'll love me, just like he does. I hope so, that's for sure.

Clare arrives just before 3pm and is carrying a large file with her. She looks tired and I offer her some iced water before we start. She quips that she'd much prefer a gin and tonic but yes, water will do.

We start by going over the statements made by Tralee Josie and Callum. I'm still shocked at the tone of Josie's comments in particular. While she and Callum are clearly putting the blame at Micky's door – they both mention his clear motive to get the P Crew gang off his back – Josie doesn't show me any sympathy. She thinks that I've been flattered by the attention of Micky and suspects we've been seeing each other on the side. She also says that she doesn't believe that my memory problems are as bad as I've been making out.

"It's my view that JJ has been exaggerating her memory problems just to get attention. I'm sure she is able to remember a lot more than she admits to and all this diary keeping stuff is just a front. She could have said no to Micky but she didn't, so that makes her just as guilty in my opinion"

I can't believe what I'm reading here and tell Clare as much. Clare shrugs and says that I shouldn't take any of this too personally. It's just Josie's opinion and people hit out when they feel angry and threatened.

"Yes well she's certainly put the boot into me, let alone Micky" I'm still plagued by a strong gut feeling that Micky isn't responsible for this, despite everything pointing towards him. But I'm reluctant to tell Clare in case she thinks it's a sign that I'm really just trying to protect someone I've had a romantic relationship with.

"When is your next hypnosis treatment with Dr Silver?" Clare asks as she neatly files away the offending statements in her bulky cardboard folder.

I point to the yellow sticker on my computer screen showing that it's tomorrow morning at 11am.

"And can I just check that you are definitely ok with the police using any information that could come out of these sessions?"

I nod, saying that I'd be more than happy if something useful could come out of it. But so far nothing has done.

After Clare has gone, I write down my feelings about reading Josie and Callum's police statements. I'm incredibly angry but also saddened that Josie could be so callous to think that I've been exaggerating my memory problems. If only she could spend a few days in my shoes, she'd know how cruel her words are.

"It's all very well Clare saying not to take it personally" I write *"but it IS personal. These are people who I thought of as good friends. So how wrong was I?"*

The next morning, I go over my diary entry with Dr Silver who nods sympathetically and suggests I try to put it to the back of my mind before we start the next hypnosis session. He laughs saying that this is something he actually wants me to forget for now.

"How about if I leave you for a few minutes with some relaxing music?" he suggests reaching across for a CD marked 'Mood Music.'

Listening to the mixed sounds of ocean waves and Gregorian chants starts to make me sleepy and I can feel myself starting to drift off. Dr Silver then returns and asks in a lowered voice if I'm ready to start the session.

"Just as well you came in when you did – a few

minutes more and I'd be in the land of nod" I say stifling a yawn.

"Well it's good that you are in a more relaxed state" he replies turning down the volume of the music. "Ok let's begin and we'll start with counting backwards from 100....99, 98, 97...."

It doesn't take long for me to find myself in that strange 'in between' state of sleepiness yet still being aware of everything around me. Dr Silver reminds me of the day of the theft and we go over my meeting with Callum and Micky in Par La Ville Park. As there is nothing in the diary about our conversation, the only image I have is of us walking through the park and then sitting down together. Dr Silver then asks me if I can recall anything after leaving the park. I concentrate hard but I'm not getting any images.

And then it comes, a sudden clear picture which takes my breath away. Noticing the change in my breathing, Dr Silver looks up from his notes.

"Actually I can see something" I say trying to hang on to the image. It's a taxi rank and I can see Callum and Micky waiting. I'm walking towards them and I can see them staring over at me.

Dr Silver makes a note and asks me if I can hang on to the image. Can I see anyone else? Am I carrying something?

Silently I use the words 'focus, focus' but already the picture is starting to blur. My arms feel heavy but I'm beginning to lose the mental image of myself. Callum and Micky are also starting to fade as if someone is slowly dissolving them away. Focus, focus. Damn it, I can't see anything any more.

The picture has gone.

"Ok never mind. It's an important image and it must have some significance. That's good JJ and I'm sure there's more to come"

Not today as it transpires but Dr Silver is pleased and I feel happy that at least something has come out of this session. Dr Silver asks me if I'd mind waiting for him to see his next patient before he drives me back home. He doesn't want me to use the bus on my own so soon after hypnosis.

As it is, I feel absolutely fine and I manage to convince him that I'll be all right to use the bus once I've had a brief rest. He tells me to call him if I start to feel dizzy or confused.

"What even more confused as usual?" I joke and he gives me a half smile before disappearing back into his office.

When I get back to the apartment I feel buoyed up and energetic, so decide to tidy around to the sound of my beloved Nina Simone. I want the place to look sparkling for Graham's mom and dad when they visit later. Graham has ordered some tapas to be delivered from a local deli and has stocked up with his dad's favourite red wine, so that side of things is already sorted thank goodness.

St George's Josephine calls briefly to ask about my latest session with Dr Silver and I tell her about the taxi picture that came to mind.

"That's brilliant JJ and it could lead to other memories. Let's meet up again soon for a proper catch up but I'll leave you to get on with things for now. Hope it all goes well tonight, I'm sure it will"

When he arrives back home, I regale Graham

with details about my taxi rank image. He says it's an exciting development and then mentions it in a brief call to Clare. By now I'm more preoccupied with what to wear and I change my outfit several times before opting for a simple blue maxi dress adorned with Josephine's jewellery presents.

As it turns out, I needn't have worried. Evelyn and Bill are dressed elegantly and casually, with a self assurance that comes with being happy in their own skin. Bill is the more outgoing one and does most of the talking. Tonight he looks even more like an older version of Graham, with similar mannerisms and ways of speaking. Evelyn comes over as quite reserved and I can sense her trying to weigh me up. I'm trying not to show how nervous I am but I notice how my hand is shaking slightly when I pour Evelyn a glass of fruit juice. I mentally admonish myself for being so silly but it doesn't stop me from feeling like someone who is 'on display' like something in a shop window.

I can see that Graham has picked up on my nervousness and he keeps smiling across at me in his reassuring way. But the conversation is stilted with the men do most of the talking while Evelyn and me eye each other up warily.

It's Graham who decides to break the ice by announcing that we have decided to move in together properly. Evelyn momentarily flinches and looks across at her husband.

Bill quickly returns her gaze and then raises his glass in a toast.

"Well, well that was quick but congratulations you two" he says clinking Graham's glass and then mine. Evelyn manages a weak smile adding that she's pleased for us. I don't believe a word of it but I return her smile while our eyes lock.

Inevitably the conversation gets around to my accident and head injury.

I go over the details and tell them all about the effects on my short term memory. I also mention my family in England and Evelyn nods and glances again at Bill. Already I can feel that she is softening towards me but is still wary, the mother guarding her one and only child. Graham may be a fully grown man and top lawyer but he is still her son and I can understand her unease.

When it comes to the accusation of theft, Graham takes the lead saying that he has absolutely no doubts about my innocence and that I've been set up by someone who I thought was a friend. He adds that the police are already pursuing this line of inquiry and that it will only be a matter of time before they get to the bottom of it.

Bill says he's sure everything will get sorted out and asks me how I've been coping with it all.

"Well it's been pretty stressful on top of everything else" I reply looking across at Graham who puts his hand on my shoulder. For a moment Evelyn looks sympathetic but then reverts to her "I'm not giving too much away" face. Bill decides that it's time for a change of subject and asks me what I think of living in Bermuda. We spend the rest of the evening discussing life on the island, its beauty and how much it has changed politically and socially over the years. It's a relief to get the subject off me and finally I start to relax.

"Well that went well" Graham says as we watch their car disappear beyond the main gates.

"Do you think so?" I reply adding that I thought Evelyn was a bit quiet.

Graham laughs and says "Ah that's just mom's way – she's not a great talker"

Not totally convinced, I tell Graham that I like them both but that his dad is probably easier to get to know.

"Well you'll soon find out" Graham says pouring himself a large glass of red wine and asking me if I'd like one.

"No, not for me – I'll leave you to clear this up while I tackle my diary" I reply playfully throwing a trash bag in his direction. "I want to write everything down about this evening while it's fresh in my mind" Graham catches the bag in mid air and tells me not to be too long as there's a great film on TV in ten minutes.

I'm just settling into my diary when Graham appears waving my cell phone.

"It's Josephine" he says handing it to me.

I'm surprised to get a call from her so late in the evening.

"Hi JJ" she says "Sorry about the time but I just had to tell you this. You know you mentioned the taxi rank memory today? Well one of my friends runs a small jewellery store that backs on to the main Hamilton taxi rank. And guess what? She tells me she has some CCTV that goes back a way. It might just show something that could help you"

I hang on to her words as their impact hits home. It might just show something.

Might.

And when I finally put down the phone, I notice that I'm crossing my fingers so hard that my nails have turned white.

Chapter 27

Location, Location

I'm back at Hamilton police station where I'm waiting to meet Paul Webster, the Bermuda police digital forensics expert. DI Robinson says that he wants to talk to me about some extra CCTV footage they have recovered from the Par La Ville Park area.

It's 9am and a cleaner is finishing off his work in the reception area. He is whistling a tune that I can't make out and is concentrating on the glass frontage of the main desk.

"Good morning ma'am" he says before resuming his low whistling sound. I nod in his direction while keeping an eye out for DI Robinson and his forensics guy.

I don't have long to wait before Paul Webster arrives on his own. He's wearing a casual polo shirt and light beige trousers and has an open friendly face. It's not quite what I was expecting – in my mind I thought I'd be meeting someone in a white lab coat.

"You must be JJ? Hi, I'm Paul" He puts out his hand and has a firm business like shake.

"Hello, good to meet you" I reply smiling and looking around for DI Robinson to appear.

"It's just me for now" Paul says "DI Robinson has been called away on something urgent. Do you want a coffee or something before we begin?"

I tell him that I'm fine and he leads me through a long corridor to a door marked BPS Digital Forensics. He presses some sort keypad code and we head into an office cluttered with computers and stacks of mobile phones lying on a work bench. It feels hot and stuffy and Paul spends a few minutes adjusting the air conditioning level.

I take a seat while he disappears into a large storage area and returns with a pile of CDs.

Noticing his slightly northern English accent, I ask him how he got to work in Bermuda in such a specialised area of forensic science.

"Oh, it's a long story so I won't bore you with all the details. But it's a second career for me after a long stint working in alternative fuels research"

"Oh so a big change then switching to police forensics?" I reply still trying to figure out his accent.

"Yes and this place is a bit of a change from Manchester as well" he says putting one of the CDs into a computer. "I've only been here for a year and I still can't get used to the heat. And from what I've heard you're new to Bermuda as well?"

It turns out that DI Robinson has already briefed him pretty well about me. So after our initial ice breaking chit chat, he gets straight down to work.

"Now I'd like you to watch this – it's from an apartment overlooking Par La Ville Park. It's not much but see what you think."

I glance at the screen and can spot me, Micky and

Callum walking towards the hot dog stall. Callum goes off to buy some dogs while Micky and me sit talking. Paul then shows me a closer picture 'grab' as he calls it and I can see us eating our hot dogs.

"Is this bringing anything back?" Paul asks clicking onto to an even bigger close-up.

"Yes, looking at this now, I can remember us being there"

"From what I understand, this was on the day that you made the first payment into the bank for Micky Doyle?"

"I can believe that" I reply staring at the screen. Seeing Micky again makes me feel sad. Only a few hours ago when I was reading back over my diary, I got quite panicky about Micky's latest disappearance. My heart started racing at the thought that he could well now be dead.

"Something has struck me while looking at this" Paul says peering at the still picture of the three of us. "From what I can see, it is Callum who seems to be doing most of the talking"

I'm not quite sure what he is getting at and glance quizzically at him.

Seeing my puzzled expression, Paul continues with his observation.

"It may not be significant but I'll mention it to DI Robinson. It's just that Micky looks a bit passive that's all, considering he's supposed to be the one setting everything up"

Funny he should mention that. In my diary I describe my niggling doubts about the assumption that Micky is responsible for setting me up. I'm still not sure why I feel this way because everything is pointing in his direction. Massively so.

Paul tells me that they have put a call out to several businesses and dwellings around Hamilton to see if they can get any more CCTV evidence.

The very last entry in my diary yesterday, referred to Josephine's jeweller friend and the CCTV at her shop which overlooks the main taxi rank. I mention this to Paul who looks interested.

He makes a note just as DI Robinson's tall frame appears at the door.

"Hi you two" he says grabbing a chair "enjoying the movies? And where's the popcorn?"

Paul laughs but I stay poker faced, not quite trusting this apparently new friendly version of DI Robinson. Every time I write about him I refer to his deadpan looks and sceptical manner. That's the image I have of him in my head and now he's coming over all smiley and jokey.

"So JJ what's this I've been hearing about your memory of a taxi rank?" he asks, ignoring the fact that I haven't responded to his jolly mood. Paul looks across, suddenly realising the significance of the jeweller's CCTV I've just mentioned.

"So you've been speaking to Dr Silver?" I reply still hanging on to my serious facial expression.

"Clare actually – she's on her way over here."

Ah so that's where he's heard it.

"JJ's just been telling me that she has a friend who knows someone with CCTV footage of the taxi rank" Paul says extracting the CD we've been viewing from the computer.

"Well now, that could be a good turn up for the books" DI Robinson responds smiling over in my direction. I still can't quite bring myself to return his smile so I avert my eyes back towards the stack of CDs piled up on the desk.

"Right then JJ, how do you fancy a trip out across the island today?" DI Robinson's expression is suddenly looking more serious.

"Trip - what do you mean trip?" I reply just as the office intercom buzzes. It's Clare and Paul leaps up to let her in.

"Ah hello there Clare" DI Robinson says ignoring my question. "Thanks for getting here so quickly."

"You're lucky that there's a break in my court case today" Clare snaps back before nodding across in my direction.

"Well I was just about to tell JJ about this trip I've got planned for us today" DI Robinson replies seemingly oblivious to Clare's brusque manner. Perhaps he's just got used to it.

He then describes how the young P Crew associate, Vernall, has shown them where Micky Doyle was holed up after he first went missing a few weeks ago. Apparently it is a disused gas station near Dockyard, Bermuda's former naval base, and the Crime Scene Examiners are pouring all over it as we speak.

"And what exactly has this got to do with JJ?" Clare asks looking across at me to glean my reaction. I shrug in a "search me?" sort of way.

"We just want to take JJ there - with you of course – to see if it triggers any memories. You know something Micky might have said? You don't have any objections do you?"

"What do you think JJ?" Clare says looking

straight past DI Robinson.

"I don't have a problem with it" I reply "but I'm not sure that I'm going to be of any use there. You have copies of my diaries and since Micky has gone missing again I've re-read them over and over. There's nothing in there, as far as I know, about a disused garage"

"Ah but you never can tell. A visual clue might just set something off however small. It's worth a go." DI Robinson stops to check his cell phone which has just signalled that he has a new text message. He seems momentarily distracted but quickly gets back to our conversation.

"Ok are you two happy to go along with this then?" He glances at Clare who nods back.

"And you JJ?" I also give him a nod back. I mean, I can't exactly say 'no' can I? It looks like we're heading out to this place come what may.

The drive to Dockyard seems to take a long time but in reality it's not much more than half an hour. We're in Clare's car and she barely says a word. She's listening intently to a radio phone-in programme about court witness protection on the island and tuts loudly when someone says something she doesn't agree with.

"It's a real problem this witness protection thing on such a small island" she announces out of the blue as if she's just realised that I'm in the car with her. "It's not easy when everyone knows everybody else. It's the same in small communities all over the world"

To be honest I haven't been listening to the show much. I'm far too preoccupied with thoughts of

Micky and exactly what may have happened to him.

"Hmm it must be a problem" I reply "I suppose that's why they've got to get this young Vernall guy off the island."

Clare doesn't respond but toots her car horn at another driver who has just overtaken us on a sharp bend.

"Crazy idiot" she yells out of her window as the car speeds ahead out of view. "You take your life in your hands being out with some of these lunatics" I wonder whether DI Robinson, driving well ahead, will spot the boy racers and pull them over.

But he makes no mention of them when we get to the run down gas station on the outskirts of Dockyard. Even in the glow of the Bermuda sunshine, it's a depressing place and it looks as though it has been in this sorry condition for some years. There are yellowing grass tufts coming up between the many cracks in the oil stained forecourt concrete. The gas pumps, long empty, have peeling paint and are rusting while the main building is decrepit and covered in graffiti.

There is police tape across the building entrance and several Crime Scene Examiners are padding around in their white protective suits.

DI Robinson ushers us past the tape and into the building. It takes a few minutes for my eyes to adjust to the darkness and the smell of gasoline is overwhelming. It's as if someone has emptied a whole canister of the stuff inside the building. There are no windows and after a while I can just about make out the outline of a table and a few chairs at the far end of the 'room' if that's what you can call it. It's more like a covered yard area and as my eyes get more used to the darkness, I can see what look like discarded sleeping bags strewn on the floor. DI Robinson flicks on a torch displaying the place in its full grimness. A torn faded Bob Marley poster sits forlornly amongst the graffiti and crumbling inner walls. The contrast with the beauty of the scenery just a few yards away is striking. We could be in downtown New York or inner city London but instead we are standing inside a decaying cavity of paradise.

DI Robinson says he'll leave us to take a look around while he has a word with the forensic team who have just finished their work here.

"Lovely place isn't it?" Clare says sarcastically holding her nose.

The smell is making me feel quite queasy but I try to ignore it as I take in the surroundings. I can imagine what it must have been like for Micky being held here and how terrified he would have been. And that smell. Now where have I heard it described before?

"Look JJ there's a chain on the wall over here – like a place where you'd keep a guard dog" Clare picks up the chain to examine it.

Dog. A guard dog. Her words trigger a momentary flash of something but hard as I try, I can't hold on to it. Damn it. I wish I could pursue the train of thought but there is nothing there.

DI Robinson arrives back carrying some small bottles of mineral water which he offers up. I gulp mine down while Clare asks whether some stains on the wall could be blood.

"We'll know soon enough once the forensics lot get the results back" DI Robinson says taking a long swig of his water.

He looks over at me to gauge my reaction to the place.

"So JJ, what do you think?"

"It must have been petrifying for Micky" I reply wanting to get out of the place as quickly as possible.

"Yes, they say that we can smell fear and I'm certainly getting the whiff of it in here let alone the stink of gas." DI Robinson crinkles his nose and coughs.

"Our police dogs get the sense that something bad has happened. The sniffer dogs have already been around and I hear that one of them held back to start with. A sure sign in my experience that something awful has gone on. And the dogs are indicating that drugs have been stashed here as well"

Clare is studying the graffiti signs on the walls while I'm still trying to ignore by growing feelings of nausea.

"Anyway, does seeing this place bring back anything Micky might have told you?" DI Robinson takes another glug of water.

Should I mention my fleeting thought after Clare mentioned the guard dog? It's not as if there was anything tangible.

"Sorry but no" I reply.

"Nothing at all?" DI Robinson looks at me sensing that I'm holding something back.

"Well ok maybe a little thing. Clare said

something about the chain on the wall looking like it was there for a 'guard dog' and I did get a flicker of something. It's as if I have heard something about a dog before but that's it. Nothing more"

DI Robinson waits for a few moments as if expecting me to come out with something else.

"That's it? Are you absolutely sure JJ?"

"Yes – now if it's ok by you, can we move outside? The smell is making me feel like I want to throw up"

Emerging back into the blazing afternoon sun is a shock and I suddenly feel faint. I hold onto one of the gas pumps to steady myself and DI Robinson asks if I feel all right. I tell him that I just need a bit more water and to get the smell of gasoline out of my nostrils.

"Ok JJ take your time. I need to make a quick call"

I can hear him on the phone while Clare says she'll head back to her car to send off a few emails.

"Just come across when you're ready" she adds clip clopping across the forecourt in her high heels.

I close my eyes and take a few deep breaths. Apart from the muted sound of DI Robinson talking, it is eerily quiet here. At night it must be deadly silent and pitch black. Poor Micky. Could this be where he has spent his last days? And did the police dog react to the stench of death?

It's not long before I hear the heavy footsteps of DI Robinson coming back across the concrete.

"Feeling better now?" he asks.

I don't have time to answer before he announces chirpily "Hey, this bit of news will cheer you up JJ.

That body washed up at Admiralty Bay – it's not Micky Doyle's. We still don't know who it is but it isn't Micky"

It isn't Micky. His words ring out as if he is yelling them through a loud speaker. Isn't Micky. I cling onto the petrol pump and DI Robinson manages to grab me before I slump down to the floor

"Are you sure you are ok?" His voice now seems further away and I try to focus on the faded gasoline sign to stop me from blacking out.

"I'm fine" I can hear myself say. "Just a bit dizzy that's all"

"Come on, let's get you back to the car then" he says taking hold of my arm.

And I can barely write as I put my first words in bold letters in today's diary.

"Thank God. Micky could still be alive"

But it's only a hope. The body may not belong to him but another young man has lost his life in a grisly way.

So what's to say that Micky isn't lying dead somewhere else?

Chapter 28

Tightening the rein

The call has gone out for information to help police put a name to the young man whose remains are now lying in a police morgue. But with the level of decomposition and parts of the body still missing, identification is proving difficult. Estimated height is around 5ft 10 inches and his build is slim. He's pale skinned and has had his appendix removed at some point in his short life. There are no other distinguishing marks and it seems that he had mousy blonde hair colouring.

Graham thinks it is going to be nigh on impossible to find out who it is.

"I bet he's not a local – probably a visitor. Chances are he's got caught up in a drugs thing and got on the wrong side of a dealer. Either that or it was just an accident"

Graham tells me that compared to some other islands. Bermuda doesn't have a big drug problem but it's still there, lurking menacingly in the background. And in such a small place any available market is ruthlessly protected.

It's a Saturday morning and we're drinking coffee with the newspapers strewn across the floor.

Already the outside temperature is in the low 80s with predictions that the weekend is going to be the hottest of the year so far.

"Do you fancy a boat trip?" Graham asks casually. "With mom and dad off island, their boat is free."

Evelyn and Bill have been invited to a friend's wedding in New York and are making a week of it. And the prospect of a boat trip away from the searing heat of the land sounds fabulous.

"What? Of course I do! As if you even have to ask"

"Well make sure you slap on the factor 50 or you'll be burned to a crisp". Graham laughs and tweaks my nose. "And get the swimming costume out – the water will be amazing"

I've been avoiding swimming due to the ankle tag that I'm still forced to wear but Graham assures me that we'll be heading out to an isolated cove so we won't be sharing the space with many people.

As we set sail, the water is an exquisite ripple mix of powder blue and pale green and is incredibly clear. In England, for most of the time at least, the sea is a murky grey colour and is always cold. That's what I remember from my dim and distant past anyway, one of those deep rooted long term memories.

The boat is a small motorised one and I sit on the rear seat while Graham is perched on what he calls 'the captain's chair'. He is navigating around the island with a confidence that comes from knowing the island waters inside out, with all the hidden gems. Apart from the ferry journey from Hamilton to Dockyard, this is the first time I've seen Bermuda from the water and the views are glorious. I'm trying to take everything in, while feverishly scribbling down snippets as Graham points out the various sights. Places with names like Fairylands and Flatts and Shelly Bay. Graham singles out the houses where various famous people have lived, or still live, including the place where John Lennon stayed when he visited the island in the summer of 1980.

We moor up in a tiny cove with a deserted beach and I can't wait to get in the water. It's like being in the best warm bath ever and is quite shallow – just about up to chest level when standing. There are quite a few colourful fish swimming around and while they are pretty to look at, I do my best to ignore them. I don't like sharing the water with shoals of fish and the idea of a 'fish pedicure' Graham has been telling me about – where your feet are softened by tiny sea creatures nibbling away at the hard skin – makes me shudder. So I try to blank them out and concentrate on luxuriating in what must be some of the best sea water in the world.

Graham, amused by my dislike of fish swimming about, has put on a snorkel and is actively seeking them out. He throws me a Lilo so that I can float on the water without worrying about being attacked by "our scaly friends" as he puts it. Just floating there, with little more than the sounds of the sea, is blissful and I can feel myself starting to doze.

The feeling doesn't last long though. Suddenly I hear splashing sounds as Graham heads towards me, holding aloft his cell phone which is in a waterproof pouch.

"It's Clare for you" he says handing me the phone from inside the protective wrap.

Talk about back to reality with a bang.

"Hi JJ – sorry to interrupt your boat trip" she says sounding like she doesn't mean a word of it.

"Just give me a minute while I sort myself out" I reply signalling to Graham to steady the Lilo as I get myself in a sitting position. He grabs the phone while I haul myself upwards trying not to fall over sideways.

"Ok Clare, sorted. I can talk properly now"

Clare clears her throat before continuing.

"Two things which I need to tell you about urgently" she says sounding tense.

"First - DI Robinson's colleague, Laura, is planning to talk to the neuro psychologist who treated you in London as well as Dr Silver over here. She wants to do this with your full co-operation"

"But why? And haven't the police already been in touch with Dr Silver anyway?"

Clare pauses for a second.

"Yes, to some extent they've spoken to Dr Silver but they now want to discuss your medical records – details about your brain injury and the effects on your memory. I think they just want to be sure that everything stacks up with what they've been told already"

It's my turn to stay silent for a few moments.

"You still there JJ?" Clare asks, before adding that she thinks this has something to do with Tralee Josie's claim that I might be 'exaggerating' the extent of my memory problems.

I try to keep my anger back but I'm finding it hard. I know only too well what Josie has said because every morning I've re-read her comments. And each time they still hurt like mad.

"Well if it helps to get them to understand what I'm going through then fine by me." I snap back thrusting my free hand into the warm water, trailing it backwards and forwards making small noisy waves at the side of the Lilo.

Clare ignores my irritation and gets straight on to her next subject.

"And the other thing you should know. They've arrested the guy in charge of the P Crew gang. Someone called Wes apparently. They raided his house this morning and he's now in custody"

"Oh - right" I reply looking across at Graham who is standing nearby examining his snorkel mask but clearly listening in at the same time. It's difficult to know what else to say to this news.

"Anyway, they want you to come back into the station on Monday morning to take a look at this Wes. Same as you did with Vernall - you'll see him but he won't see you. They want to know if you might recognise him from somewhere"

So yet another visit to my new home from home, Hamilton police station. Only a few hours ago I counted up the number of times I've been in there and it's been four visits in the past three weeks alone.

Still, the name Wes seems vaguely familiar. At least I think it does until I try to remember why. Then I draw a blank.

I let out a sigh before telling Clare that I'll be

there.

"It's 10am then – let Graham know if you can't write it down now" she says.

"I don't go anywhere without a notebook and that yes, I'll be on time" I'm finding it hard to keep the exasperation from my voice.

"Good – have a nice weekend" she replies crisply "and tell Graham that I'll catch up with him properly on Monday. Bye for now"

I don't want the conversation to spoil our boat trip but in reality it does, damn it. Graham keeps trying to cheer me up but my mind won't let go of the fact that the police want to talk to my doctors and are taking seriously Tralee's Josie's spiteful comments.

And where the hell have I heard about this Wes guy?

After we get home – with me still introspective and poor Graham doing his best to drag me out of it – there's an email waiting from DI Robinson. This time the tone is formal.

"Just to confirm your appointment at Hamilton police station at 10.00am on Monday. I will be there with my colleague Laura and I expect us to need at least a couple of hours. Regards, DI Robinson"

Two hours. Surely it won't take that long to look that this Wes? I then notice that I've got another of my hypnosis sessions booked with Dr Silver at 12.00pm on Monday. If they need me at Hamilton station for that long, there won't be enough time to get to Dr Silver's.

Graham suggests that I give him a call.

"Ray won't mind taking a call on a Saturday and

it's better than running late on Monday" he says giving me a supportive hug.

As usual he's right and Dr Silver actually seems pleased to hear from me. I tell him about my conversation with Clare earlier and he reassures me that it will be made clear to the police that my short term memory problems are genuine and profound.

"The thing is JJ, you've learned quickly to compensate for your brain injury and you've been incredibly conscientious with your diary keeping. You've also retained a good visual memory which throws people sometimes. This sort of condition is difficult to get a handle on but it is sure hard to fake. Loads have tried but they are always caught out in the end"

This makes me feel a bit better and Dr Silver suggests that we leave my next appointment until 2.00pm to allow for any delays at the police station. After making the change to my notes, I get the urge to ring my mom for a chat. I still haven't told her that things have become more serious between me and Graham and that we're pretty much engaged now.

Graham gives me a peck on the cheek and says that he'll fix up some dinner while I'm on the phone.

"Say hi from me to her. And try not to let all this police stuff get to you. Not easy I know, but worrying the weekend away isn't going to help either"

Wise words but as he says, a lot easier said than done.

Mom lets out a long screech when I tell her about

Graham and me. Then she calms down as the news sinks in.

"But this has happened so quickly. Are you sure? I mean he seems a lovely lad and a lawyer too. But still…."

"Mom I'm as sure as I can be" I reply. I know what she means about speed and the old JJ would have been much more questioning. Is this new 'caution to the wind' JJ the result of my brain injury? Or is it just that I now realise how fickle life can be and that things can change in the blink of an eye? Either way, deep down I know that I'm making the right decision about Graham.

"You do realise this means that me and Jeff have to visit now? No excuses. We've got to meet Graham and his parents" She pauses, waiting for my reaction.

"Mom I'd rather get this theft business out of the way first"

It's not what she wants to hear and she's not giving up this time.

"Well that could take ages and I don't want to wait that long. No, we're going to come and visit soon. I'll get on the internet tonight and see what deals there are"

I know there'll be no stopping her now. I tell her that August is uncomfortably humid and it might be best to leave things until September. It's just a delaying tactic but she seems mollified.

"I suppose it will be a bit less expensive in September too" she replies before firing off a barrage of questions about Graham's parents. By the end of the call I'm beginning to regret having rung her but that's mom for you. Irritating but at the same time it's lovely to hear her voice.

Monday morning and here I am waiting behind the police glass screen for Wes to appear. His full name is Wesley Caesar apparently and DI Robinson quips that he's probably been nicknamed Julius at some point in his life.

"Nasty piece of work – has a police record as long as your arm" he adds glaring as Wes walks in behind the screen handcuffed between two officers.

He's tall and has the bulked out build of someone who knows his way around a gym.

"Pumped up with steroids" DI Robinson mutters before telling me to take my time and to have a good look.

Wes is grinning widely and obviously knows the score – it's clear that he's no stranger to being paraded in front of an invisible person. One of the officers tells him to keep a 'goddam straight face' but he ignores him and carries on grinning inanely. But the smile doesn't extend to his eyes which look cold and calculating. And then he lets out a large spit which hits the screen and I flinch backwards. The two officers scream at him to behave himself but he just starts laughing loudly and menacingly. DI Robinson now has a face like thunder.

"Do you recognise this punk JJ?" he asks me looking like he's about to run behind the screen and punch the lights out of Wes.

I take another long stare. His face does look familiar and I know I've heard someone somewhere mention his name.

"Yes I think I've seen him before" I reply adding

that the name is triggering something as well.

"Any idea where you might have seen him?" DI Robinson asks glaring back at the still grinning Wes.

But I haven't I'm afraid. Clare gives DI Robinson a look that says "don't push it sunshine" and he shrugs adding that it was worth a go.

Behind the screen Wes is being pushed towards the door by the two burly police officers. As a parting shot he winks at the camera and gives out another loud laugh. DI Robinson's face is bright red and one of his fists is clenched as if he is about to thump the glass partition.

He calls in Laura, who explains why she needs to speak to Dr Peters who treated me in London and to talk further to Dr Silver.

"It's just a formality, especially after the accusations being bandied around by Josie James and her fiancé in Ireland"

Ah - so Callum is taking the Josie line then; that I'm exaggerating my memory problems.

"And they both think I'm pretending?" I ask feeling the anger welling up again.

"Not pretending as such – just over playing it" Laura replies in a matter of fact voice. Her tone does little to improve my mood.

"Well ask away" I snap back. "I've got nothing to hide on that front"

Laura nods and we spend the next hour going over chunks of my diary entries. Clare stays quiet and is making copious notes.

"Now if you do get a memory of something – however small – you must get in touch straight away whatever time of the day or night " DI

Robinson says as we finally get up to leave the room.

I'm glad to get out into the outside world. Clare offers to give me a lift to Dr Silver's but I tell her that I'm happy to get the bus.

"Ok good luck with Dr Silver today and by the way, congratulations to you and Graham on setting up home together"

I'm momentarily thrown by Clare's comment but thank her anyway.

"I expect you'll be having a big party sometime" she says before driving off in her open topped gleaming red MG sports car. Like Clare herself, the car screams "look at me I'm a successful professional" and I notice her waving to a couple of people as she zips down the road.

When I get to Dr Silver's, his consulting room is especially cool with the air conditioning set to its highest level. It's a welcome contrast to the heat outside but it takes me a few minutes to get used to it. Today the relaxing music is a mix of panpipes and what sounds like a waterfall. With the combination of these soothing sounds and Dr Silver's reassuring voice, it doesn't take long before I'm ready to begin this latest session.

"So JJ today I want you to go back to the day of the theft – to go back to your meeting with Callum and Micky in Par La Ville Park."

I try to visualise myself walking towards the park. To help me with this, Dr Silver reads out my recent diary entry about viewing the CCTV images of the meetings in the park.

At first there is virtually nothing. A flash image

of the park entrance. Then a glimpse of a hot dog stand. Occasional facial images of Callum and Micky looking concerned.

But wait. Concentrate, concentrate.

Then some words. Not pictures this time but words. Callum is doing all the talking, gesticulating. He's telling me something. But what? Concentrate.

I hear him now. He's saying that I Josie has had to fly back to Ireland. Something about her having flown out the night before.

The words seem disconnected, a bit garbled even but there's no doubting the message. And no doubt about who the messenger is.

I can hear Dr Silver's keyboard clicking as he takes down my words.

"JJ this is good. Just keep focusing on that conversation"

I stay with the mental image of Callum but he's now just making mixed up noises. His mouth is still moving but nothing is making sense anymore. It's as if I'm trying to listen to a conversation a long distance away.

Far, far away.

But Dr Silver is delighted with this latest memory and asks if it is ok for him to pass it on to Clare and DI Robinson.

"Of course" I respond feeling awake but still not one hundred per cent there.

Dr Silver laughs and says he'll ask me the same question in a few minutes when I've had a chance to re-adjust to reality.

"It'll be the same answer doctor"

He grins and gives me a cheery 'thumbs up' sign,

before turning his attention back to his computer notes.

Graham is already home when I get back to the apartment and before I can tell him about my retrieved hypnosis memory, he announces that he has some intriguing news.

"Sit down before I tell you" he says steering me towards the sofa. I laugh telling him not to be so bossy, that he's not in court now.

"Well here's the thing" he says now looking deadly serious. "A crime reporter on the Bermuda Sun has received an anonymous email this afternoon saying that Micky Doyle is alive. According to the tip off - which the police think is real - he's holed up in a secret location for his own safety."

So still alive then and by all accounts in hiding on the island. Part of me is delighted, relieved even. Yet another part is telling me that Micky is still in danger.

Out of the blue, the large grinning face of Wesley Caesar looms at the front of my mind and I get an overwhelming urge to capture it on paper before it disappears. Possibly forever.

Chapter 29

Every Picture Tells A Story?

After the recent flurry of activity, things now seem to have gone a bit quiet with the police investigation. It's been over a fortnight since I went to view P Crew gang leader, Wesley Caesar, at Hamilton police station. And while DI Robinson is undeniably interested in my recovered memory about the conversation with Callum, there's been little contact from him.

"It's a good sign JJ" Graham tells me as he is speed reading a weighty legal document. "It means they are doing some serious digging and the focus is shifting away from you"

From my deep rooted childhood memories, I recall my mom telling me that men are useless at doing more than one thing at a time and that women are the archetypal multi tasking sex.

Well that certainly isn't the case with Graham. He seems to be able to read, speak and make notes at the same time. And I can't believe how quickly he can zip through his massive case notes. With the amount of diary reading I have to do, I'd love to be able to read as speedily as that. But according to Dr Silver, that's an ability I'm unlikely to master with my brain injury. It doesn't stop me wishing though and I remind myself to tell mom that I've found the exception to her rule.

On the subject of mom, she has now booked plane tickets for her and Jeff to visit in early September. It's only five weeks away and the date has pride of place in my diary and calendar. While I'm looking forward to seeing them again, I'm also apprehensive. What will they think of Graham? And will they get on with his parents?

Pauletta has offered to put mom and Jeff up in my old flat, which has not been rented out since I left. She refuses point blank to take any money but mom has made plans to take her out for some slap up meals and is bringing some presents over from London. I've warned mom that Pauletta doesn't rate too many restaurants on the island, preferring to do her own cooking but I know that will go in one ear and out of the other.

"I've got them some lovely bits and pieces from Harrods – they'll adore that" she told me last night. I've taken to jotting things down when mom rings and there are usually several pages by the time we've finished our conversation. I know from last night's phone call that she has already spoken to Pauletta and thinks they will get on famously. Poor Dave – he'll have even less opportunities to speak once mom and Pauletta get together.

It's raining hard today and the humidity is sky high. But the deluge is needed after weeks of drought which have left water levels extremely low.

The highlight of today is lunch in Hamilton with St George's Josephine. It's been a good few weeks since we've seen each other, although we have spoken on the phone a number of times. I see from last time we talked, she was excited about her jewellery shop friend having some CCTV of the main city taxi rank on the day of the bank theft. But so far I haven't recorded any updated news about this. I remind myself to ask her about it today.

The bus into Hamilton is full of rain soaked tourists and locals looking a bit bedraggled and sorry for themselves. The tourists are sticking stubbornly to shorts and tees despite the weather, while the locals are wearing full waterproofs and some of the older women have shower caps covering their hair.

To lighten the mood, the female driver is humming 'Singing In The Rain' in between chats to elderly man who is sitting in one of the front bucket style seats. They obviously know each other and are gossiping about a relative who is due to go into hospital for a gall bladder operation. Her humming and general banter raises smiles from some of the tourists as they hang on to the bus straps for dear life. I'm grateful to have a seat, even though I can barely move because a hugely overweight woman has just plonked herself down beside me. She's texting away on her cell phone and every so often I can feel her chubby arm jabbing into me.

I've arranged to meet Josephine at the Onion Packet restaurant and when I get there she is already sitting inside perusing the menu. There's a cruise ship in today, so the place is heaving with mainly American tourists and everyone is wedged indoors because no one wants to sit in the normally coveted outside area. No point in having a great harbour view while the rain is lashing down.

We decide to order straight away to avoid a long wait for our food and I can sense that Josephine is excited about something. Once the waiter has disappeared she leans across the table and drops her voice.

"Listen JJ, I have some good news for you. Well at least I hope it is good news" She takes a sip of her lemon tea and smiles broadly.

"The friend I have who runs the jewellery shop up the road? Did you manage to write down what I told you about her?"

"You mean about her having some CCTV pictures?" I reply, moving a bit closer across so I can hear her a bit better.

"Exactly JJ" She lowers her voice again and looks across to see if anyone else is listening. Satisfied that they aren't, she continues in a barely audible whisper.

"I need to keep my voice down because I'm not really sure I should be telling you this. But hell – it's too good to keep to myself. Anyway, Bernadette – that's my friend – has handed over her CCTV to the police but she had a peek herself before she did. And from what I can gather there is a picture of you heading towards the taxi rank carrying a large package. She knows it's you because I've shown her a photograph"

It's now my turn to check out the room and mercifully nobody seems to be interested in what we are talking about. Already I'm beginning to wonder whether the CCTV pictures are going to do me any good or will they just make things look a lot worse?

Josephine raises one eyebrow as if reading my thoughts.

"Don't look so worried JJ. Trust me, this will be good. Bernadette says two men are waiting by the taxi rank and after talking to you they take the package and head off in the cab"

Ok, this is now looking much more promising.

"And are the men Callum and Micky?" I ask, my head spinning at the thought of what this could mean.

Josephine takes another sip of her lemon tea and leans across even closer to me.

"Bernadette doesn't recognise one of the young men but she does recognise the other as Micky Doyle, the one who works as a bar tender at Finnegans"

So Micky was at the taxi rank then. Well that's just put paid to my nagging doubts that he was involved in the charity theft. But what I really want to know is whether the other guy is Callum and if it is, then could this mean that the whole thing was cooked up between the two of them?

I tell Josephine as much and she says that she'd put a bet on the second guy being Callum.

"And did Bernadette say whether the CCTV has got the cab registration number?"

Our waiter arrives with the food, so I have to wait an agonising few minutes before Josephine can answer.

"I'm not sure about that – I'll ask Bernadette later. But what they have got could be gold dust don't you think?"

I nod trying not to get too excited. There are still unanswered questions and I don't want to get my hopes up too much just yet. I'm also wondering why the police haven't said anything yet to me or Clare.

"Well she only handed over the CCTV yesterday so the police are still probably looking at it as we speak " Josephine bites into a slice of her vegetarian pizza, wincing because it is piping hot. She fans her mouth and takes a gulp of water.

"My, that topping is practically molten. Anyway JJ, do you know that CSI television programme?"

"Yes, it used to be one of my favourites back in London" I reply doing a quick heat test of my own toasted sandwich and deciding not to dive in just yet.

"Well JJ you'll know from that programme how it's always the forensics that catches people out. And the camera, as the saying goes, doesn't lie"

Hmm. I'm not so sure about that one. Pictures can be interpreted in different ways and an innocent action can be made to look bad. It just depends on who is doing the looking and what they read into it.

"Anyway JJ keep what I've just told you to yourself. Now shall we change the subject? I want to hear all about this plan for your mom and brother to visit"

The rest of the lunch is spent chatting to Josephine about the best places on the island to take them. Jeff isn't bringing his new girlfriend, so I'll have to think of some 'teenager friendly' things for him to do.

"That shouldn't be too difficult" Josephine laughs gesticulating across to the seafront. "With all these beaches it's a great place for a young man to hang out. I bet he'll have a great time eyeing up our beautiful bikini clad young women"

I'm sure she's right but I'll still have to organise some nights out for him. Graham will know the best clubs, so I suppose we'll just have to bite the bullet and take my little bro to where the younger action is. Mom will be much easier to sort. She'll just want to do some exploring and to hit the designer shops on Front Street.

"My, she'll get a shock at the prices in Bermuda" Josephine says with a rare frown on her face. "I try to buy as much as I can on my visits to New York"

Before we head off, Josephine tells me that she'll introduce me to her jeweller shop friend Bernadette "Once all this nonsense about the missing charity money is over" And she reminds me again not to say anything about what she's told me, not even to Graham.

"I promise I won't say or record anything down about it" I tell her before we hug and go our separate ways along Front Street. I get a feeling that I've been down this 'don't tell' path before but frustratingly I can't pin it down.

Walking back towards home, I pass the taxi rank and it occurs to me that any one of them could have driven Micky and the other guy away with the charity stash. A waiting cab driver smiles over.

"Need to be taken anywhere sweetie?" he asks, adding that it would be a privilege to transport such a beautiful young lady wherever she wants to go.

I politely decline and he tells me to "have a great day anyway honey" Now that the rain has stopped, steam is rising up from the pavements. I notice a well dressed man waiting outside a designer handbag shop and he is engrossed in a newspaper article. The headline catches my eye.

"New Police Appeal - Missing Bartender."

I dive into a nearby general store and buy the paper. I don't want to wait to get home before reading it, so I sit down on a bench by the ferry terminal to scan the main story by the Bermuda Sun's crime correspondent.

"Police today have issued a new appeal for missing bartender, Micky Doyle, to come forward. This newspaper has passed over an anonymous email sent to our office by someone who is shielding Micky. The email says that the bartender is 'safe and well' but is in hiding on the island for his own protection. A police spokesperson says that Micky is wanted for questioning in relation to a serious crime and that anyone shielding him will be prosecuted for hindering an ongoing police investigation"

The article has a quote from an Assistant Police Commissioner saying that harbouring a wanted criminal suspect is in itself a serious offence and that anyone doing so should "think long and hard" about the consequences.

It features a recent photograph of Micky taken by a bar customer. He's smiling, giving a 'thumbs up' gesture to the camera and looking as though he hasn't got a care in the world. It was probably taken just before Micky disappeared again, which I know from my notes was less than a three weeks ago. I wonder where he is now and which part of the island he is hiding in? Even on such a small island I'm sure there are lots of places to conceal a person. And it's intriguing that the police are only referring obliquely to a 'serious crime' rather than the charity theft.

I'm so absorbed in the piece that I nearly jump out of my skin when someone sits down alongside me.

"Hi JJ, thought it was you"

I take a few moments trying to recognise who it is.

"Sorry, JJ, me being stupid. It's Paul Webster from the police Digital Forensics team"

Ah, yes of course. Although my visual memory is fairly intact, linking the face to the person – especially if I haven't had regular contact – is much more hit and miss.

"Anyway, I'm glad I've seen you JJ. I've just been viewing some CCTV of the taxi rank. And there are strong images of you walking towards it carrying the bank parcel. There's more as well but I can't tell you anything else just yet. I'm sure DI Robinson will be in touch later though"

I have to give the impression that all of this is brand new information and that I haven't already just heard it – and more – from St George's Josephine.

Paul says that he has to dash but adds that this latest CCTV footage is "highly significant"

Almost on cue my cell phone rings out and it's DI Robinson.

"Where are you JJ?" he asks sounding as though

he is running somewhere.

"Just outside the ferry station" I reply watching Paul Webster as he zips across Front Street.

"Good. Well stay there. I'm on my way down"

A gaggle of tourists head past me towards the ferry boat, laughing as they try to dodge the puddles of rain water on the road. How I wish my only concern was trying to avoid a bit of Bermuda rainfall. Instead I'm scanning the horizon for a senior police officer to appear, hoping for all the world that he isn't coming to re-arrest me.

And then I notice that a large rain drop has landed on the smiling thumbs up newspaper shot of Micky Doyle, running down the page like an oversized inky tear.

Chapter 30

The Net Closes In

DI Robinson is out of breath by the time he gets to the Ferry terminal and his greying hair is soaked and flattened by the heavy rain. He is scowling and mutters something about having to "make the journey on foot" because his police car is in for a service. I've moved under the covered passenger waiting area which is packed with people waiting for the next ferry to Dockyard.

"Trust me to get a day when it's tipping it down to have my car off the road" he says, brushing past an elderly couple in matching plastic rain coats to join me.

We wait for the rain to ease off before heading to the Lemon Café next to Par La Ville Park. DI Robinson finds us a seat at the back of the café before going to the counter to buy some coffees.

"It's good to get out of the station for a while" he says balancing two large cups and a piece of fruit cake.

"No time for lunch today JJ. It's been mad" He takes a large bite out of the cake before swigging his coffee noisily. He still hasn't told me why he is in such a hurry to talk but I can guess it has something to do with the taxi rank CCTV. I must try not to put my foot in it about my earlier conversation with Josephine.

DI Robinson has chosen our seat well because there is no one on either side of us to listen in. He manages to demolish most of his cake before cutting to the chase.

"I saw Paul Webster on the way here and he said he'd mentioned the taxi rank CCTV footage to you?" He is looking for confirmation, so I nod but don't say anything. I really do have to be careful after what Josephine has just told me over lunch.

"Well you are all over it and carrying that large parcel of readies. Did Paul say anything about what else was on there?"

"No" I reply truthfully. It's clearly a test to see if Paul has told me something he shouldn't have. In which case, it's a definite 'not guilty'.

Di Robinson takes out a note book and I can see that there is a long list of what look like number codes. But his handwriting is too small and untidy for me to make out what is written alongside the list.

"I'll go over this properly with you and that solicitor of yours. She's in court this afternoon but I've let her know that I'm speaking to you informally"

He goes through the shot list and confirms what I was expecting. The two men waiting are Micky and Callum. He glances up to glean my reaction and I manage to remain poker faced. If he'd looked up a second earlier, he'd have seen me wince at the mention of Callum.

"Callum takes the parcel off you and then they both make off in the taxi. We're doing a number plate enhancement and we should be able to trace the driver pretty quickly"

He takes another large gulp of coffee before continuing.

"Now we notice that Callum handed you another bag. Do you know what it could be?"

At the moment I have absolutely no idea. DI Robinson pulls out a still picture grab and I can see me holding what I now recognise as my overnight bag.

"Oh that's just a small bag I own. I guess they were just minding it for me that day"

DI Robinson stares hard at me for an uncomfortable amount of time.

"And why would that be?" he asks his eyes boring right through me.

"Right now I don't have a clue. But I can re-check my diary later and that might explain things more"

He gives me another penetrating stare and says that he thinks that would be a good idea.

This isn't a formal question and answer session but I'm beginning to feel uneasy. Di Robinson seems to be fixating on this bag, as if it's got some sort of importance. Whereas I just want to know more about the cab journey and where Callum and Micky are heading.

"Are there any other street shots of the cab journey?" I ask trying to deflect the subject off my own bag.

"We're checking that out but the main thing is to trace the cab driver. We'll also be talking to Callum and his fiancé again pronto. Now if any of this triggers more memories, you just give me a call day or night. Ok?"

I nod and promise him that I'll go through my diary again for that day, to try to explain why my overnight bag is on the CCTV pictures. There's bound to be a clue or explanation buried in there somewhere. At least I hope there is.

On the way home, I try to take in the significance of Callum taking the bank parcel off me before disappearing with Micky in the cab. Right now Callum is thousands of miles away in Ireland and Micky is apparently in hiding. And I can't help but think how this is going to play out between Callum and Tralee Josie. Certainly it doesn't look good that her "lovely fiancé" seems to have cooked something up with Micky behind her back.

For a moment I actually feel sorry for her but then her words, re-visited this morning, come back to me.

"I'm sure she is able to remember a lot more than she admits to and all this diary keeping stuff is just a front"

Well serve her right for doubting me. I'd have to be an Oscar winning actress to pull this one off. Still, before all this happened, I did like her and part of me hopes that we'll become friends again. One day perhaps, once the truth comes out.

Graham is already home when I get back and has heard all about the CCTV findings. He's excited and thinks that it will only be a matter of time before they arrest Micky and Callum and then "the whole sorry story will come out"

"You'll be out of the woods before you know it"

he says giving me a hug before doing a silly dance around the room. I can't help but laugh at his antics, even though I don't nearly feel as confident about things as Graham does. I know the taxi rank CCTV is a good find but things can still be twisted to make it look bad for me. Talking of which, I must take another look at my notes about the day of the bank theft to fathom out why Callum handed me that damned overnight bag.

When I finally get around to looking – only after Graham has insisted that we have a glass of wine on the terrace to celebrate the CCTV breakthrough – my head is spinning a little but things do start to fall into place. I can see now that I'd gone back to Paget that day to collect some bits and pieces from my flat. So that explains the bag. I text DI Robinson to put him in the picture and he replies with a terse 'thank you', obviously not needing anything more at this stage.

The newspapers the next day are full of more headlines about Micky. It seems that after yesterday's police appeal, the Bermuda Sun crime desk received another anonymous email claiming that Micky is innocent of any crime and is horrified that he is being seen as a suspect. The email goes on to say that he is in hiding for his own safety and insists that he is being fitted up for something he didn't do. There is still no mention of the nature of the crime and for the readers it must all appear a bit cloak and dagger. I guess there must be a reason why the police are not saying exactly what they want to question him about.

I'm still reading the piece about Micky when

Clare rings. She doesn't sound too happy about the chat between myself and DI Robinson yesterday and says she only agreed to it because she was in a rush to get back into court.

"But no more of these little chats with him without me being there" she adds before moving on to what she has really called about.

"Thought I should let you know that Wesley Caesar, the gang leader, has been quizzed about Micky Doyle's disappearance. He's coughed to taking him away the first time – saying he just wanted to put the frighteners on him – but he's denying point blank that he has had anything to do with the bank money. Of course he could be lying but he's even offered to do a lie detector test"

It hardly comes as a surprise that Wesley is claiming no knowledge of the stolen money. After all, he would hardly roll over and put his hand up to the theft as soon as the police started asking questions. But offering to take a lie detector test? Now that is more interesting and Clare seems to think so too.

"When do you think they'll go back to question Callum?" I ask, still wondering how Josie is going to react to the news about the CCTV.

"From what I gather, DI Robinson and his colleague Laura are both planning to fly out to Ireland later today. They want to just turn up so as not to alert him and Josie to anything" Clare seems to be talking while flicking through some notes – I can hear the pages turning in the background. Another multi tasking lawyer, just like Graham.

"Oh, and another thing" she adds over her still

rustling paperwork. "They think Josie may have had something to do with as well. At least they're looking at the possibility"

Now this is a puzzling piece of news. Why on earth would they suspect Josie?

"Well she may have kept herself literally out of the frame" Clare replies a bit distractedly, as if she's just read something that has caught her eye. "But Callum is her fiancé and Micky is their best friend. And the police are keen to know how the charity account cheque book and payment slips got out of her office in the first place – it seems that this is strictly against bank protocol"

So now Josie, Callum and Micky are all suspects. And of course so am I, however optimistic Graham and St George's Josephine say they are. New evidence may be stacking up but I'm not out of the water, not by a long way.

"Do you have any more hypnosis sessions booked with that Dr Silver of yours?" Clare asks lurching into a change of subject.

I glance at my diary and there is nothing booked in until next Monday. I can see that so far I've had four sessions and the last one – where I recalled a snippet of conversation with Callum – has been the most productive.

"Yes one next week" I reply double checking the diary again just to make sure.

"Laura has already interviewed him about you" she continues and I can still hear her flicking through pages in the background. "And he thinks there might be more recovered memories to be had. If so, that could be really valuable extra evidence.

Anyway, I'll have to dash now – I'm due to interview a client and I'm already running late"

Before I'm able to ask anything else, she has hung up and clearly she had been mugging up on her notes on this so called 'client' while on the telephone to me. The conversation has certainly given me a lot to think about and I can imagine the shock Tralee Josie and Callum will get when DI Robinson turns up on their doorstep in Ireland. I still can't get my head around the fact the police think Josie could be involved. Why would she want to risk her whole career for $300,000? Yes, it's a lot of money but not enough to ruin your whole life for. But then if she and Callum thought their best friend Micky's life was in real danger, perhaps they felt they had no choice?

And if any of this is true, was I just a convenient stooge with a dodgy brain to be used and thrown to the dogs once the dirty deed was done?

Questions, questions. I go back to the newspaper article about Micky and it is intriguing that he is claiming innocence of any crime. Yet still scared witless enough to be in hiding. And then there's gang master, Wesley, who is also swearing that he knows nothing about the money and confident enough to go for a lie detector test.

I log onto the online version of the newspaper to see if there has been any update on the story. I see there is a new police call for Micky to come forward so police can speak to him and they are promising "full protection."

It's accompanied by yet another picture of Micky. I recognise it as a grab from the CCTV footage taken in Par La Ville Park, cropped to remove any shots of me or Callum.

But this time around there are no thumbs up or smiles for the camera. Just the expression of a man carrying the weight of the world on his shoulders.

Chapter 31

Family On The Island

September 20 has been ringed in my diary for weeks and today is the day. I'm doing some last minute tidying before Graham gets back and we head off for the airport. Yes, in two hours mom and Jeff are landing at Bermuda's L F Wade airport and as the time draws nearer, I'm feeling more nervous. Crazy, I know, to be feeling this anxious about seeing my family again but there you have it.

I just hope that mom likes Graham. I can't see any reason why she won't and she has already spoken to him a lot on the phone. But meeting someone face to face is different and I'll be glad to get the initial introductions over with. Then there's the meeting in a few days time with Graham's parents. Now that one I'm even more nervous about.

The plan is to bring mom and Jeff here first to see the apartment. Then we'll drive them over to Pauletta's place where they'll be staying in my old flat. Pauletta and her husband Dave have planned a BBQ on a Portuguese theme and I hope mom and Jeff are up to it after their seven hour flight.

Nina Simone is on the background as I try to

calm my nerves. The weather has cooled down a little since the heat of July and August but it is still 80 degrees with high humidity. Knowing mom she'll have packed jackets and cardigans "just in case" because it is hard for British people to believe that the temperature doesn't drop in the evenings. Jeff will arrive with no more than a few pairs of shorts, T-shirts and maybe some jeans. He has already said that he wants to spend time surfing, so he'll be pleased that he's staying just minutes away from Elbow Beach.

After the recent flurry of police activity, things have gone fairly quiet again. As far as I know, the call for Micky to come out of hiding hasn't worked. And I've got nothing in my diary about the outcome of DI Robinson's trip to Ireland with his colleague Laura. But I've no doubt that I'll be hearing something back on that soon.

Satisfied that the place is tidy enough to pass muster, I look over the itinerary that Graham and me have come up with for mom and Jeff's ten day visit. It includes a boat trip, a couple of visits to Dockyard, a day in St George's to meet Josephine and her father, dinner with Graham's parents, Horseshoe Bay and an afternoon at the Crystal Caves - an incredible network of deep caves discovered back in the day by some young boys who were searching for their lost ball. I've tried to factor in enough shopping time in Hamilton for mom and beach time for Jeff.

There's the possibility of a theatre performance one evening and a night club visit for Jeff. It's certainly a jam packed ten days and I'm sure it will be exhausting but exhilarating.

Graham arrives home early and has brought two bottles of champagne to take to Pauletta's BBQ. While he's getting changed, I sit on the terrace watching a large passenger boat as it moors up. A group of well dressed people get off and look as though they are heading for a swanky venue in Hamilton for the evening. I can see the sun glinting off one of the women's expensive looking bejewelled handbag which matches her sparkly evening shoes.

"What are you gawping at then?" Graham laughs as he takes a seat beside me. He's poured himself a light beer and leans across to see what I'm looking at.

"Ah they'll be off to the film premiere – there's a big movie director in town tonight for the opening. There's a reception afterwards and he'll be doing the rounds. Hell that one looks like she's off to meet the Queen. A bit over the top eh?"

He's pointing to the woman with the sparkly shoes and handbag who seems to be having trouble walking across the road and keeps stopping to check her footwear.

"She's be better taking those off and walking barefoot" Graham says imitating her wobbly gait. "Let's hope she doesn't have too much to drink tonight in those ridiculous shoes"

By the time we get to the airport, the waiting area is crowded with people anticipating the arrival of their loved ones or work colleagues. There's a mix of smartly dressed business types and more casually attired people who look like they've just got back from a day on the beach. Graham and me are sort of in the middle – smart casual which is the norm for most locals. And already that's how I'm starting to see myself, even though I've only been on the island since May.

The flight from London arrives right on time and within half an hour I spot mom, dressed in a floral two piece suit and carrying the obligatory cardigan. Jeff is dragging a trolley containing their two large suitcases and is wearing a pair of baggy jeans and a tee shirt with a large Union Jack flag on the front.

As soon as mom sees me, she rushes over and bursts into tears. We hug each other and I can feel my eyes welling up too. Jeff is hanging back a little and Graham shakes his hand before introducing himself.

"Hi, so you must be the little brother Jeff I've heard so much about? Welcome to Bermuda"

Jeff gives Graham a small shy smile before I extricate myself from mom and rush over to give my brother a hug. Meantime Graham introduces himself to mom who is still in floods of tears.

"Hey Carol – we meet at last after all those phone calls. How was your flight?"

Out of the corner of my eye, I can see mom measuring up Graham and I think she likes what she sees. The next few minutes are a blur of family news and catch ups, with Graham helping Jeff lug the suitcases back to the car park.

No mention of my being dragged into a bank theft yet, which is fine by me.

"Hey Carol – this is a heavy one! What have you got hidden in there then?" Graham makes an exaggerated puffing noise as he lifts mom's case into the rear of the car.

"Oh you know what we women are like – at least three outfits for every day with all the accessories to match. It mounts up doesn't it JJ?"

I laugh and tell her that she had better not do too much clothes shopping in Bermuda then and she pretends not to hear me. I sit in the back seats with mom, while Jeff goes in the front with Graham.

As we make our way back towards Hamilton, Graham points out all the sights. It's a beautiful evening and the sun is reflecting off the white roofs showing off the pastel coloured houses to perfection.

"Oh it's so pretty – but why are the roofs white?" mom asks moving across the seat to get a better view. I can see the small beads of sweat already forming across her face and ask Graham to wick up the air conditioning.

Graham tweaks the air level, while telling mom about lime washed roofs collecting water and deflecting heat. Jeff is staring out of the window with his mouth open as if he can't quite believe that he is here. He looks like he has grown up a lot since I last saw him and I wonder whether he's already missing his first proper girlfriend, Sophie. It's something I'll ask him about later when we get some time on our own.

When we get to the apartment both mom and Jeff are dumb struck.

"This is just fantastic – like something from a film or one of those glossy magazines" mom says her eyes scanning the place trying to drink in all the details. "What do you think Jeff – gorgeous eh?"

Jeff nods and heads across towards the terrace. I know he'll be bowled over by the view and he let's out a loud gasp once he sees it.

"Mom get yourself over here. It's to die for."

Mom goes onto the terrace and stands there transfixed.

"Wow, wow" Jeff mutters taking in the view from all sides. Mom is still seemingly overwhelmed, so Graham suggests we have a cocktail on the terrace.

"I'll have a gin and tonic" mom says entranced by the view. Like me, Jeff opts for a soft drink even though he's been legal to have alcohol for nearly a year now. For a teenager, he's a sensible lad.

Inevitably the conversation turns to "my predicament" as mom puts it, so I guess it's time to get it over with.

"They seem to be taking ages to sort this mess out" mom says after we've given her a quick update on the latest developments. "It's bloody obvious you've been set up and ridiculous that you are still forced to wear that silly ankle tag"

"Well these things do take time" Graham replies diplomatically. "And the police need to be sure that they have got the right people"

"Hmm well that – what's his name? – Micky looks as guilty as hell from what you've told me. And that Callum bloke is probably up to his neck too" Mom resorts to her disapproving sniff habit and it is clear that it's time to change the subject. Seeing the expression on my face, Graham comes to the rescue.

287

"Oh look at the time. We'd better be getting over to the BBQ - Pauletta will be getting into a state"

Mom downs the rest of her drink and I can see that her cheeks have turned a rosy pinkish colour, meaning that she's either too warm or that the gin is having its effect. I suspect it's the latter.

Pauletta has put on a spectacular spread and has invited several of her friends along. As mom has predicted, they get on well from the off and no one can get a word in edgeways. Still it gives me a chance to have a chat to Jeff on my own.

"So how are things with Sophie?" I ask as he tucks into a huge piece of Portuguese spicy chicken which has just been handed to him by Dave wearing his 'Men Like It Hot' apron.

Jeff gives Dave a thumbs up saying the chicken is "ace" before answering my question.

"Oh things are great sis. Sophie's just the best – really beautiful but with some brains as well. Wish she could be here but she's got two psychology exams to do. Shame"

Jeff pulls out a photo of him and Sophie from his jeans pocket. I've already got pictures of them both which I look at every day but she seems different in this one.

"She's just had her hair cut shorter" Jeff adds noticing my confusion. "It suits her doesn't it?"

With her new pixie cut style, Sophie looks older and is undeniably very pretty.

"Looks like you've done well for yourself little bro" I joke nudging him in the chest. "Shame she's got to put up with you"

Jeff laughs telling me that I'm a cheeky cow,

poorly head or not. It is lovely having him here to banter with and it makes me realise just how much I've missed him and mom.

Jeff suddenly turns serious and brings up the subject of the charity theft.

"How are you coping with all that sis? I mean it can't be easy being here in a new country with a new guy and having all that to deal with as well. And on top of your memory problems too. You must have been a very bad girl in your former life that's all I can say"

That's Jeff for you. Tempering the serious with the jokey and a bit like Graham in that respect.

"Well it hasn't been easy" I reply laughing at my own understatement. "But you know there have been so many good things that have happened to me here as well. Meeting Graham and St George's Josephine for a start. And friends like Pauletta and Dave here"

Graham smiles across at us and I can feel my heart melt. He really is the most amazing man and I still can't quite believe how lucky I have been to find him.

I tell my little bro as much and I can see that he understands. Before meeting Sophie he'd have pulled a face and made a "I think I'm going to throw up" gesture at any display of affection. But not now. Jeff is getting all grown up and I think I like it.

The BBQ is still in full swing when Graham and me decide to make our way home. Mom looks a bit tipsy but it could be tiredness as well. Jeff is manfully trying to stay awake but I can see that he's flagging. It will be the early hours of the morning in London now and they'd have been in bed ages ago.

"Well that's gone well. Your mom's great and Jeff has a wicked sense of humour" Graham says as we get into the car. I'm pleased how the evening has gone and that everyone seems to be getting along. Let's just hope that Graham's folks see my family in the same way.

I'm not sure why, but I wake up in the middle of the night bathed in sweat and the nightmare about my accident has reoccurred. I haven't had this dream for a long time and I try to calm my breathing so that I don't wake Graham up. He's dead to the world so is oblivious to my distress and I try to lie as still as I can, while wondering what on earth has triggered this.

When the alarm clock finally signals that it is 8am, I'm a bit bleary eyed after my interrupted night and fall straight back into a deep sleep. I'm then woken up by Graham cursing that he's slept through the alarm and is running late. Although he's booked some time off while mom and Jeff are visiting, he has to make a brief court appearance on their first full day here.

"I'll be through by 11am and we can head over to St George's then" he says grabbing his briefcase and taking a quick swig of black coffee. He gives me a kiss and then sprints over to the car, waving as he sets off.

My ritual morning diary read puts me in a better mood as I re-live all the details about last night's BBQ and the successful introduction of Graham to my family. Graham took lots of pictures and it is lovely to see everyone looking so happy. I smile as I spot one of mom looking a bit unsteady on her feet, with a silly grin on her face.

It's 10am so probably safe to give Pauletta a call. She answers the phone quickly and sounds very chirpy considering the busy night she's had.

"Morning JJ, and a beautiful one at that. I'm just preparing some breakfast for your mom and Jeff"

"So they're up already? I thought they'd still be sleeping in"

"No, they've been up for over an hour and your mom is unpacking her things. They've brought us a lovely coffee set from Harrods and a beautiful flower vase. So kind of them to do that" I can hear Pauletta clattering cutlery in the background and I tell her that I'll call back when they've had breakfast.

"How are they looking?" I ask.

"Fine but they'll be even better after one of my breakfasts. See you later JJ – I'll tell them you called"

By the time Graham and me get over to Paget, a little later than expected, mom and Jeff are sitting on Pauletta's lawn enjoying the sun. It's mid day and exactly the time you should be keeping well out of it, but not mom and Jeff. They are the classic English visitors abroad and want to be basking in the sunshine whatever time of the day it is.

"I hope you've got some good sun cream slapped on Carol" Graham jokes as we wend our way across Pauletta's large front garden.

Mom laughs and says that in her day, people used to just put on olive oil and that "all this sun factor nonsense" didn't exist.

"That must have stunk to high heaven" Jeff says crinkling his nose at the thought.

Pauletta appears with a jug of freshly made lemonade which she insists that we drink before heading off.

"So what do you think of your accommodation then?" I ask mom once Pauletta is out of ear shot.

"It's not as grand as yours but it's comfortable enough" She drops her voice slightly. "But there are quite a few ants around so I'll be getting some powder to see them off"

Ah, the ants. They are a pest in Bermuda even as late as September and are a scourge in the earlier summer months. Graham laughs and asks mom if she's spotted any lizards yet. Mom looks a bit worried and says that no, she hasn't, thank god.

Jeff quips that he thinks lizards are "really cool" and mom gives him a disapproving look. I can see that it will take them some time to adapt to this sub tropical climate of ours.

When we get to St George's, Josephine is waiting on her doorstep with her dad Clarence. Immediately I can see the resemblance, although Clarence's face is etched with deep wrinkles while Josephine's is virtually crease free.

"Dad, this is JJ who I've been talking to you about" Josephine lightly propels him towards me and he extends his long boney hand. As I clasp it, his skin feels dry and slightly cool but his shake is firm. His smile is as enchanting as Josephine's.

It takes a few minutes to get everyone introduced but the atmosphere is relaxed and jovial. Mom is wearing a jaunty straw hat which Josephine admires, remarking that she's got a similar one herself. She suggests that mom and Jeff have a quick tour of her house and studio, while Graham and me sit in the garden area with Clarence. Josephine's dog, Mutt, comes bounding over and Graham heads off to play "fetch the stick" with him.

Clarence's speech is slow and he has a pronounced Bermudian accent with an even heavier emphasis on the 'o' sounds than Josephine. But like her, he is easy to talk to and it is clear that Josephine has told him all about me.

"Now this memory problem of yours – it has got you into some real bad trouble I hear?"

I nod, wondering just how much information to give him about my involvement with the police.

"Josephine tells me that the police are questioning a few people. The truth will out and I know that the Lord will be on your side" He makes a cross sign and suggests that we pray together that something good will happen. He takes hold of my hand before praying for the Lord "to look after me in my times of troubles."

It seems strange praying in this way but surprisingly comforting. Graham is still engrossed in his game with Mutt, who is running around quickly for an old dog. Then I see an excited looking Josephine coming towards us, with mom and Jeff trailing behind.

"Hey JJ I've just heard from my friend, Bernadette, who runs the jewellery shop. And she tells me that the police have managed to trace the taxi driver from the CCTV pictures. Isn't that great news?"

Clarence smiles over at me before whispering under his breath

"See - the power of prayer has worked already. Thank you Lord. Thank you"

Chapter 32

Smoking Out Micky

Josephine's news about the taxi driver being traced dominates the conversation for the rest of the afternoon. I'm trying hard at playing the role of the excited victim of a miscarriage of justice who is about to be vindicated. But I can't keep down that inner voice that keeps telling me to hold fire on the celebrations for now. It might just be self protection, the voice of reason telling me that it ain't over until it is over. Whatever, it is powerful and insistent and I can't ignore it.

It's not long before I get the predictable phone call from Clare, telling me again what I already know.

"They've got the driver JJ. He dropped Micky off at the supermarket at the far end of Front Street and then took Callum back to his apartment. The driver remembers the bulky parcel but didn't ask Callum anything about it. He says it looked like something he could have purchased from a store"

I can see Josephine at the far side of the garden showing mom and Jeff her various exotic species of plants. Graham is deep in conversation with Clarence while Mutt, thoroughly exhausted from his earlier exertions, is snoozing on the grass.

"Well aren't you excited?" Clare asks when she doesn't get the gleeful reaction she has been expecting.

"Yes, of course I'm pleased" I say trying to dampen down that inner doubting voice. "It's just that, you know, I don't want to get my hopes up too much. Just in case…"

"In case of what?" Clare asks sounding more than a bit exasperated.

"Oh I don't know – I haven't had any recent update from DI Robinson about what's gone on in Ireland. And Micky's still in hiding. There's still pieces of the jigsaw missing, that's what I really mean"

"Well I can give you one bit of news there" she replies suddenly resuming her earlier upbeat voice. "Micky has been back in touch with that newspaper guy and he's seriously thinking about meeting up with the police. He just wants some guarantees about his protection first. But you won't be reading any headlines about that – it's being kept under wraps for now."

It sounds as though Micky is getting close to revealing himself and hopefully the full story will then finally come out.

"And DI Robinson and Laura are due back from Ireland tomorrow" Clare adds sounding even chirpier. "So that bit of the puzzle should start to make a bit more sense too. I expect they'll be on to me as soon as they land"

Once off the phone, I pull Graham to one side to give him the latest news. Like Clare he's incredibly upbeat about it and he thinks there will be an arrest warrant out for Josie and Callum.

"And let's see what Micky comes up with once he's given himself up. It's my guess you'll be out of the woods very soon sweetheart, you wait and see" He puts his arms around me and for a few blissful moments we kiss, oblivious to the world.

"Urgh – get a room you two!" Jeff is bounding over, followed by Mutt, with an exaggerated look of disgust on his face.

Graham laughs and tells him that he should show more respect for his big sister, while I grab him around the chest playfully just like I used to do as a kid.

"Ouch – that hurts sis. Mercy, mercy" We're play fighting like two youngsters and if it wasn't for the heat and the tropical plants, we could be back in the Islington garden of our childhood.

Our antics have caught the attention of mom and Josephine who are looking across and giggling between themselves. Mutt is now jumping up between me and Jeff, trying to get in on the action.

"Hey you two – behave yourselves" mom yells over putting on a pretend angry face. Already she and Josephine are making their way across the lawn carrying armfuls of flowers and plants.

The rest of the afternoon is filled with a tour of St George's and a late lunch at the English style tea shop. Mom is in her element telling Josie that the tea and scones are the best she's ever tasted.

"Not as good as the Hamilton Royal hotel in my view" Josephine replies while Clarence declares that the best eating place in Bermuda has to be "Lenny's

Shack" at the back of town.

"Good old fashioned plain cooking, none of this fancy stuff" he adds stirring his tea and nodding across the table to reinforce his point.

"Oh pop, Lenny's closed months ago. You know that" Josephine says eyeing her father affectionately.

"Ah well, I still think it had the best food in Bermuda. Anyway, his son Kyril says they might reopen it in memory of the old man"

"What Kyril cook? You are joking, right?" Josephine laughs out loud before regaling us with the story of the time Kyril put on a birthday BBQ and nearly burned down the family home.

I can see that mom is starting to flag as the jet lag is kicking in. Jeff looks jaded too and keeps rubbing his eyes.

"Time for us to start making tracks I think" Graham says also noticing that mom is having trouble keeping her eyes open.

After dropping mom and Jeff at Pauletta's place, we head off to buy food for the meal we are planning tomorrow night to introduce mom and Jeff to Graham's folks.

'Keep it simple' is Graham's mantra so we opt for grilled fish steaks and salad.

"Does your mom like wine?" Graham asks as we head towards the drinks counter.

"No she's an occasional gin and tonic girl only" I reply, suddenly remembering a Christmas all those years ago when mom got sick after drinking too much red wine. As far as I know she hasn't touched it since.

"Really - she only sticks to one drink?" Graham

sounds incredulous and throws in an extra large bottle of gin into our trolley. He still has a lot to learn about mom that's for sure.

"And what about Jeff? Is he allowed to drink anything grown up?"

"I don't think he's that bothered. But we could get some light beers in just in case"

"Let's get some stronger ones in as well. Your little brother might feel like it after spending the evening with all us old folks"

It has already occurred to me that Jeff could be bored rigid by spending another evening with people a lot older than him. Perhaps we'll need to arrange that visit to a night club over the next few days to make up for it.

As it turns out, I needn't have worried. After the first slightly awkward introductions, it's clear that Jeff is getting on like a house on fire with Graham's dad Bill. Mom, on the other hand, isn't faring so well with Evelyn. And there are a couple of hilarious misunderstandings which I'm still giggling about later as I record them in my diary.

The first relates to language. Although everyone speaks English here, it is predominantly American English. So post boxes are 'mail' boxes. Rubbish is 'trash' and pavements are 'sidewalks'.

At one point Evelyn is lamenting the way some people just drop their cigarette ends and trash on the sidewalks instead of putting it in the 'cans'.

"Ooh I know just what you mean" mom replies "people should put their ciggie butts inside their empty drinks cans before throwing them in the bin. Much tidier"

Evelyn looks as though mom is speaking a foreign language and doesn't know how to respond.

"I think by 'cans' Evelyn means 'bins' mom" I say trying not to laugh. "People should put their ciggie ends in the waste bins"

Mom reddens a little and my attempt to explain things just leaves Evelyn even more confused. Best to change the subject I think.

Next there is the subject of fashion. Mom is of the school that the brighter and garish the colours the better. If it is floral and loud then mom loves it. Evelyn, on the other hand, likes muted neutral colours that blend into the background rather than stand out.

"I can't wait to hit the shops properly in Hamilton" mom tells Evelyn, adding that she "loves the bright pinks, yellows and oranges" that she has seen in some of the windows.

"So exotic Evelyn, don't you think?"

Evelyn, dressed head to toe in the palest of blues and greys, clearly doesn't agree but she is far too polite to say as much. So she shifts on her seat uncomfortably trying to think how to respond.

"Well Carol, bright colours suit you. As for me, they just drain my colour and make me look even paler than I am"

Mom responds with one of her sniffs, telling Evelyn that a bright scarf, bag or shoes would still look nice and would 'lift' her outfit. The implication is that Evelyn's outfit is a bit dowdy and it hangs in the air like a bad smell.

I retreat into the kitchen area trying to think of a way of separating mom and Evelyn before they insult each other even more.

Graham follows me with mom's empty glass.

"I think Carol needs a top up" he says waving the glass and leaning across to grab the gin bottle. I'm not sure it's a good idea.

"Hmm, make it a small one" I whisper, adding that I'm not convinced mom and Evelyn are getting along. Graham shrugs and tells me that they'll be fine once they've tiptoed around each other's egos. He's missed out the word 'big'.

By the time we return with mom's drink, Evelyn has moved across the room to join Bill and Jeff leaving mom looking a bit deflated. They barely exchange words for the rest of the evening while in a short space of time Jeff has ingratiated himself with everyone.

"Guess what sis? Bill and Evelyn have invited me out on their boat. Isn't that great?" Jeff is smiling broadly and looks like he's about to punch the air.

I don't bother to ask whether they've invited mom as well – I think the answer is fairly self evident.

It seems that mom has already made it clear that she hates boats and that she's read all about "the Bermuda Triangle thingy." Apparently it is this little witticism that has forced Evelyn to make a hasty retreat back to the company of her husband and Jeff. Well that and mom's continued "advice" to Evelyn on "sexing up her outfits with bold splashes of colour" Oh dear.

The next morning I can see the funny side of things and Graham is sanguine saying that there'll be plenty of time for the two moms to make amends. He's doing a great impression of them both when the apartment door buzzer is pressed hard and loudly.

"Ok I'm coming" Graham shouts "don't worry we can hear you"

Graham returns with an exhausted looking DI Robinson in tow alongside Paul Webster, the police digital forensics guy.

"Your cell phone seems to be switched off" DI Robinson announces without even saying so much as 'Good Morning.' As it turns out it isn't - the battery has just gone flat and I quickly hook it up to the charger while Graham disappears to make some coffee.

"Right JJ, I only got in from Ireland last night so I'm feeling a bit groggy " DI Robinson rubs the back of his neck and just about manages to stifle a yawn. When Graham arrives with the coffee he grabs a cup gratefully and throws in three lumps of sugar.

"I need the energy. Now JJ, I need you to listen to this carefully. Have you had any communication from Josie or Callum recently?"

"Shouldn't Clare be here?" Graham asks on his way back to the kitchen.

DI Robinson tries to hide his irritation at being interrupted but fails to do so.

"I'm not formally interviewing JJ. Just passing on information. If you want to sit in I've got no objection but I need to be back at the station before 9.30am"

"Ok I'll sit in then – just as an observer" Graham says putting down his coffee tray. "And I'll let Clare know later"

"Fine by me" DI Robinson snaps and returns his attention to me.

"Now JJ - you haven't had any recent contact with Josie or Callum?"

"No, there's nothing in my diary and you're welcome to check my phone or computer" I reply glancing across at Paul Webster. I'm guessing that's why he's here.

"We might do that later, but I take it that you'd put something in your daily diary if you had heard anything?"

I catch Graham's eye and he nods as if to say that it's fine for me to answer.

"Yes, I would put such a big event in my diary. Of course I would. And no, there is nothing in there"

Satisfied. DI Robinson downs what is left of his coffee and accepts another cup from Graham.

"Fine. Let's leave it at that then. You should also know that Josie and Callum have disappeared and we are liaising with the Irish authorities to see whether they have left the country. Seems like they have done a runner"

First Micky, and now Josie and Callum have disappeared as well. I can barely believe what I'm hearing. DI Robinson then invites Paul Webster, who hasn't said a word so far, to tell me what he knows about the airport CCTV he has been examining.

"We're recovered all the airport CCTV and flight passenger records. We now know that Callum and Josie left Bermuda on the same flight which was a few hours after the bank theft" Paul pulls out a detailed flight document and also a still grab from the airport CCTV system.

He passes me a copy of the CCTV grab and I can see Josie and Callum walking across the main airport concourse. Both are wearing heavy jackets and are carrying substantial pieces of hand luggage.

"As you see they have bulky looking coats and bags" Paul remarks showing me a second close up where I can clearly see the faces of them both.

DI Robinson puts down his coffee cup and leans across to take another look at the photos.

"We searched the house in Ireland for the jackets and hand luggage but there was nothing. All their stuff was cleared out"

Unable to keep his lawyer's hat off, Graham asks if the police suspect that the stolen money has been stashed inside the unseasonably heavy jackets and hefty hand luggage.

DI Robinson refuses to be drawn on this simply answering that "all lines of investigation are being explored"

"So that's a yes then" Graham quips and DI Robinson doesn't have a chance to answer before his cell phone rings out. He disappears into the kitchen to answer it, while Paul Webster files away the CCTV stills.

Graham is intrigued by digital forensics and is quizzing Paul about the growing importance of this new investigatory branch of science, when DI Robinson reappears. His face is flushed and he can't keep the excitement from his voice.

"We'll have to be off now. That was the editor of the Bermuda Sun on the phone. Micky Doyle's been back in touch with their crime guy and he's ready to meet up with us today. You ok to drive Paul?"

And with that they are off. So Micky is back on the horizon just as Josie and Callum have vanished off the face of the earth.

I feel like I'm walking down an ever increasing twisting path and I've no idea where it will lead. Or whether I'll ever make my way out of it.

Chapter 33

Run Hit and Jump

Mom and Jeff are nearing the end of their stay in Bermuda and today mom wants to hit those designer shops in Hamilton. Jeff, on the other hand, is off on his promised boat trip with Evelyn and Bill.

"I'd much rather be on the water than traipsing round shops" he says as he clambers into the front seat of our car with Graham. It's another hot and humid Bermuda day and mom is carrying a portable air fan which she keeps putting up to her face. She's developed a reddish tinged tan and you can see the contrast with her pale English skin under the straps of her bright pink sundress. Jeff has also caught the sun and his dark hair has lightened in parts giving it a streaky appearance.

"OK are we ready to be off then?" Graham asks, looking back at mom.

"Can't wait" mom replies opening her handbag to fish out a tissue. She dabs her face and ups the air level on the miniature fan. It blasts her carefully styled hair backwards and she tuts loudly, turning the level back down. Poor mom, she really is finding the sub tropical heat hard cope with at times. Whereas Jeff seems to have been born to it.

It's now been four days since the visit from DI Robinson, although I have been getting updates from Clare. It seems that the focus is firmly fixed on the hunt for Josie and Callum. Apparently they made their way to London and then onto the Eurostar cross channel link to France. After that the trail has gone cold but I gather that the Irish police and Interpol are now involved.

The Irish newspapers have got hold of the story and have run a number of pieces about what they are calling an 'international manhunt'. Mom says it will be a matter of time before the English press take an interest and she still thinks that she should give an them an interview about me, her poor brain injured daughter, who has been dragged into all of this.

"No mom, I don't want to be plastered all over the newspapers" I snap back at her. Mercifully Graham agrees.

"Carol, I'm with JJ on this. Leave it to the police to sort things out. Going public at this stage won't help and could make things a whole lot worse. Take it from me as a seasoned lawyer – keep a low profile for now"

Mom gives her customary sniff and the conversation comes to an abrupt end – at least for the time being.

As for Micky Doyle, he is still negotiating with police through the crime desk of the Bermuda Sun newspaper. According to Clare, his emails are proving impossible to trace and even the clever Paul Webster has been unable to crack them. The sticking point seems to be the type of protection Micky will get if he meets with the police. He also wants assurances on the security of the location for that first crucial interview.

Meantime, I've tried to focus on the remaining days of mom and Jeff's holiday as best I can. And today we're meeting St George's Josephine in Hamilton for mom's much anticipated shop. Josephine has also arranged afternoon tea at the Hamilton Royal hotel and Graham has promised he'll join us for that part. But first he's going to drop Jeff off at his parent's boat and is planning on a few hours sailing before hooking up with us.

"Enjoy yourselves and don't flex that plastic too much Carol" he jokes as he drops us off outside the grand City Hall building where we've arranged to meet Josephine.

When she does arrive, flustered from trying to find a parking space, she is armed with a long list of shops and an itinerary that looks exhausting. There's got to be at least twenty stores of that list of hers.

"Well I've gone for broke Carol, but we'll see how we get on. Now, have you two got water and something to cover your heads?"

Mom has her sunhat but I've got nothing, so Josephine reaches into in her voluminous shoulder bag and produces a white silk scarf.

"Here JJ put that on – it's not a day for walking around without head protection"

Sometimes Josephine reminds me of a benign but strict school teacher and I know it is best just to take her advice. I twist my hair up inside the scarf and tie a knot at the back. Goodness knows what it looks like but mom says it suits me, adding that all I need is a gleaming open topped sports car to set it off.

It's clear from the first half hour of our trip that Josephine's plan is going to the wall. We've barely set off when we bump into one of her friends which triggers a long chat and introductions to me and mom. And just as we arrive outside one of the main department stores, Josephine spots someone else she knows. This time it is "Auntie Lucille" one of her many relatives. Cue another long exchange before we finally get through the door.

Ignoring Graham's advice, mom doesn't so much flex her credit card as makes it do a triple somersault. First there's a designer bag that has been reduced by 60% and still costs several hundred dollars. Then there are several pairs of shoes, dresses, jackets and tops. By now her card isn't just releasing sparks from being swiped so many times, it is threatening to combust. As for me, I've only managed a couple of pairs of shorts and a shirt for Graham.

Even though there are three of us, we can barely carry our bags by the time Josephine realises that it's time for us to start making our way to the hotel. We squash the bags into the car 'trunk' as Josephine calls it, before heading off. We've just turned out of the car park when Graham rings me to say that he'll be running a little late.

"Got carried away with the sailing but Jeff is having a whale of a time. He's a natural"

He laughs when I tell him how much stuff we have got.

"Just as well we're heading back in my car then.

See you later sweetheart"

I don't even have time to finish the call when there is an almighty bang. Mom and me are thrown violently forward and Josephine is leaning hard on the car horn.

"You stupid idiot! What do you think you are doing?" Josephine is craning out of the window and glaring at the driver behind who has slammed right into the back of her car. Mom and me are dumbstruck and I can hear Graham's voice yelling out of my cell phone which has landed somewhere on the floor.

"JJ, JJ. What the hell happened? JJ - can you hear me? What's going on?"

I feel around my feet and manage to locate the phone which has rolled under the front seat. Josephine is now out of her car and after a quick check to see that we are ok, she is off to confront the young man in the car who has slammed into us.

Mom is rubbing the back of her neck and already I can feel a lump developing where my forehead hit the back of Josephine's driver seat.

I quickly let Graham know what has happened and that we are fine.

"I think you should still go to the hospital to be checked out, especially given what's happened before" he says after I tell him about my bruised forehead and mom's neck. I can hear raised voices outside and Josephine is waving her fists at the young man as he bends down to inspect the damage to the two cars.

"Is Josephine ok?" Graham asks as I open the car door to get a better view of what is going on. It's clear that both cars have been badly dented, with the young man's one coming off a lot worse.

"Give me a minute and I'll let you know" I say, telling mom to stay put for now. She is still rubbing at her neck and looks to be in a state of shock.

I'm still clutching the phone when that familiar smell of hot tarmac and rubber hits my nose. I hear the thud of the phone as it drops from my hand and Josephine's raised voice suddenly seems a long way off. Then there is a creeping blackness as if the sky has suddenly darkened over. Somewhere in the distance I can hear Graham's anguished voice.

"JJ? JJ?"

When I come around, I'm once again in an ambulance and for a moment I think I've been transported back in time.

"Don't worry young lady. You just fainted. We'll get you checked out with the doctor"

Out of the corner of my eye, I can see mom and Josephine peering across with worried looks on their faces. Mom is wearing a neck brace and a paramedic is holding her hand.

"Mom, Josephine, you two all right?" I manage to ask before realising that I can't pull up my head to look at them properly.

"You'll have to keep still" the second paramedic says touching my arm gently. "We've strapped you down until the doctor has checked you over. It's just a precaution"

"We're both fine JJ. You just rest there. We'll be at the hospital soon and Graham and Jeff are on their way" It's good to hear Josephine's reassuring voice and she gives me a small wave from the other side of the ambulance. She is smiling broadly but I can see that it isn't her usual genuine beam. Her eyes look fearful and concerned.

When we get to the hospital, Graham and Jeff are waiting at the entrance. They both rush over and Graham takes hold of my hand.

"Sweetheart, you gave us a scare" he says planting a kiss on my cheek.

I smile and give a weak smile across at Jeff who is looking teary.

"I'm fine honestly" I tell them before the paramedic whisks me along a wide white corridor and into an examination room.

The next few hours are a blur of checks and tests and I'm told that I'll have to stay overnight for observation. Mercifully Graham is allowed to stay with me. My ankle tag has been a bit of a sticking point with the medical staff and after some discussions with DI Robinson, they've been allowed to remove it. It seems odd not having it on and Graham gives me a foot massage which makes me relaxed and sleepy. Just as I'm about to nod off, I remember that I haven't done my daily diary.

"Don't worry honey, I'll fill you in on everything tomorrow. You just get some sleep"

And with those words I'm off. For the first time in ages I haven't finished my day with a mound of written words, a detailed narrative of my time over the past few hours.

And like the removal of the ankle tag, this seems strange but liberating. Perhaps this really is a day I should forget forever – like snipping out an unwelcome scene from a film.

But then again, maybe not....

Chapter 34

Now and Yesterday

When I open my eyes, it takes a while to take in my surroundings. Graham is slumped in the hospital bedside chair, fast asleep and snoring lightly. The room is cool, despite the bright sunshine streaming through the bottom of the window blinds. I can hear muffled voices from behind the door and the noise of trolley wheels clattering along the outside corridor. There are vaguely familiar smells of cleaning chemicals, coffee and toasted bread. It's all seems so recognisable and yet strange at the same time.

I lie still for a few moments trying to make sense of everything. My head is throbbing and I gingerly feel the raised bump on the top of my left eyebrow. It must look a sight so it's just as well Graham is still asleep.

I gently raise myself up into a sitting position trying to be as quiet as possible so that I don't wake Graham up. Poor bloke, he looks dead to the world.

Then I'm struck by something. An incredible, magical something.

I know why I'm here. I really do know. It was that car incident yesterday, the one we had on the way to the Royal Hotel after the shopping trip. The one where the young guy ploughed into the back of Josephine's car, throwing mom and me towards the front seats. The one where I ended up fainting and getting this prize bump on my head.

Yes, it's all coming back. Details, clear details.

And know for a fact that I haven't even written anything down. I can even remember Graham telling me, just before I fell asleep, that there was no need to worry about doing my diary. He'd remind me. Well no need now. It's all there.

I get a vision of mom in a neck brace inside the ambulance. I wonder how she's feeling this morning? I can recall her and Josephine heading off in a taxi last night with my upset looking little brother. Wow, this quite is amazing.

While I'm on a roll, I go through the things we bought yesterday. I remember the pale blue stripped cotton shirt I bought for Graham and I can even see everything in mom's huge pile of shopping. This really is something else, a thing to savour.

A nurse pops her head around the door and Graham wakes up with a jolt.

"How are you feeling this morning Miss James?" She ignores Graham who is rubbing his eyes and trying to adjust to the light.

"Fine" I reply smiling across at Graham. He grins back stretching out his legs and then wincing at the effort.

"I'm not sure about him though"

The nurse laughs adding that it's nothing that a good cup of coffee won't sort out and asks what I'd like for breakfast.

315

"Toast and lots of it" Graham replies even though she hasn't asked him.

"I'll have some fruit salad as well if you have it" I add "and some tea please instead of coffee"

The nurse nods and darts back behind the door. Graham plonks himself on the bed and gently touches my bruised forehead.

"Hey, morning sweetie. That bump has come up good and proper. So how are you *really* feeling Miss James?" He gives me a kiss telling me to move across the bed so he can join me.

He's nuzzling my neck and we're giggling like a couple of teenagers when the nurse arrives back with our breakfast. If she's embarrassed, she doesn't show it and asks if we'd like her to throw open the blinds.

"Yes please" I reply trying not to laugh as Graham pulls a silly face in the background. He's behaving like a naughty schoolboy and it's hard to believe that he is really the hot shot Hamilton lawyer. But in truth I wouldn't have him any other way.

Mom and Josephine arrive early, just as we are about to start breakfast. I still haven't had a chance to tell Graham about my exciting news - that I can remember everything from yesterday without prompting. It'll just have to wait for now.

Mom is carrying a basket of fresh fruit and is still wearing her cumbersome neck brace.

"Didn't sleep a wink last night what with this thing and worrying about you" she says planting a kiss on my cheek and turning my head up towards the light so that she can inspect my bruise.

Josephine and Graham decide to make a quick exit to stock up on coffees, leaving mom and me alone for a few minutes.

"So how are you mom – and where's Jeff?"

"Oh Jeff's still in bed. The sailing yesterday and the shock of the accident have taken it out of him. I'm fine, just a bit of a sore neck. Anyway, it's you I want to know about. Have you had any of your test results back yet?"

"It's too early mom, we've only just had breakfast delivered. But I'm sure it will all be ok"

"I hope so after all you've been through. Josephine told me that the young man behind the wheel had been drinking and she could smell the alcohol on his breath. Disgusting"

This is news to me and I'm shocked to hear it. Mom also tells me that he wasn't insured to drive either and that the damage to Josephine's car is substantial.

"At least we managed to rescue our shopping which miraculously wasn't ruined – it got off better than you and me JJ" She feels her neck as if to reinforce the point.

Her mention of the shopping reminds me of my own good news.

"Actually mom I discovered something amazing this morning…"

I don't have time to finish my sentence before Josephine and Graham are back with a tray full of drinks. Josephine is also clutching a large paper bag full of 'goodies' as she puts it, winking across at me.

"So what's this thing you were about to tell me about?" mom inquires as soon as she's been handed her coffee.

Graham and Josephine glance up expectantly.

"Well, I don't want to get too excited just yet but this is a big deal for me. The thing is, when I woke up this morning I could remember about yesterday, the shopping, the accident – all of it. And I didn't write down anything. It might sound silly but I even remembered that I *hadn't* written up my diary"

No one speaks for a few seconds before Josephine gives out a huge whoop.

"Hey JJ - that's great. Fantastic! Have you told the doctors?" She's already at my bedside and before I know it I'm enveloped in a big Josephine hug and the scent of her heavy floral perfume.

Graham gets me to recall everything again, knowing full well that he hasn't talked me through yesterday's events. It seems that he didn't want to go over things before I'd had breakfast and woken up properly. Funny, that was my plan too – until mom and Josephine turned up early doors.

"Well I can certainly vouch that I haven't had a chance to talk through what happened with JJ" he says, suddenly sounding like the serious lawyer that he is.

Mom looks thoughtful.

"Do you think the accident, the impact of it, might have triggered your memory? I mean it was a shocker wasn't it?" She looks across at Graham and Josephine to see their reaction.

"I think we need to discuss this with a doctor first Carol" Graham responds still wearing his serious lawyer expression. "It might just be a one-off. We should try Ray to see what he thinks"

"Ray...?" Mom looks confused until Josephine tells her that it's Dr Silver.

"This might sound silly but can you remember anything about the day before yesterday?" Josephine asks grabbing hold of my hand and squeezing it hard.

Try as I might, there is nothing specific aside from yesterday's memories. But those are clear and precise.

"I'll give Ray a call and get him to drop by" Graham announces before disappearing into the corridor to make use of his cell phone.

While we're waiting for Dr Silver to turn up, I use Graham's lap top to check my emails. There's one from DI Robinson and copied to Clare.

"Hi JJ – Sorry to hear about yesterday's car accident and I hope you are feeling ok. Please bear in mind that we'll have to refit your ankle tag as soon as you return home. Also just to let you know that we have now agreed to meet Micky Doyle later today at a secure location. I may need to speak to you as soon as we have interviewed him and I'll be in touch about that. Regards, DI Robinson."

Again it strikes me that with no access to my memory diary, I can understand what DI Robinson saying. Somehow I know that Micky Doyle has been missing on the island for some time and that DI Robinson wants to interview him about the bank theft. I can sense though, that I'm not getting a complete picture and out of habit I'm itching to read my memory diary. But Graham has advised that I don't look at it until I've spoken to Dr Silver.

"Ray will want to know how much you can recall

without it" he says taking the laptop away to stop me accessing the electronic version of my diary. So to amuse myself, I spend the next few minutes writing down a list of everything I can recall about yesterday. And it turns out to be quite a list.

I don't have to wait long before the man himself appears, dressed in his tennis outfit with a racquet case slung across one shoulder.

"Just on my way to a game when I got Tucky's call" he says throwing himself down on one of the chairs. "So where is he?"

"He's just popped home for a shower but will be back soon" I reply trying not to be too distracted by Dr Silver's toned and tanned tennis legs.

"Right then, let's hear all about these new memories of yours. Fire away"

We're still going through everything when Graham arrives back looking refreshed and spruced up.

"So what do you make of this Ray?" he asks after they've exchanged banter about who is the better tennis player.

"Fascinating" Dr Silver responds scanning my detailed list of yesterday's memories.

"This is the first time JJ has been able to remember anything significant from the day before. Yes, there's been the odd thing here and there but nothing like this. But we won't know more until we've experimented. What I now need JJ, is for you to stop doing your diary for a few days. I know that will seem strange but it is the only way we'll find out if this latest accident has somehow stimulated the short term memory part of your brain"

I tell Dr Silver about broadly understanding the details of DI Robinson's latest email.

"Yes, that's all good. So what I'd now like you to do is to voice everything on this little machine about what you remember from the day you arrived in Bermuda. Doesn't matter if it is not in any particular order. Just speak into this and say anything that comes into your mind"

He hands me a small recording device and a sheet with instructions on how to use it.

"It's dead simple – you just press that button and the red light will flash to say it's recording. Then just speak into the little microphone here"

He gets me to try it out and I'm surprised to hear the sound of my own voice. I'm struck by how different it sounds on the machine to the one in my head.

"I'm used to hearing my own voice on tape all the time, so you'll get used to it" Dr Silver replies giving me one of his handsome smiles.

Just as he is leaving, a hospital doctor arrives with the results from my head scan. Dr Silver asks for a quick word with him and I can hear them talking in low voices in the corridor. Graham is checking out my recording device and messing around with the various controls. How does that expression go - boys and their toys? Jeff would be doing exactly the same thing if he were here now.

The hospital doctor returns clutching a large sheet of paper which looks like some sort of complicated graph. He explains that I've got severe bruising but no other additional damage.

"We can see evidence of your original injury but

apart from getting a bad bump everything else looks ok. You've had no headaches or dizziness?"

I tell him that there's been nothing like that and the only pain I have is when I press against the bump.

"Well it won't look pretty for a few days but all things done, it could have been much worse. So we'll get another doctor to look you over one more time and if all is ok, you can head off home"

I'm delighted to hear it and can't wait to get back to the apartment.

"Shame your mom has got to wear that neck brace for the last few days of her vacation" Graham says as we are packing up my things to head home.

A second doctor has just finished checking me over and has declared that I'm fit to leave the hospital.

"When are they due to go back?" I ask with no clue about when they will return to London.

"In two days time – not long now. Oh and I suppose we'll have to get the ankle tag back on before we leave here. You'll have to contact DI Robinson about that"

Damn it. It feels great not having that thing on, so I'm not looking forward to getting it back. But I don't have time to make the call before Clare's number flashes up.

"Hey JJ how are you? I've heard all about the fender bender yesterday with the drunken driver"

Fender bender. It strikes me as a funny way to describe a powerful car shunt. Sounds almost inconsequential.

After telling Clare that I've got away with a giant

bruise – omitting the retrieved memory bit – she moves on to what she's really called me about.

"It's about Tralee Josie as you like to call her. The publicity in the Irish newspapers has caused a bit of a stir. Her former employer in Ireland has told the police that she left under a bit of a cloud, with thousands missing from an account she was in charge of. That's why she took off to Bermuda apparently. It was all kept hush hush at the time to avoid a scandal"

Left under a cloud. With thousands of Irish money vanishing. Fled across the Atlantic to Bermuda. And this my very own namesake, Josie James. A namesake I didn't even know existed until a few months ago.

A namesake who has now completely vanished from the face of the earth.

Chapter 35

Putting The Pieces Together

In an ideal fairy tale world, this latest bump on the head would have worked a miracle. It would have put things right. You know - the notion that sudden trauma and shock can trigger all those 'lost' memories.

In that ideal world I'd now be able to recall everything from the day before and would be able to dispense with my diary writing. Forever.

Oh for that shiny ideal world.

But hey, this is reality and in the real world neat solutions just don't happen. Of all people I should know this but I'm ever the optimist, always hoping against the odds. Anyway, to all intents and purposes, nothing has changed. The short term memories I got back after the car shunt in Hamilton have stayed with me and I can still recall everything about that particular day. But it seems to have been a one-off, an aberration. I tried Dr Silver's suggestion of not writing down anything for a few days just to see what would happen. And guess what? Without prompting from Graham I could recall very little. A few snippets and fleeting images but that was it.

So it's back to the detailed diary keeping, back to my 'normal' life, having been given a tantalising glimpse of what could be.

What used to be.

Mom and Jeff returned to London a few days ago and I'm now compiling a collection of photographs from their stay. I smile as I see mom's pink face and slightly tipsy expression at Pauletta's BBQ party. There are pictures of a grinning happy looking Jeff on board Bill and Evelyn's boat. As I arrange the photos in my album, I realise how much I miss them and at the same time I get an intense image of mom at the airport, tears cascading down her face and wearing a neck brace.

Another flash back memory I'll record for Dr Silver.

And today I'm feeling particularly distracted because later on I've got a crunch appointment with Clare and DI Robinson at Hamilton police station. As I remind myself about the latest developments in the police inquiry, I can feel my heart start to thump and my throat turn dry. Micky Doyle has come out of hiding and is in under police guard at a secret location. He's given his side of the story and they now want to run it past me. The very thought of this fills me with anticipation but fear as well.

Graham is sitting outside on the terrace and I can hear him chatting away on his cell phone. I signal to him and make a 'do you want a coffee?' sign, raising a pretend cup to my lips. He smiles back and gives me the thumbs up.

But by the time I finish making the coffee, he is back in the kitchen saying that he has to head out to the office.

"Sorry sweetie, forget the coffee. One of our guys has just rung in sick and I've got to cover for him. I'm not sure how long I'll be but give me a call when you've finished at Hamilton station"

Within minutes he is flying out of the door, blowing a kiss and shouting back that he'll make sure Clare gives me a lift there. Damn it. I'd rather be making the journey with Graham but I doubt I'll see him for the rest of the day now.

So what does a girl wear for a crunch police meeting? Formal and sombre? Or comfortable and casual?

I'm just getting ready, having finally decided on a crisp business like white shirt and tailored trousers, when I hear the phone ringing out. I assume it is Clare and just manage to get there before it rings off.

But it's not who I think it is. Instead it is mom calling from London sounding sleepy, even though it's early afternoon her time.

"Haven't been able to sleep properly since I landed back JJ. I'm still in Bermuda time and it's freezing here. So how are you?"

I tell her about my imminent police appointment but I can sense that she's distracted

"Not to worry mom, I'll let you know how I get on. How are things with you and Jeff?"

Mom sniffs loudly, so I know there is some news coming.

"That's partly why I rang you. That little cow Sophie has dumped Jeff. The lad is in bits"

What? Sophie? For a moment I have to think who

she is talking about.

"You know – Jeff's girlfriend? *That* Sophie, the little bitch"

Ah yes, now I get it. Jeff must be devastated.

"Left him in the lurch she has. As soon as he got back from Bermuda she told him it was all off. Apparently she's met somebody else. Me? I couldn't give a toss as I never liked her much anyway. But I'm worried about Jeff. He won't eat or do anything other than lie around moping in his room"

"Can you get him to speak to me mom? Perhaps I can make him feel a bit better?" I still know how bad I felt when my very first boyfriend, Jack, dumped me all those years ago. At the time I thought it was the end of the world and I would never get over it.

"Well I'll ask him JJ, I already have in fact. But he says he doesn't want to talk to anyone at the moment, not even his big sis"

Poor Jeff. As I speak, I can see his smiling photo captured just days ago on Bill and Evelyn's sailing trip. Little did he know what was facing him when he returned to London.

I tell mom to try to persuade him to talk to me later on.

"Good luck with the police meeting" she says before adding that she's going to cook Jeff his favourite brunch to cheer him up. If only life were that simple. It will take a lot more than fried bacon, egg and a side of baked beans to sort out my little bro over this one.

I'm waiting suited and booted when Clare zips up the driveway in her gleaming red convertible.

"My, you look smart today JJ" she says giving me a look of approval.

"Thanks Clare. I'm taking a leaf out of your book"

She smiles, straightening her jacket and then smoothing her hair. But there's no need – by some miracle it has managed to stay in place despite the open top car.

When we get to Hamilton police station there are no spare parking spaces, so Clare drives off in search of one along the road.

"You go on ahead into the station JJ and I'll be with you once I've found a space"

The police receptionist nods at me when I tell her I'm here to see Di Robinson.

"And here's the man himself!" she replies as he appears through the main door.

He looks exhausted, with dark rings under his eyes and dark stubble on his chin. Whatever he's been doing, it hasn't involved much sleep.

"Well you look bright and perky today JJ – wish I felt the same. Where's that solicitor of yours?"

He laughs when I explain that she's gone off to look for a parking spot.

"Ah – that'll take a while then" He turns to the receptionist and tells her to send Clare up to room 212 when she gets here.

The room turns out to be a large conference one, with a huge board room style table and a giant screen showing the police service logo.

"We use this for press briefings but it's the only spare room we've got today. There's a visit on with some bigwigs from the FBI. That's why there's shortage of parking"

When Clare finally arrives she is red faced and angry.

"You might have told me there was a damn FBI contingent here. I've had to park several blocks away" She's glaring across at DI Robinson and I can see that he's in no mood to take any flak from her today.

"Well forgive me for forgetting to mention it Miss Thompson - but I've had a busy few hours interviewing Micky Doyle and haven't even been home yet. Sleep well last night did you? Because I didn't, that's for sure"

Taken aback by his tone, Clare looks down at her shoes like a schoolgirl who has been chastised by the head teacher.

"Ok, sorry. I know you've been busy. So shall we just get on with things and then you can go home to sleep? And tidy yourself up"

They certainly now how to wind each other up. It's like being caught between two warring factions and you can cut the atmosphere with a knife right now. DI Robinson slams a chair down for Clare and spends a few minutes fiddling with a recording machine. Clare raises her eyes to the ceiling, and while he isn't looking she points to DI Robinson mouthing the word "prat" across at me. I can see this is going to be an interesting interview.

"Right. We'll get started. I'm recording this for official purposes, so if you could both confirm who you are…."

And so we begin the interview with DI Robinson and Clare still glowering across the table at each other.

"I'm going to take you through the interview notes I did yesterday with Michael Doyle, otherwise known as Micky, at a secret location. You can interrupt at any time and I'll be asking you questions about key parts of his interview. Ok?"

DI Robinson peers across at me. I nod back just wanting to cut to the chase. Clare pointedly turns to a new page of her note book and has her pen poised at the ready.

"And just so you know JJ, I'll advise you if I think you shouldn't answer a question or if I consider it is inappropriate" She says this without looking up from her notebook.

This time DI Robinson doesn't rise to the bait but gives us both a fixed stare before continuing.

"Ok let's get going then. Here are the headlines from Micky Doyle's interview. He has told me that he feared for his life after a gang leader – Wesley Caesar - accused him of stealing goods supposedly worth $250,000 dollars. We now know those so called 'goods' were Class A drugs."

DI Robinson pauses to clear his throat before continuing.

"According to Micky, a parcel was handed over to him by Wesley Caesar. Micky said that he thought it was high end American clothing and that Wesley had asked him to pass it over to a 'friend' who wanted to avoid paying duty on it. Apparently Micky had already done this on a number of previous occasions and was paid well for his efforts. He claims he was acting purely as an intermediary for Wesley and believed him when he said it was clothing"

Clare's cell phone vibrates and she rummages in her bag to switch it off. DI Robinson glares at her and carries on reading.

"Micky insisted that he had nothing to do with this package going missing. He merely left it in his usual hiding place ready to hand it over to Wesley's associate the next day. Wesley didn't believe this and then demanded payback. You ok, following this so far?"

I nod looking across at Clare who is feverishly making notes.

"For the record, Ms James has just nodded that she has understood what I've said so far. Shortly after the parcel disappeared, Micky was involved in a bike accident which resulted in the loss of a leg. And more recently he'd been snatched off the streets and held captive for the best part of two days by people associated with Wesley's gang. They told him that they'd been responsible for the motor cycle crash. This left Micky in a state of terror and he'd been saving up as many dollars as he could to make some sort of payment to Wesley. Enough to get him off his back for a while until Micky could plan an escape from the island"

"Er, can I stop you for a moment?" Clare puts down her pen and stares hard at DI Robinson.

"For the record Miss Thompson has just interrupted" DI says with more than a hint of irritation in his voice.

"Could you try to pace yourself a little? It's just that I'm having difficulty keeping up with my notes" Clare flicks her pen to reinforce her point.

"Noted, Miss Thompson. So to continue, Micky is confiding all of this to his best friend Callum O'Toole. Then Callum comes up with an idea to help Micky out"

DI Robinson pauses again to take a swig of water.

"I'll read out exactly what Micky Doyle says about this episode, so you'll have to excuse the language" DI Robinson says picking up a printed document with the police logo visible across the top. As he reads, I try to imagine Micky speaking but I'm having difficulty remembering the sound of his voice.

"It was all Callum's idea for me to get JJ to put my saved up money into the children's charity account . He said it made sense. That way I wouldn't be tempted to spend the money because it would be safely tucked up in an account that I couldn't get at. And when I'd saved up say $5,000, I could pay Wes something to get him off my case. Then I could plan my escape back to Dublin. He said that he knew his fiancé Josie wouldn't go along with this plan as she could lose her job but that we could get JJ to pay the money in. After all they both shared the same name didn't they? So it was easy. He said to me, who would know? The bank charity account people wouldn't know that 'JJ' wasn't his 'Josie' because she didn't go in there that often. And he said that he knew where his fiancé kept the charity bank account paying in slips and cheque book, so he could get to them without her suspecting a thing. Callum told me to think about it. He said if I played the sympathy card, JJ would go along with it and with her memory problems keeping the whole thing a secret wouldn't be difficult"

Hearing him talking about me like that is upsetting. But what comes next is worse. Much worse.

"I now know that this was just a way of setting me and JJ up. I thought this fecking best mate of mine was trying to do me a favour. Trying to get me somewhere safe to park my money - until I could get myself out of Bermuda. Some frigging mate he was. No, it was just a way of introducing JJ to the bank, to soften her up, so she would then do what he really wanted – to withdraw the $300,000 charity ball money. Can you believe that he even persuaded me to get JJ to put in another $1,000 of my savings on the same day he sent her in to get the fecking big charity wad? Then he drops me off in Hamilton, cool as you like, before hot footing it back to his place with the stolen loot and all the time me thinking that he's genuinely off to deliver it to the charity HQ. And meantime his frigging fiancé was back at their flat waiting for him – not in Ireland with her sick sister as he told me and JJ. So they flee the island with the charity wad and then try to pin the whole thing on me and JJ, their supposed friends. Sick bastards"

DI Robinson pauses and looks up at me. He must be able to see how upset I am. Clare has stopped writing and asks if I'm ok. In truth I'm lost for words.

If what Micky says is true, everything is starting to fall horribly into place. And it puts Tralee Josie slap bang in the centre stage. She must have planned to steal the very money her bank helped to raise. This was nothing to do with Micky or the gang threats. Micky's problem was just a way of pinning the blame on him as he had a clear cut motive to steal. And I was dragged it because I had the same name and a handy short term memory problem.

Josie must have come up with this sick plot but cleverly managed to distance herself from everything. And to think that I sought her out as my namesake and thought of her as a true friend. My mind spins as I'm left wondering exactly when she conjured this whole thing up? Was it on the first day I met her and Callum, recorded so enthusiastically in my diary? Or did it happen much later, some time after I'd been 'conveniently' introduced to Micky?

"Shall we take a quick break here?" DI Robinson says glancing across at Clare who gives a curt nod.

"For the record, we're now taking a break at 10.15am". He switches off the tape adding that he'll leave us for a few minutes to consult and "take a comfort break if you want"

Left alone with Clare, I'm still too stunned for words.

"Does any of this actually ring true JJ?" Clare asks getting up to stretch her legs.

I pause for a few moments before answering but when I do I'm surprised by the clarity of my response.

"Yes Clare it does. Everything is now making some kind of sense. It didn't before but it does now. I think Micky is telling the truth"

If Clare agrees with me, she is giving nothing away. Then DI Robinson returns with an animated look on his face.

"After we're finished in here, which won't be

long, would you be ok to be interviewed alongside Micky Doyle?"

Clare looks as though she is about to say something but I get in first.

"Yes absolutely" I reply "absolutely"

Chapter 36

Backwards and Forwards

When I next clap eyes on Micky he is sitting in a pokey office deep inside the police station. There are two armed officers on guard outside and they move across to let Clare and me inside. The room is stuffy and DI Robinson asks one of the officers if we could have a rotary fan to make things more comfortable.

I'm shocked at the sight of Micky. He's seems to have lost a lot of weight and looks gaunt and dishevelled. I guess he is so ghostly pale because he has hardly been out of doors lately.

"Hi JJ" he says getting up to greet me. "A fine mess we've got ourselves into here eh?"

He is smiling but his eyes are dull and he looks shell shocked. My instinct is to give him a hug but clearly this is no friendly reunion. DI Robinson is a man with a mission and he now wants to crack on with things.

"Right Micky, I've just gone over everything you've told me with Miss James. It's all been a bit of a shock for her as you can imagine and I'd like to fill in a few more details. Can you both confirm that you are happy to proceed?"

We nod keeping our eyes firmly fixed on each

other. Micky smiles across again and this time I return it.

DI Robinson takes us through everything one more time and I can now understand why Micky and Callum were so insistent that I didn't write anything down about our meetings. It's a classic case of secrets and lies, with a dollop of short term memory problems thrown in for good measure.

"Sorry JJ but I honestly thought you were just there to help me out over this Wesley business. I'd no idea what they were really planning, that's the truth. I hope you believe that"

Yes, I believe him. I really do.

And by the time we are finished, DI Robinson is already planning to narrow the net in the search for Callum and Josie.

"We know they have been in Barcelona and they can't hide themselves forever" he says "the world isn't that big"

I can see Micky wince at these words.

"What will happen to you now?" I ask Micky, who is staring down at the table looking even paler and wan than he did earlier.

"Feck, who knows? I'll have to get out of Bermuda but I'm not sure where I'll go. This lot have promised me anonymity" He looks across at DI Robinson who nods and says that everything will be sorted. It's clear that Micky wants to believe him but I can see real fear in his eyes.

"I'm so sorry JJ for dragging you into this mess I really am. If I could turn the clock back…." He tails off with his voice cracking.

And then it's all over. We shake hands

awkwardly and I know that I'll never see him again. I want to cry but no tears come. Instead I just watch as Micky is led away, his frail frame wedged between two burly minders. I'm sad but relieved as well. A long nightmare is finally coming to an end and DI Robinson tells me that I'll no longer be required to wear my electronic ankle tag.

"Come on, let's go and meet Graham" Clare says as we head off into the late afternoon sunshine. "I think we should all have a celebratory drink JJ – God only knows you deserve it"

Funny but I don't feel in a joyous mood. Yes, it's great that the truth is finally coming out, as everyone kept saying it would. And yes, it's wonderful to be free of that awful ankle tag with its implied guilt until proven innocent.

But Micky has been as much as a victim as I have and there is no happy ending for him wherever he ends up.

And as for Tralee Josie and Callum, there is absolutely nothing to celebrate about trust betrayed. In Josie's case she has trampled over everybody, including the children's charity, just to get what she wants. Presumably a new life for her and Callum with a handy $300,000 to set them up.

It seems a pathetic amount to cause so much pain and suffering to those left behind.

"Actually if you don't mind Clare I'd rather just head back home" I reply punching in Graham's number on my cell phone. Clare shrugs.

"Suit yourself but trust me you should get out there and start living your life to the full and but this nightmare well and truly behind you"

I ignore her and leave a simple message on Graham's cell answer phone.

"Hi Graham – it's sorted. Everything makes sense now and I'm cleared of any involvement in the theft. Call me as soon as you can"

Then I dial the number of my other namesake, St George's Josephine.

A namesake who has been such a force for good in my life.

So fast forward a year later and how are things now with my self labelled 'poorly head.' Best first to describe what *hasn't* changed.

I still have a good visual memory of faces and places I see regularly. This confuses people, me included.

I can recall some intense emotional experiences. I know I love Graham with all my heart and I can visualise the beautiful parts of Bermuda, even if I can't always remember exactly where they are located.

When I try, I can remember most of my childhood and adult years, my family and friends from that time and I can recall in vivid detail the events leading up to my accident in London. I still have occasional dreams the accident and these are accompanied by the sounds and smells of that day.

Incredibly I can still do graphic design and can paint detailed images from memory, like my drawing of the young man with the snake tattoo.

I know how to use a computer, cell phone and can follow instructions on how to work things.

I can remember the names of close friends and acquaintances people and their relationship to me.

I can recall most of what I've done today but by tomorrow it will have disappeared, apart from a few intense flash back moments.

But then ask yourself this question - how much do you really remember about what happened yesterday without the help of a diary?

And now for what I believe has changed over the past twelve months.

Despite everything, my relationship with Graham has gone from strength to strength. Adversity can sometimes kill off relationships but in our case it has brought us closer together. And it won't be too long before I'll be changing my name to Mrs Tucker.

I've got to know my future in-laws, Bill and Evelyn, much better and they are more relaxed around me now I'm no longer accused of literally taking money from the mouths of babes. I doubt Evelyn will ever see me as the perfect daughter-in-law but we're getting along.

While I'm not seeing Dr Silver on a regular basis, I've agreed that he can write my case up for his long term research into brain rehabilitation. He tells me that I've made good progress but we both know that there can be no accurate predictions for the future, no miracle cures.

Graham doesn't know what the old JJ was like before the accident but as each day goes by, I can feel a little bit of her coming back. The feistier more confident me is slowly re-emerging. "Small steps" as Dr Silver says.

St George's Josephine is my surrogate Bermuda mom and because of her I'm doing more painting and drawing. While I regret ever making the call to Tralee Josie, Josephine has more than made up for the wickedness of my other namesake.

Now I see this beautiful island as my spiritual and physical home. Yes, even paradise has its problems but it fits me, JJ, perfectly. England will always be my place of birth but Bermuda is where my future lies.

As for what happened to me on the island, I won't be able to put that behind me until after the court case. Tralee Josie and Callum were finally found lying low in a small Spanish village and according to DI Robinson they'll be hauled back to Bermuda to stand trial. Over $250,000 of the stolen money has been tracked down and will be paid to the children's charities once the trial is over.

The next time I'll face the two people I thought of as friends, will be inside the imposing Bermuda Supreme Court building - just a short distance from where Josie worked and not far from the Hoagie's jazz club where I went with Callum all those months ago. I've still got no idea how big a role Callum played in the grand plan but I suspect it was no more than a bit part, done to go along with what Josie wanted. When I think of Josie now, the words cold, calculating and clinical come to mind. Someone in a beautiful guise who is capable of trampling on anyone to get her own way. Someone without a conscience.

Micky Doyle won't be appearing in court because he has been given a new identity and is living permanently undercover somewhere. But his evidence will help to put away Josie and Callum as well as gang leader, Wesley Caesar. He not only stands accused of dealing in Class A drugs, extortion and kidnap but is also being held responsible for a number of violent attacks on rival gang members, including the shooting I witnessed at Hoagies. And for that the wider community will be grateful to Micky Doyle and the young tattooed gang associate turned informer, Vernall Smythe.

As for the young man found washed up on one of the islands more beautiful stretches of water, no one has come forward to report him missing and his untimely death remains yet another Bermuda mystery.

Ok, it's time for the biggest question of all. If I had a way to turn the clock back to my life before the accident, would I do so? My answer is a resounding no. I'm a different person today but a better one I think.

My dicky brain, as I affectionately call it, is part of me now but so is Graham, the lovely St George's Josephine and this amazing little gem of an island.

If asked to use my graphic artist skills to sum up where I am in my life, I'd create the triangle symbol so closely associated with this part of the world. But it wouldn't be one tinged with fear and dread. Mine would be big, bold and sparkling.

It's been the strangest twist and turn journey to get to this point but I've finally reached an incredible destination. And in doing so, I've discovered my very own Bermuda 'triangle' of happiness.

About the Author:

Maggie Fogarty is a Royal Television Society award winning television producer and journalist, making TV programmes for all the major UK broadcasters. She has also written extensively on health and social affairs for a number of national newspapers and magazines. In April 2011 her story 'Namesakes' was a finalist in the Artists and Writers/WAYB short story competition.

'My Bermuda Namesakes' is her debut novel and grew out of the original short story. It was written during a year long stay in Bermuda where Maggie's partner, Paul, was working as a digital forensics consultant. During her time on the island, Maggie wrote a regular guest column for the Bermuda Sun newspaper. The couple now live in a Grade 2 listed building in the South West of England in the grounds of a former naval hospital. Before moving there, they lived on the outskirts of Birmingham, in the UK English Midlands, where Maggie was born and grew up.

15683302R10186

Made in the USA
Charleston, SC
15 November 2012